For Ian Wibberley
With thanks for your help, expertise and patience.
It can't have been easy!
Well done, Big Wibbs

PROLOGUE

'Another bloody dead end!'

Detective Inspector Nikki Galena slammed the car door and glared back at the peeling paintwork of the shabby, terraced house. 'Did you see their faces? Their body language?'

Detective Sergeant Joseph Easter slipped his notebook back into his pocket and turned the key in the ignition. 'I didn't have to. The atmosphere was thick enough to choke on. But you can hardly blame them. That bastard isn't just threatening them, he's targeting their families as well. Think how you'd feel if something happened to one of your loved ones and you thought you could have prevented it? I totally understand why they don't want to talk to us.'

Nikki took a deep breath and then let out a long sigh. 'I don't know. How the hell are we expected to get people to cooperate when they are terrified out of their wits? There has to be someone who will stand up to Stephen Cox and just give us something we can use against him. He's back in the area with a vengeance, and he's into everything! Not just drugs, but money laundering, people trafficking. You name it and if it's illegal, Cox crawls to the surface.'

Joseph was perplexed. 'I cannot understand why he'd want to come within a hundred miles of this place. Police and villains throughout Greenborough want him gone. And considering the Leonard family has a contract out on him, well, it beats me.'

'I'm beginning to think that monster is superhuman. We knock him down, and he gets up again.'

'And if he really is back, he's stronger than ever.'

'But can we bloody nail him? Can we . . . ?' Her next words were torn away from her as an earth-jarring thump shook the car.

'What the hell was that?' Joseph gripped the steering wheel. He stared, open-mouthed, at a dust cloud that was beginning to rise up from behind the buildings at the end of the narrow cul-de-sac.

'Oh my God! That's the main road! The dual carriageway through the centre of town! Back up, Joseph! Get us out of this rabbit warren!'

As Joseph revved the engine and jammed it into reverse, Nikki grabbed her radio.

The voice from the control room sounded taut, hyped up. 'We've already got it, ma'am. Reports are flooding in. Massive RTC at the Blackmoor Cross traffic lights. Articulated lorry versus pedestrians.'

'We're located in the Carborough Estate, just behind it. It felt like an explosion!'

'Eyewitnesses say that the vehicle has crashed into that restoration project on the north side of the carriageway, next to the college.'

It was term time. The sixth form college would be heaving with kids. Thank God the truck had missed the school. Then with a dawning horror, she visualised the location more clearly. What should have been a row of sturdy, Tudor buildings, were at present an unstable mass of wood and brick, encased in a cocoon of scaffolding and supported by a framework of acrow posts. Her mouth went dry and she said, 'Show us attending, control. We are one minute away.'

Ahead of them was a double line of stationary vehicles. 'Shit! We'll never get through this.'

'There's a space over there. Ditch the car. We'll do better on foot.'

Joseph spun the car into the impossibly small space and killed the engine.

Together they leapt out, and skirting hot exhaust pipes and bonnets, raced toward the scene.

* * *

The usual hubbub of the market town of Greenborough had been replaced by the scream of cutting gear and the shriek of sirens and two-tones. The air that usually had the salty smell of ozone from the tidal river, mixed with hotdogs and fresh baked bread, reeked of diesel fumes and the dry, choking clag of brick dust.

'Over here!' Nikki called out to a green-clad paramedic, then knelt back down beside the terrified woman and murmured, 'It's okay, it's okay. The ambulance is here. Try to keep calm, they'll help you.' She squeezed the woman's hand reassuringly, then as the medic dropped to one knee and began his assessment of her injuries, Nikki moved on deeper into the devastation that an hour ago had been a prestigious rebuilding project.

'Ma'am!' Joseph appeared out of the gloom, his clothes covered in dust. A tall fire officer accompanied him, picking his way through the rubble to keep up. Nikki vaguely recognised the man and nodded briefly. 'Any idea what happened?'

His expression was grim. 'Don't quote me, Inspector, but the doctor who came out from A&E reckons that lorry was being driven by a dead man. He's pretty sure that the driver had a catastrophic heart attack and died at the wheel.'

Nikki let out a long, slow breath. 'How many fatalities so far?'

'Four at present, including the lorry driver, but,' he shrugged, 'God alone knows what the final count is going to be. We've managed to secure the wagon, it's all this bloody debris from the building that's the problem now. I wondered if you'd deploy some of your . . .'

Before he could finish, Nikki's radio crackled with her call sign. 'Ma'am, we've had an unconfirmed report of a problem with a damaged building in Ironworks Passage. Are you in the area?'

'Affirmative, control. DS Easter and I are about a hundred yards from there. Show us responding. Roger and out.'

The fire officer growled, 'This is far worse than we first thought. I'd better come with you.'

When they got there Nikki looked along the passage, a cut-through from the college to the market square. 'Doesn't look too badly damaged.'

The fireman appeared to believe otherwise. 'Careful, ma'am. I'm not sure how stable these walls are, and it's a very narrow alley here. If they come down on us, we'll all be brown bread.' The fire chief went ahead, casting a professional eye over the structures on either side of them. Broken glass crunched underfoot. 'Luckily this is the back of the shops and storehouses and not the front. Damn great sheets of plate glass would have been lethal.'

'Look.' Joseph pointed ahead of them to a large gaping hole in the brickwork of one of the old buildings. 'I guess that's what they are talking about. What is this place?'

Nikki moved towards the opening. 'It's a storeroom for the pub, I think. The wall has collapsed, and part of the floor by the look of it. You can see into the cellar.'

'Don't worry, ma'am, I'll get a team down here to check it out.' The fire officer's radio spluttered with static. 'Damn! The signal's crap down here. I need to get away from these high buildings.' He moved back the way they had come in and called out as he went. 'And *don't* go down there, it's far too dangerous.'

Nikki looked at Joseph, raised one eyebrow and said softly, 'Oh dear, the man says it's *far* too dangerous. You reckon?'

Together they stared into the darkness of the cellar. The debris from the collapsed wall had formed an almost gentle slope of rubble, down to the floor.

Joseph stepped forward and frowned. 'If someone was working down there they may need urgent assistance.' He looked at her, his frown changing to a wicked grin, 'And apart from that, don't you just *hate* being bossed around by Trumpton? Shall I go first?'

Nikki was about to return his smile when she heard a noise. It was a whimper, a small animal-like cry. 'Joseph! Someone *is* down there! Come on.' Supporting each other, they inched down the landslide of crumbling wall. 'For God's sake, be careful. If someone is hurt we could make things a whole lot worse for them if we start an avalanche.'

'I'm almost there.' He held out his hand to her. 'Yes, it's safe down here. There's solid ground.'

Nikki stepped down beside him and they stared around into the shadows. 'Hello? It's the police! Where are you? Are you hurt?'

There was nothing but an eerie silence, broken occasionally by the ominous creaking of the damaged building. Nikki felt an insidious shiver of fear creep down her backbone. The dim, shadowy basement was crushingly claustrophobic, and she feared she was about to be buried alive. And that was not all. Even though they had only been down there for a matter of moments, dark memories of an old case rose from the past.

'Hello?' Joseph's voice brought her back to the present, and they stood side by side and waited. There was a trickling sound as a small shower of debris slid to the floor, and then something else. Another whimper.

'Damn! I can't see where it's coming from.' Nikki slowly moved forward, desperately wishing she had thought to bring the torch from the car.

'Look! Over there! I think it's a woman! She's partially protected by that upright timber post.' Joseph began to ease his tall frame over a pile of broken beer crates and splintered shelving, then Nikki heard him curse as he found his way blocked.

Nikki moved around the other way. 'Okay, Joseph. It's clearer this way.' As she fought her way to the half-buried figure she spoke as calmly as she could manage. 'Hang on in there! We're near you now! We've got you.' After a moment or two she was able to slide down beside the unmoving woman. A pale hand protruded from beneath a lump of masonry. Nikki felt for a pulse, then sighed with relief. It was weak, but hell, it was a pulse.

'Ma'am,' Joseph held out something to her. 'It's not much use, but take my Maglite.'

'Thanks.' She reached out and grasped the small metal pocket torch. 'Do you think you can get back to the street? The radios won't work in this hellhole and we really need help here.'

'Yes, of course. On my way.'

'Tell them she's semi-conscious. Suspected crush injuries, and her legs . . .' Nikki shone the slim beam of light towards them, saw the white shard of bone protruding from the bloodied flesh, and bit hard on her lip. 'Just get the medics, and hurry.'

As he began to extricate himself from the chaos, Nikki leaned closer to the woman, talking softly to her. 'I'm Nikki, I'm a police officer. Can you tell me your name?'

There was the slightest hint of a murmur, the cold fingers moved and an eyelid flickered in the torchlight.

Nikki gently brushed a swathe of blood-soaked hair from the girl's face, and gasped in horror. 'Helen! Oh my God! Helen!' She swung round towards the disappearing figure of Joseph Easter and screamed, 'Hurry! For heaven's sake, hurry!'

CHAPTER ONE

ONE YEAR LATER

'Okay, which one?' Nikki held up two dresses on hangers and glared at Joseph.

'The blue one. Definitely.'

'Why? What's wrong with the black one?'

'If you want to wear the black one, why ask me?'

'I don't *want* to wear the black one, I just . . .' Nikki sank down on the sofa next to him. 'I don't want to go. I hate parties!'

'We can't let her down, now can we?'

Joseph sounded so calm and reasonable that Nikki wanted to hit him. 'Look at you! A smart suit, shiny shoes and you manage to look like you've just stepped onto a red carpet. It's so *easy* for you.'

'Actually it's not.' He sat back and sighed, 'I hate social gatherings as much as you. Small talk is not my thing, and if you throw too much alcohol into the equation, the conversations get mind-numbingly inane.'

'More like *insane*,' grumbled Nikki. 'Maybe it's the job. When we were beat bobbies we saw too much "Whoopee, it's Friday night! Let's get hammered!" and then had to clear up the aftermath.'

'And as I recall, most of it finished up splashed across our boots.' Joseph pulled a face. 'Happy days!'

'I never saw the point in spending a fortune on overpriced drinks, then barfing them up in the gutter an hour later.' Nikki looked down at the two dresses. 'You really think the blue one?'

'Absolutely.' He grinned at her then tapped his wrist-watch. 'And we should be leaving in five minutes, Cinderella.'

'Oh Lord! Well, at least I'm showered. Won't be a min-ute.' Nikki jumped up and ran upstairs to her bedroom. 'I still don't want to go,' she called back down.

As she hunted for some shoes that would match, she heard Joseph's footsteps on the stairs. She realised he was sitting on the top step so that he could continue talking to her. 'You don't have to sit out there, Joseph. I am decent.'

'I'm fine here. You keep moving. We don't want to be too late arriving.' There was a silence and then she heard him say, 'And I think you are right about the job. It changes things, your priorities — what's important to you and what isn't.'

Nikki stood in front of the mirror and frowned at her-self. The woman who looked back was not DI Nikki Galena, but some stranger in a posh frock. 'I really don't get out enough,' she muttered to herself, then called out, 'I agree. Sometimes I feel guilty if I'm doing anything remotely like enjoying myself.'

'Me too. It's a case of "Why am I standing here with a glass in my hand and laughing with my friends, when some old lady is being mugged or a child is being abused." We have to have some down time, but it's not easy to find a balance.'

'You surprise me, Joseph,' Nikki said. 'You are so,' she struggled for the right words, 'so centred and in control of yourself. You have a sense of peace about you, even in grim situations.'

'Ever heard about the swan? All serene on the surface, and paddling like hell under the water.'

'Rubbish. You know exactly how to control your emo-tions. Not like me — Detective "Shout first, think later"

Galena.' She gathered up her bag and stepped out onto the landing. 'Will I do?'

Joseph stood up, an appreciative smile on his face. 'Very nicely indeed, ma'am. It will be a pleasure and an honour to escort you.'

'If I thought you were taking the piss, DS Easter, I'd clock you one with this bloody handbag.'

'You look great, and I mean it. Now let's go put on a show for Helen, shall we?'

* * *

As they drove along the lanes that led from Cloud Fen, Joseph asked, 'So what has Helen called her new clinic?'

'Newlands. I think it's after her grandparents' old home. Childhood memories, and all that.'

'And it's on the Westland Waterway? That's one classy address! I took a statement down there after a robbery. It had river frontage, three storeys, and it was *seriously* upmarket.'

Nikki let out a groan. 'Tell me about it. I am going to feel totally out of place! And can you imagine the kind of people who will be there? Weirdos and oddballs! No, worse! *Rich* weirdos and oddballs.'

Joseph laughed. 'Helen is an aromatherapist, not a Voodoo priestess! Her clients will be ordinary people like you and me. And she's your friend, Nikki. She'd be devastated if you weren't at her opening party.'

'I know, I know. Why do you think I'm suffering in high heels and a fixed grin?' She smiled at Joseph, 'And of course I wouldn't let her down, this is just as much a celebration of her surviving the accident as it is the opening of her own clinic.'

'Well, I'm driving, so you let your hair down for once. Chill out and have a few drinks with an old friend, okay?'

'Message received and understood. Just don't let me get buttonholed by any oddballs.'

* * *

9

'Nikki! Joseph! You made it! Knowing what your dreadful shifts are like, Andrew and I were taking bets on whether you'd have to cry off.' Helen Brook stood at the open front door. She was a tall, slim woman with huge, bovine eyes and a heart-shaped face framed by short dark hair cut into a wispy uneven style. 'I'm *so* pleased you are here.'

Seeing the wide smile and perceiving Helen's genuine pleasure, Nikki felt a stab of guilt at complaining so bitterly about making the effort. 'We wouldn't have missed it for the world,' she lied, and felt Joseph's elbow nudge her ribs. 'And look at you! No crutches? No stick?'

Helen stepped forward and hugged them both. 'Finally I've ditched them. And now I feel halfway to normal again.'

Nikki hugged her back. 'Well, you look incredible.'

'Physically I'm doing great, but inside I'm not too sure. That's the really hard part.' The bright smile dimmed.

'Hey, enough of that! What would you tell your patients? You know better than anyone, the bones are the easy bit, but the mind takes a whole lot longer. But you'll get there, Helen, I promise you. If ever there was a fighter, it's you.' Nikki held her at arm's length and grinned at her. 'And now, lead me to the goodies! The sausage rolls, the nibbles, the cheese straws, the vino!'

Helen laughed. 'You're right. Some welcome! Come on in and meet everyone. I still can't believe we've actually got everything together at last.'

'So when do you open, officially?' asked Joseph.

Nikki noticed a slight hesitation before Helen answered.

'Oh, I've just got a few things to sort out before I can take off full-time. I'm already seeing a few of my old regulars from the Willows Clinic where I used to work. You know, special clients, ones who suffer if I neglect them for too long.'

'This place looks fantastic, Helen!' Nikki slipped an arm through her friend's and they moved into the spacious hallway. 'So what does Andrew think of it all? I haven't seen him for ages.'

Again there was a hesitation and Nikki heard the vaguest sound of alarm bells ringing in the distance. *She's nervous, and I don't think it's anything to do with this party.*

'Oh, he's over the moon, naturally. And he's so supportive. He said to apologise to you. He'll be here soon.' She gave a short laugh, 'Usual thing, something came up just as he was about to leave work.' Helen turned to Joseph. 'And I'm giving you a warning. He's found some fantastic IT program that he wants to talk to you about. Something that he's certain will revolutionise your police computer. That's if it needs revolutionising of course. Anyway, I'm apologising in advance. You know how passionate he is when it comes to his beloved computer systems.' She ushered them towards the kitchen. 'Now, what are you two drinking?'

Nikki watched Helen as she poured their drinks. She was talking far too fast, her voice much too bright. Something was decidedly wrong.

Joseph whispered to her. 'You're being a detective again, Galena, not a jolly partygoer. What's the matter?'

'Sorry? Oh, it's nothing. Just thinking.'

Helen handed her a glass of cold white wine and Joseph a tumbler of juice.

'There are some really interesting people here that I'd like to introduce you to . . . oh, sorry, that's the door. You circulate, I'll catch you up in a minute.'

'Saved by the bell,' murmured Joseph. 'You looked horrified at the thought of meeting those "interesting" people.'

'I hoped it didn't show.'

'Well, I noticed. If you don't fancy mingling, let's go have a sneaky nose around this amazing place.'

For the next half hour Helen caught up with her guests, and apart from a few polite words here and there, Nikki successfully avoided any deep, meaningful conversations.

Joseph brought her a top-up, sat down on a stylish new sofa and looked around. 'This must have cost an absolute fortune. Apart from its location on the river, it's been refurbished from top to bottom, by skilled craftsmen from the look of it.'

Nikki shook her head. 'Plus all the treatment room stuff, the massage tables and gallons of expensive aromatherapy essential oils. *And* that gorgeous conservatory that leads to the Japanese garden. But then again, I guess the compensation for having practically lost your legs, having half your head caved in and being scarred for life could be considerable, couldn't it?'

Joseph nodded. 'It has to be that, doesn't it? The last I heard, Andrew was struggling financially, so he's probably not making much of a contribution.'

Nikki sipped her drink. 'I don't think that's the case anymore. He's had some sort of promotion, or so Helen says. With lots of overtime, which means lots of wonga, so maybe his luck has changed.' Her brow wrinkled in distaste. 'What on earth are you eating?'

'Sushi. It's delicious.'

'I'll take your word for that.' She picked up a large chunk of ocean-green calcite crystal from the table and stared at it. She passed the glassy rock specimen from hand to hand and felt the coolness of it on her skin. 'I really like these crystals. They are supposed to relax you, aren't they? Maybe I should get one?'

'Unless they sell them in industrial sizes, like by the hundredweight, I doubt there will be one big enough.'

'Smart-arse. I'm well known in some circles for my calm diplomacy and gentle manner.'

Joseph spluttered into his drink. 'Not any circle I've ever been in.'

Nikki's smile faded and she said, 'Joseph, do you think Helen is okay? She seems a bit, well, uneasy, don't you think?'

'Ah, now we come to what is really worrying you. You've felt like that since Helen opened the door, haven't you?'

'Well spotted, Detective. But what do *you* think?'

'She's twitchy, and pretty on edge. I thought it might be because of the stress of being the perfect hostess, well, more

12

to the point, the *lone* hostess. If you think it's more than that, go talk to her, she's just left a group of people. Get her to yourself for a moment or two.'

'Okay, and as I just saw Andrew's Beemer draw up, why don't you hunt him down and keep him occupied while I see what I can find out.'

For a moment she watched him as he made his way across the room. Joseph had said that he hated small talk and social gatherings, but it didn't look like it. He had the ability to seem at ease in any situation. Mixing with villains or VIPs, it made no difference to Joseph. She envied him his chameleon quality, because she was always the same. Whatever she was wearing, Nikki the police officer was never off-duty. She exhaled, then crossed the room and sat down close to Helen. 'Okay, sister. Spill the beans. What's wrong?'

For a moment there was silence, then the cheerful veneer crumbled. 'Nikki, I'm so worried. I think I'm being followed.'

The DI slid deftly in to replace the good friend. 'Is there somewhere we can talk without being overheard?'

'Maybe it's time I showed you the Japanese garden. I'll get our coats.'

A few moments later, they sat huddled together on a wooden bench beside the water garden. Brightly coloured fish flitted between the gently moving fronds of underwater plants. Their orange and scarlet was iridescent in the glow of the sensor lights.

'Okay. Do you know who is watching you?'

Helen shook her head. 'I've never seen him close to. It's more that I sense someone, rather than actually see him. He's a shadowy figure that disappears when I try to look at him. It's creepy, but I know he's there.'

'Where have you seen him?'

'Here mainly, over by the river walk and in that wilderness of a garden through the gate over there.' She gestured to a big heavy wooden gate set in the wall behind them. 'And at the Willows Clinic, and in Tesco's car park.' She bit her lower lip. 'And once when I took a walk along the river at the Tumby Fenside bird reserve, I swear I saw him there too.'

'What does Andrew think?'

'Oh, you know Andrew. He's got microchips instead of blood. He's unbelievably clever, but he hasn't got a clue when it comes to anything like this.'

'You mean he thinks you are imagining it?'

'Probably. But that's not all, Nikki. I . . . I need to ask you something about the accident.'

Nikki frowned. 'Sure. What's bothering you?'

'When you found me, I was alone, wasn't I?'

Where the hell was this going? 'Yes. You were quite alone. Why?'

Helen stared into the clear cold water. 'I've been remembering things. Just little things. The doctors said it might happen.'

Nikki would have to tread warily. 'And have you remembered something that's worrying you?'

'I don't understand, Nikki. You say I was alone, but I'm sure someone else was there, speaking to me. I remember someone in the darkness. They said, "Is anyone there?"'

'But that was me.'

'No it wasn't. This was just after the wall collapsed. Long before you found me.'

Nikki looked at her intently. 'Surely it was all a bit of a blur, Helen? You were so badly hurt. It must have been me, or maybe Joseph.'

'It was a man's voice, but not Joseph. And you two kept saying, "Hello!" and "It's the police. Where are you? Are you hurt?"'

It was exactly what they'd said. 'So what else do you remember?'

'Not much, just a huge feeling of relief that I was not alone.'

Nikki leaned forward and touched her friend's hand. 'Helen? This has to be some kind of memory glitch. Joseph and I were first on the scene, and I promise you, you were

14

alone. There was no one with you. That basement was cleared afterwards, no traces of anyone else were found. If it wasn't Joseph or I that you remember, maybe your mind needed to invent someone, someone to comfort you? I'm sure it's something quite simple and you shouldn't worry too much about it. To be honest, I think we should concentrate on whoever is following you, don't you?'

Helen's voice was low, almost a whisper. 'I can't help thinking that they are connected in some way.'

'What, the accident and being watched?'

Helen abruptly released Nikki's hand, and began to ease herself up from the bench, obviously in pain. 'I'm sorry, Nikki, I can't do this right now. I'm sure you're right and I'm just being silly and confused about it all.'

'I never said you were being silly, Helen, but the mind can play tricks. You were in an unbelievably traumatic situation.'

'I must go. I haven't even seen Andrew yet, and I have guests to attend to.'

Nikki watched her friend limp back through the garden to the conservatory. This wasn't the time to go after her, but no way was she going to leave it there. Helen's fear was no flight of fancy. It was very real.

When Joseph found her fifteen minutes later, she was still staring into the fish pond and wondering who the hell would want to follow Helen Brook.

CHAPTER TWO

It was ten minutes before the shift was due to end, and the whole day had been spent following up ifs, maybes, and could-haves regarding Stephen Cox. Nikki swallowed two paracetamol and tried to get back into reading a report from uniform about another "possible" sighting. She yearned for something concrete, something definite to work with. Cox seemed to have haunted her whole life as a copper. He was an evil man with no compassion, and years ago he had caused both her and her family untold heartbreak. Everywhere he went, people suffered, and there was no one that Nikki would rather see behind bars. She groaned. Her headache however had nothing to do with Cox, or the wine from the night before, and everything to do with what her friend had told her. She pushed the report to one side and tried to recall when she and Helen had first met. It was before her daughter Hannah had been hospitalised, at some kind of fundraiser, she couldn't remember for which charity. All she knew was that she and Helen had been thrown together manning a stall selling raffle tickets. Which was *so* not her thing. Luckily Helen had seen the funny side to her grumbling and complaining, and in a very short time Nikki had made a friend. Over the years, she had neglected Helen, like all her other friends. She had let the job take over her life, and then Hannah had occupied her every waking hour. Nikki had become an angry loner. It had been a bad time, and one she might not have survived, if not for the arrival of Joseph Easter. And then somehow Helen made contact and managed to find a way back into her life, and Nikki had a friend again. 'Hen's teeth,' she murmured. A friendship like Helen's was rare indeed.

'Nikki? Before you go, can I have a moment of your time?' Superintendent Greg Woodhall stood in her doorway.

'Come in, sir. I was wool-gathering, if I'm honest.'

Greg closed the door behind him, then sunk down into a chair. 'I've got a problem, and I'm going to pass it on to you.'

Nikki gave him a half-hearted grin. 'Thanks a bunch, sir. What have you just let me in for?'

'Now, I assure you this is not a permanent restructuring of CID staff. I, er, need you to do a little short-term babysitting for me.'

'Sorry, sir, the kindergarten is in the next street. This here is the cop shop.'

Greg chose to ignore her. 'There has been an incident within DI Gill Mercer's team and I have to relocate two officers. One has decided to use up some outstanding leave, and the other is coming on loan to you for a while.'

Nikki instantly became serious. She'd already heard some of this on the grapevine. 'You're talking about DC Eric Barnes, aren't you, sir?'

'I am. And I already know that he and your DC Cat Cullen do not get along, so it won't be easy, but frankly, Nikki, you are the only senior detective that might be able to bring him into line.'

Nikki stared at the superintendent, and wondered how he kept his skin so smooth and unlined, considering the flak he had to take on a daily basis. Like the flak she was about to dish out with her next breath. 'Sir! We have a tight-knit team with an excellent arrest rate and a bloody brilliant record. I do not want that unpleasant young man stirring things up with us, like he has in the Mercer team.'

'He's intelligent, sharp, and has a talent for lateral thinking.'

'He also has a talent for bringing out the worst in others, and he does it with all the charisma of a heap of camel dung.' Nikki stood up and began to pace the office. 'How the hell am I going to explain this to Cat? She's already had one run-in with him and they weren't even working together. Eric Barnes is a loner; he's just not capable of working as part of a team.'

Greg looked seriously at Nikki. 'And I cannot afford to lose him. It's complicated, but his family are very well connected, and I've been given something of an ultimatum from up high. We need to rein him in, and I'm afraid the job of doing it just fell in your lap. DC Dave Harris is back tomorrow from sick leave, but he's on two weeks' light duties after his operation, so he will be mainly office-bound. Eric can be his legs, okay?'

'Have you told Barnes yet?'

'I'm on my way to see him now before he goes home.'

Nikki knew there was no way around this one. At least it was a temporary arrangement. 'Okay, I'll go fill Joseph in. I'm going to need every one of his extensive negotiation skills just to stop Cat poisoning Eric's coffee.'

'Or vice versa. I get the picture.' Greg stood up. 'Do your best, Nikki. He does have considerable potential, but only if someone can manage to knock some sense into him.'

Right, and I might finish up knocking more than sense into him, Nikki thought grimly. *This is just what I need right now.*

* * *

Helen Brook shifted uncomfortably in her chair and decided that television was just not worth watching anymore. It was either repeats, sometimes even a repeat of a programme you had seen the day before, or reality crap. If you had told her twenty years ago that they would be making long-running TV series about street cleaners, vermin control companies, estate agents and people who suffered from sad psychological conditions like hoarding, she would have said you were mad. She switched off a show that seemed to feature a man knocking on people's doors and offering the owners good money to take away junk, stood up and made her way to the kitchen. If she stayed in one position for too long, the muscles in her injured legs still throbbed and ached. She knew that she should be working, there were still preparations to be made for the clinic, but she just felt so low.

She made herself yet another non-caffeinated herbal tea, took it into the lounge and sat in darkness in a big leather recliner, looking out of the front window and across the river. She should also be thinking about getting some supper, but she really wasn't hungry. This job of Andrew's was becoming a real problem. His bosses seemed to think he should drop everything, day or night, and rush to the office to sort out their constant computer problems. Last night's call had come just as their guests were leaving and, like a sheepdog to the whistle, he'd gone. The same thing had happened earlier. The phone rings, Andrew leaves. Damn him! And more to the point, damn his bloody job. The extra money was great, but it wasn't worth all the emotional upheaval it caused. They had no reason to worry about money, she had enough for both of them, but Andrew didn't see it that way. He didn't want to sponge, he wanted to pay his way, and she could hardly knock him for having decent values. However, his high ideals meant that he'd been in France for the week when she was due to move to Newlands, and now he was chasing back and forth to the city, when she needed him most. And talking to Nikki had not helped. In fact it had made it worse. Her friend's obvious concern for her had made it seem suddenly real, and her fears intensified.

Andrew always said that to be successful at work you should always be able to do something that others couldn't do. Make yourself indispensable. Well, he seemed to be making a pretty good job of that. Sometimes she wondered if Seymour Kramer Systems had any other trouble-shooters working for their sodding global network.

A sudden feeling of loneliness washed over her. He seemed to be away so often, and she missed him more with every trip. Surely she had never felt this insecure before the accident? Sometimes it seemed that the Helen Brook who, a year ago, had walked happily into that alleyway, had never come out. A different woman now inhabited her body.

She looked across at her front garden and saw silver diamonds of frost glistening on the grass. She dearly wished the winter was over. She hated how it got dark so early and was still dark when you got up in the morning. After being in that cellar, she was not a fan of the dark.

A thin, hungry-looking cat moved silently along the top of a wooden fence and she watched it drop down and make its way across the road to the wall that edged the river walk. She kept watching its progress until it disappeared, and then she froze.

A shadowy figure appeared, visible for a fraction of a second, then gone.

Helen slowly replaced her mug on the side table, shrank back in the chair, and sat perfectly still. She held her breath and stared fixedly at the spot where the shape had been. There was a sudden rush as a truck thundered down the road, cutting off her view of the river wall. It sent Helen crashing back into the awful darkness of a year ago.

Unable to move and barely able to breathe, something sticky covered her face, but she was unable to wipe it from her eyes. She heard herself whimper in the darkness, but other than that, and a roaring sound inside her head, it was oddly quiet. She tried to call out but only managed to cough up some brick dust from her throat.

'Is someone there?' A man's voice said.

Helen felt herself begin to shake. She wanted to answer but nothing came out. Then again she heard it.

'Hello? Are you hurt?'

She managed a small moan, then waited.

'I'm sorry, I can't get to you. My legs are trapped. Are you badly hurt?'

She wanted to cry with relief. She did not know what had happened, but at least she was not alone. Thank God!

Another vehicle whistled past her house, and she found herself back in her leather chair, rocking back and forth, shaking and hugging herself. Whose was that voice? She put her hands to her face and clamped her eyes shut. This was no mental glitch. It was a full-blown memory in the form of a horrible flashback. What the hell was happening to her? One thing was for sure. That was not Joseph's voice.

Tears formed and slowly ran down her cheeks. She wanted Andrew. But as Andrew was God knows where, she rang the only other person that she trusted.

CHAPTER THREE

Nikki and Joseph were preparing to leave work and discussing how they would deal with their unwanted new arrival, when she heard the muffled sound of her mobile ringing in her shoulder bag. She pulled it out and saw *Helen* was the caller. A tiny shiver went down her spine.

'Nikki here. Helen? Are you all right?'

Her friend's tone said it all. Helen Brook was far from all right. 'Hang on in there. I was just going home anyway. I'll be with you very soon.'

Exactly ten minutes later, Nikki sat across the table from Helen and tried to understand what had frightened her so badly. Helen had already admitted that she never actually saw anyone watching her, just a shadow over by the river walk that could have been anything. Her problem was the flashback.

Her friend was cocooned in an over-sized sweater that must have been Andrew's, and sat fidgeting anxiously with the long sleeves. 'I don't understand. All the other things I've remembered have been true, so why imagine someone else being there?'

Nikki shifted in her seat. 'I don't know. I wish I did. Do you think that maybe it was more a dream than a flashback? Maybe you dozed off for a minute or two?'

Helen laughed dryly. 'I do know the difference, Nikki. Believe me, if you'd ever experienced something so horrible that it has to come crashing back when you least expect it, you'd know exactly what I mean.'

Nikki knew all too well, but she wasn't going to tell Helen that she still suffered panic attacks after one of her own "horrible" experiences. She swallowed hard and pushed the past back where it belonged. 'I'm so sorry,' she said softly.

'Oh, Nikki, it's not your fault. It's me. I'm just afraid to remember.'

Nikki got up, walked around the table and put her arm around her friend. *This really should be Andrew,* she thought. 'You shouldn't be on your own right now.'

'I know. But Andrew's job is so demanding.'

Bugger Andrew! 'Would you like me to talk to him for you? If he thinks a police officer is taking you seriously, maybe he'll climb out of his computer for a moment and see the real world.'

Helen's eyes brimmed with tears. 'Would you? I know he loves me, Nikki, but sometimes he's just on a different planet. He's always had to struggle. And now, for the first time in years, his company has recognised his talents and actually backed that up with a solid pay cheque. He wants to make a difference, give us a good life together.' She smiled wanly at Nikki. 'You'll never believe this, but after all this time, he's asked me to marry him! I really shouldn't criticise him when he's making such an effort, and I know I probably sound selfish, but I just want him here with me.'

'Of course you do. So would I, if I were going through something like this.' Nikki sat back down. 'How about I make you a hot drink and maybe a sandwich? I'll stay with you until you feel a bit better.'

'I don't want anything to eat, thank you, Nikki, but please do stay for a while, if it's not holding you up?'

Nikki stayed for two hours, and endeavoured to keep the conversation light and away from talk of anything scary; like shadowy figures lurking in the dark. Then she looked at the clock and said, 'I suppose I'd better go. I have something of a difficult task to carry out tomorrow, and I get the feeling that I'll need my wits about me. When's Andrew due back?'

'Around eleven.'

'Okay, I'll ring him then, if it's not too late?'

'Oh no, that would be fine, he's a real night owl. Thank you, Nikki, and please, can you keep it just between us regarding the engagement? It's under wraps for the present.'

'Of course,'

'And don't give him too much of a hard time, will you? He's a good man and he means well.'

Well, actually, Helen, he's acting like an arsehole, and I might just tell him exactly what I think about his stinking priorities. 'Trust me, Helen. I'm a copper.'

* * *

As Nikki drove home she wondered whether it would be a good idea if Helen saw her neurologist again. A slight shiver moved between her shoulders when she remembered those awful days after the Blackmoor Cross crash. Days when it had been touch and go whether Helen would live. Then, when they knew that she would survive, their immediate relief had been replaced by the terrible concern that she would be brain-damaged. Other than the kind of damage her own lovely daughter had suffered, Nikki didn't know too much about head trauma. She did know several police officers who'd had their lives wrecked by psychological problems following serious head injuries. She quietly prayed that this was not what was happening to Helen.

Perhaps she should moderate her planned conversation with Andrew. Maybe a bollocking wasn't the way to go. She of all people should understand how a job can take over everything. Much as she'd like to give him a real Galena-style tongue-lashing, the concerned friend would probably be the most effective option. Then again, perhaps she'd just play it by ear.

Nikki unlocked the door to Cloud Cottage Farm and felt warmth surround her. She hung up her jacket, flung her bag on a chair and wandered through to the kitchen. From the window she could see across the fen to where Joseph lived. The lights were still on in Knot Cottage. She went to the fridge and took out an opened bottle of Sancerre and poured herself a glass, then took it through to the lounge.

Joseph answered the phone on the second ring. 'Home at last?'

'Mmm, but far from happy. Helen should not have to cope with these blasted flashbacks on her own, it's not fair.'

'And are you going to be the one to tell Andrew?'

Nikki glanced at the clock on the mantelpiece, 'In about thirty minutes.'

'I'll set up a no-go zone around Cloud Fen, shall I?'

'Not a bad idea. Thing is, I don't want to lose it and make things worse.'

Joseph exhaled. 'Tough one. He clearly needs to be told, but half the time he's away with the fairies. I'm sure he doesn't intentionally want to hurt her, but he's on a completely different wavelength.' He paused, 'Have you eaten tonight?'

Nikki had to stop and think. 'Uh, no, and it's getting too late to start cooking now.'

'You never cook, Nikki Galena. All the food in your kitchen comes with microwave instructions printed on it, is that not right?'

'No! Well, maybe, although I do cook a rather good omelette,' she added huffily.

'Whisking up an egg does not constitute cooking. Now go look in your fridge. I've left you a salad Nicoise with some cling film over it. It should go nicely with the glass of Sancerre that is clasped tightly in your right hand.'

'Can you see through walls?'

'Now that would be useful in our line of business. Go eat, then phone Andrew. You can fill me in on how it goes at work tomorrow. Night.'

'Thank you for the food, Joseph, and goodnight to you too.'

Nikki ate, drained her wine glass, then with a long intake of breath, picked up the phone again. *Here goes nothing*, she thought.

Andrew sounded surprised to hear her voice, and Nikki was relieved that Helen had had the sense not to warn him to expect her call.

'It was great to see you the other night, Nikki. Has Joseph mentioned anything about that fantastic piece of kit I found for him? It's a diamond of a package, it could—'

'Yes, I know, revolutionise the national police computer system, and I'm sure he'll talk to you about it again, but that's not why I've rung you. Look, I know it's late, but the fact is that I'm really worried about Helen.'

'What do you mean, worried?' He sounded genuinely puzzled.

'She's frightened, Andrew. She thinks someone is following her and I don't think you are taking it seriously enough.'

Andrew stifled a cough. 'Eh, well, yes, but she's never actually seen anyone, has she? She's just stressed out, Nikki, with the clinic opening and all that. She's exhausted.'

'And do you believe that being tired has triggered the flashbacks too?' Nikki fought to remain civil.

'I . . . I don't know. Maybe?'

'And the memories? They have only just started to surface, haven't they?' In the silence that followed Nikki could visualise Andrew's craggy, handsome face, screwing up in confusion. 'She needs you right now, Andrew. Hell, I know I can't lecture you on the dangers of letting your career ruin your home life, but when I said she was frightened, I meant it. She's terrified. And fear escalates when you are alone.'

'You really are concerned about her, aren't you?'

Hallelujah! Light dawns! 'Very much so.'

She heard him exhale loudly. 'Right, well, I'll ring up and get the locks changed. A friend of mine will sort that for me.'

It's a start, thought Nikki, *but she needs more from you.*

'And I'll look into getting a security camera for the front and back entrances. That would give her some peace of mind, wouldn't it?'

'Good idea, Andrew, and your technology is a great help, but do you know, I think she'd appreciate you taking a few days off even more. Like, had you thought of just being around for her?'

This time the silence was heavy. 'Things are . . . are rather awkward for me right now. *Of course* I want to be with her, but I have to take call-outs. Anyway, I'll get the security sorted first thing tomorrow, I promise.'

Nikki knew that other than driving over and nailing him to the floor, it was the best she'd get from Andrew tonight. 'Okay, but while you are sorting those locks, I think you should think about whether Helen should go see her neurologist again, just to keep him in the picture. He needs to know about these anomalies.'

'Bloody hell, Nikki! Helen's been doing so well. She's just a bit stressed over the clinic opening, that's all. I don't want to overreact and frighten her even more.'

Nikki thought that Andrew wouldn't overreact if his trousers were on fire, and right now she was talking to the proverbial brick wall. 'Well, I'm sure you'll do the right thing, Andrew. Give Helen my love. I have to go.'

She replaced the receiver, rubbed hard at her tired eyes and muttered, 'He's a sweet guy, but he's also such a wanker! If anyone is going to help that woman, it will have to be me.'

CHAPTER FOUR

The morning mist had still not cleared the fields as Joseph made his way to work. It was one of those days when he felt eternally grateful that he lived on Cloud Fen, and that Greenborough police station was only fifteen peaceful minutes' drive from home.

A silvery, watery sun was staining the steel-grey sky and lighting up the hazy landscape. A heron flew silently across the lane ahead of him and he slowed down to watch its graceful flight towards the river. Sometimes this odd water-world in which he found himself seemed almost unreal, a fantasy film set, or a dreamscape. He would never have believed that he could feel so at home here, but he did. He had lived all over. In towns, in cities, in army camps, in the desert and in the forest, but that had all been travelling, exploring and working. The fens had become home. For the first time in many years, Joseph had a sense of belonging, and he liked it.

He negotiated a tight bend and smiled smugly to himself as he heard the travel announcer on the radio describe a four-junction tailback on the M25. Yes, living on the marshes had its merits, and this wonderful drive to work was one of them.

He yawned and wondered what the day would bring. Nikki must have left early as her car had gone when he drove past Cloud Cottage Farm. He hoped it had nothing to do with Helen Brook and her mysterious, and possibly imaginary, stalker. His calm expression gave way to a worried frown. Something told him that Helen's fears were real. After all, Nikki was good at reading people, and if she was concerned about her friend, then he should be too. He decided that if the day turned out to be fairly quiet, he would suggest they took an hour out and went for a stroll around Helen's garden and maybe that of the next-door neighbour. Peeping Toms often left tell-tale signs where they had hidden themselves. It would be worth looking for footprints, cigarette ends, sweet wrappers, broken branches, anything to prove that someone had been where they shouldn't have been. Although it would confirm Helen's worst fears, it would also confirm she wasn't imagining it all. And, he thought almost angrily, perhaps it would make Andrew sit up and take notice.

As Joseph drove towards the main road to Greenborough he marvelled that for once he wasn't agonising in some way or another over his daughter Tamsin, or his ex-wife, or Nikki Galena. It seemed that for the past few years, the people he cared about most had been intent on causing him as much angst as possible, but suddenly all was quiet. Tamsin had moved back to England and taken a conservationist job working as a project manager in Woodland Creation outside Cambridge. Joseph smiled. It was good to have her around, even if she did spend most of her available free time with PC Niall Farrow. His smiled widened. Now that was really something. Tamsin Easter going out with a police officer! He could only guess what her mother was thinking. He chuckled softly. But then Laura was pretty busy herself at present, settling into a permanent position with the WHO in Geneva. And Nikki? Well, he guessed they had reached a plateau in their relationship, and while many people questioned it, it worked for them. They looked out for each other, as colleagues, neighbours and friends. Joseph knew that wouldn't last forever, someone would come along one day, either into Nikki's life or his, and the whole thing would change. But for now, what they had together was enough. In fact, it was fine. They had both suffered broken marriages and disastrous affairs, so for them the status quo was practically domestic bliss.

So right now he could afford to worry about someone else. Someone like Helen Brook. As he drove through the security gates and into the station car park, he decided that if they were busy, he'd still make it a priority to make a trip to the Westland Waterway, even if he had to do it in his lunch break. Helen deserved some answers.

* * *

Cat sat opposite Nikki and chewed ferociously on her bottom lip. She wasn't taking the news about Eric Barnes particularly well. In fact she was heading for melt-down.

'Why us, boss?' she asked for the third time. 'The man's a liability.'

Nikki exhaled. 'I know, but I really do not have any say in it, Cat. I'll try to keep you two apart as much as possible, but if the job demands it, you'll simply have to work together.'

Absent-mindedly, Cat touched the scar that ran down the side of her face. Nikki had noticed that she did this when she was upset or thinking hard. The surgeons had done a brilliant job after she was injured on duty, but there was still a long uneven line from her eyebrow down to her jaw. 'Maybe I could take some leave?'

'You feel that strongly about working with him?' Nikki looked at her shrewdly. 'What exactly happened between you two?'

Cat sighed loudly. 'I'd rather not go into it, ma'am.' She pulled a face. 'Let's just say that he has a problem with women. I don't think anyone ever explained to him about gender equality in the workplace.'

'Then he's going to love having me as a boss, isn't he? DI Gill Mercer is a pussycat compared to me, and even she had to throw him out of the playground.' She gave Cat a tired smile. 'Stick it out, kid, it's not forever. The team needs you. *I* need you. And your lovely old mate Dave is back today, hernia all repaired. He really will need you.'

'I know,' Cat grumbled. 'It's people like Dave who make the team what it is, not loners like Eric.' She stopped and thought for a moment, then added, 'But yeah, thinking about it, why should he push me out? This is *my* team, not his.' She looked at Nikki, her old determination returning. 'Sorry, boss. I had a bit of a wobble there, all better now.' Her grin was back, 'But if he steps out of line, I might just have to do him some damage. Okay with you?'

Nikki was relieved at Cat's turnaround. 'If he steps out of line you'll have to fight me to get at him first, and that's a promise. But seriously, Cat, he is here to learn something. Gold Braid wants him reined in and hobbled, and it's my job to do that. Don't give him any ammunition or he'll use it on you. I want to go home each night with unruffled feathers and dream sweet dreams, all right?'

'I'll be a perfect angel, ma'am.' She smiled angelically, and added, 'While I'm counting off the days until he goes.'

Nikki was about to reply when her door opened and Joseph stuck his head in. 'Thought you'd want to know that Dave's here. I'm gathering up the Welcome Back party.'

'Brilliant. We are finished here anyway.' Nikki touched Cat's shoulder and whispered, 'I mean it about the ammunition. Just keep your cool and don't rise to the bait, okay? I know you can do it.'

Cat nodded. 'Got it, ma'am. Just call me Frosty.'

* * *

At ten o'clock, Helen was halfway through doing an essential oils order for the new clinic, when the phone rang. 'Newlands Clinic, how can I help you?'

The phone crackled for a minute, then went dead. She stared at the handset, then switched it off and returned to her list. She needed Melissa, Chamomile Roman, Clary sage, Tea-tree, Eucalyptus . . .

It rang again. This time Helen felt a tingle of anxiety as she answered, a feeling that intensified when she heard the howl of a disconnected line, followed by silence. This time she punched 1471, only to hear that the caller had withheld their number. She replaced the handset. 'Andrew? Where are you?'

There was no answer. Mild anxiety escalated to something else. 'Andrew!' Helen hurried out of the treatment room and climbed the stairs to the lounge. It was empty. The kitchen and bathroom were the same. But he'd been on the phone to the locksmith just before she went to place her order, so where was he? She limped across to the window, just in time to see him coming through the back gate, his coat pulled up around his chin and his mobile phone clamped tightly to his ear. Relief and concern flooded through her as she waited for him to come inside.

'Cold out there, sweetheart.' He hung his coat in the hall cupboard, then turned and looked at her, 'Hey! You look awful! Whatever's the matter?'

'What were you doing, Andrew? Why were you outside?'

He stared at her blankly. 'Checking that jungle that our neighbour laughingly calls a garden. You could hide an elephant in there and no one would know.' He blinked a few times. 'Why?'

'I had two anonymous calls, and I couldn't find you.'

He hurried across and put his arms around her. 'When, babe?'

'Just now.'

He frowned, 'Like dirty calls? Heavy breathers?'

She shook her head against his chest. 'No, but there was someone there, I know it. Then it went dead.'

Andrew gently pushed her away and looked at her with undisguised compassion.

'You silly baby! You've been getting all upset over nothing. That was my office. They just caught me on my mobile while I was outside.'

'Are you sure?' Helen asked.

'Absolutely. One of our field agents needed to speak to me. She had a dodgy signal, nothing more sinister than that, I promise.'

Tears threatened to spill from her eyes, so she turned away. How could she be so overwrought over a missed call? What on earth was the matter with her?

Andrew placed his hands on her shoulders and gently drew her back against him. 'Look, why don't we forget what we were doing and go and chill out in front of the television? Let's watch a hammy film or some reruns of something funny, huh? I'll make a pot of coffee and we'll have a bit of "us" time until the locksmith gets here.'

Helen nodded mutely. A black cloud of depression was descending over her, and with it came a feeling that something was in motion. It was something that a few new locks would not stop. She wanted nothing more than to snuggle down on the couch with Andrew, but all the time she would be on edge, just waiting for the office to ring again, and Andrew would be gone.

This was ridiculous! She physically shook herself. This was helping no one.

'That would be lovely, darling. We don't get much down time together, so my order can wait. You make the drinks and I'll see what's on.'

During the second half hour of the Big Bang Theory, Andrew fell asleep, his arms still wrapped tightly around her, and Helen started channel hopping.

A kid's cartoon. A cookery programme. A search for crap in your attic. A police car chase. A war documentary. She paused there, listening to the monotone of the narrator. "The bombing continued throughout the night. Thousands of families were made homeless as the bombs rained down on the once beautiful city . . ."

The darkness crashed around her like a heavy suffocating blanket, and she fought for breath. Her nostrils were clogged with dust, and her chest felt as if every rib were broken. She coughed painfully.

'Is someone there?'

This time the voice was familiar to her, but again she couldn't speak.

'Hello? Are you hurt?'

From her resting place, half-covered by fallen debris, she knew exactly what he would say next.

'I'm sorry, I can't get to you. My legs are trapped. Are you badly hurt?'

She swallowed hard, and stuttered, 'I think I am. There's blood, and my legs, I can't feel them! I'm frightened, what hap—?'

'You're alive! That's what counts, and I don't know what happened.' There was the sound of movement and then a muffled curse, followed by, 'What's your name?'

'Helen," she groaned. The effort of talking was costing her dearly.

'Hello, Helen. I wish I could get to you.' There was another series of scrabbling sounds, then a small cry and more cursing. 'Talk to me, Helen. Tell me what you look like.'

'Fucking awful!' she managed.

The laugh was gentle. 'I didn't mean now, I mean normally. Are you blonde, brunette, or ginger maybe?'

She knew what he was doing, trying to keep her conscious, but she just wanted to close her eyes and sleep. 'Brown hair, brown eyes, broken legs, I think.' A small fall of loose rubble stopped her, and she began to cry.

'Keep still! The rescue services will get to us soon. Just try not to cause anything to move, okay?'

'Damn it! I can't move at all!' Her cry sounded slightly mad, even to her own ears.

'Sshh, it's all right. Listen, as soon as they get here, they'll sort you out. Just try to take some deep breaths and relax.'

'Who . . . ?' The tiredness overcame her. She heard him talking, but could not understand him. Just a few words here and there through the fuzzy state of bewilderment that she found herself in, then the pain became almost too much to bear.

'Helen! Helen! Talk to me!'

She struggled to keep her eyes open, and something like awareness crept back into her mind. 'Thank you, for being there for me.'

She heard a long sigh on the other side of the collapsed wall.

'Did you tell me your name?'

There was a long pause, and after a while she realised that it was not him, but the fact that she was still drifting in and out of consciousness.

'I'm losing you, Helen, aren't I?' The voice was soft and full of pain.

Her head throbbed and she could no longer answer him.

'I wish I could have helped you, but you are going to die too, just like her.'

Somehow she fought to hold on. Die? What was he saying? Somehow, despite all that had happened, she had never even considered the thought of dying. Sleep, yes, but dying? She strained to hear the man, whose voice was now little more than a whisper.

'You sound so nice, Helen, but you wouldn't like me if you knew me. You see, I've just left a woman in my bedroom. She's dead, and I killed her.'

Helen heard screaming. Terrified, agonising screams. Who was it?

'Helen! For God's sake, darling! It's me, it's Andrew. What on earth is wrong?'

As she realised what was happening, she burst into tears. The screams had been her own.

* * *

Nikki stared at the memo that her office manager, Sheila Robbins, had placed on her desk.

'They've pulled a body from the Westland River, ma'am.' Sheila raised her eyebrows. 'That's three in six months and all in the Halbeck area of town.'

'Gang-related again?' Nikki asked.

'Well, from the ID found on him, he has a name that I can't pronounce, and seems to have been involved with some Russian migrants that one of the other CID teams were interested in, so drugs or people smuggling would be my guess.'

It was an increasing worry for Greenborough. The impact of migration on local policing had been immense. Taskforces had been set up and extensive recommendations made. There were offices within her own police station that Nikki had never even set foot in, but she knew they were exclusively operating to produce facts and figures and intelligence about the effects of the large influx of migrant workers. She knew that old Greenborough folk didn't walk some of the streets at night, and that a chunk of their budget was taken up by translation costs. She knew that she was spending increasing amounts of time at 'Good Relations' public meetings, trying to find solutions to the challenges that population change had brought into her town. She also knew that the old market town and its hundreds of acres of farming land needed the migrant workers to survive, and most were hard-working, decent people. It was a double-edged sword.

'Am I needed at the scene?'

Sheila shook her head. 'The river retrieval unit has it under control. DI Mercer has taken the shout and she has a doctor there. The body should be on its way to the morgue fairly shortly. I just thought you should know.'

'Thanks, Sheila.'

The office manager returned to her desk, and Nikki glanced down at a daily paper that she had left behind. Greenborough had been named one of the worst crime spots in the country. *Great,* she thought. *Just great!*

It was tempting to ball up the rag and throw it in the bin, but she supposed she should see what the world was being told about her town. She picked it up, but her phone rang and she was temporarily saved.

'Whoa! Hold it, Andrew! Slow down. Now, have you called a doctor?'

She listened silently to his uncharacteristic outpouring. Finally he seemed to run out of steam. 'I should have listened to you, Nikki. I'm so sorry. Could you come, do you think? It's you she wants to talk to.'

'Keep her calm, Andrew. Tell her I'm on my way.'

Nikki grabbed her bag and called for Joseph. She kept her voice low. 'It's Helen. She's had some sort of traumatic flashback. Andrew is beside himself with worry. Are you free to come with me?'

He nodded quickly. 'We'll take my car. Let's go.'

CHAPTER FIVE

By the time Nikki and Joseph arrived, Helen was considerably calmer. Nikki noticed a slight tremor in her hands, but her voice was steady.

'It was a memory. No doubt about it. He was with me in that cellar. A man was with me. I recalled everything he said.'

'What triggered it?' asked Nikki.

'A history programme on the TV, about the bombing of Dresden.' She swallowed. 'One minute I was watching the screen, the next I was back in that cellar.'

'Well, that's an understandable trigger for a flashback. And where were you, Andrew?' Joseph asked.

'Right here on the sofa, my arm around Helen. I was exhausted and I went to sleep. I woke up to hear Helen screaming. She'd slipped down onto the floor and was shivering like it was twenty degrees below. She was terrified.' Andrew looked more disturbed than Helen. He sat fiddling with his hands, looking plaintively at Nikki and Joseph.

Nikki was looking at Helen. 'So what did this man say that has frightened you so much?'

Helen's lip quivered. 'He confessed to a murder. He must have thought I was dying, or maybe dead already, because he told me he'd killed a woman.' Her eyes widened. 'Nikki, do you understand me? He confessed to killing someone!'

Nikki remained calm. 'Did he tell you who he'd killed?'

'Just said a woman. He'd left her in their bedroom.'

'Did he tell you his name?'

'I think he did, but I can't recall everything. I was semi-conscious some of the time and often completely out of it.'

Nikki knew that when she and Joseph had scrambled down into that hellhole, Helen was almost unresponsive, and quite alone. She racked her brain for something constructive to say. 'Helen? On the phone, Andrew said something about you wanting me here officially. So, apart from being here as your friend, what is it you want me to do?' *Egg shells, or what?*

Helen's expression was difficult to read, but Nikki saw anger there. Through taut, thin lips she said, 'Don't you get it? I am reporting a murder. I want you to follow the procedures. I'm also telling you, *officially*, that one year later he has found out that I am still alive and he's bitterly regretting using that cellar as a confessional! He's out there, Nikki. He's watching me, and he's going to kill me.'

* * *

Outside, Joseph shook his head slowly from side to side. 'I'm sorry. Earlier I was convinced that she had a stalker, or at least a peeping Tom, but now I think Helen needs help, and not the kind that Greenborough Police has to offer.' He unlocked the car and they both flopped heavily into their seats.

'I don't understand it,' Nikki said. 'She made an almost miraculous recovery. Lord, you saw the state of her twelve months ago! She got on top of everything, even got herself back to work. Now she's a wreck.'

'Perhaps she never really addressed all the issues, and they're catching up on her.'

Nikki shook her head. 'No, I'm sure it's not that. You don't know her as well as I do. She's one of those people who just copes with things. Whatever life throws at her, she gets on with it. She's very much like you, all beautifully balanced and calm. She used to teach yoga and meditation before she specialised in aromatherapy. I'm sure it's this thing about someone following her that's sent her off the rails. She nearly bit my head off in there, and that's not Helen. All this is so out of character, but whatever, she really believes what she just told us.'

'So, do you think it's some kind of mental aberration, or a real memory?'

'I don't know, but she's not an idiot. If she thinks she is being watched, then that's good enough for me. We are too close to all this to think clearly. What would we do if a member of the public, someone unknown to us, made a serious claim?'

'We'd check it out.'

'Exactly. So that's what we'll do. We start at the beginning, at the crash site. And we also see if anyone else suspects a prowler in the area of the Westland Waterway.'

Joseph took a deep breath. 'You're right. It's certainly worth making some enquiries. I'll get Dave to check the day book on the computer when we get back, see if anyone else has reported seeing anything suspicious in her area recently. And Cat, or our new boy, can fish out the old accident reports on the crash.' He looked across at her. 'Yes, this is the way to go. Study the facts.'

Nikki nodded as she pulled her seatbelt across her. 'After what Helen's been through, she deserves us to do our job properly. So I'm going to try to forget that she's my friend and inject a bit of clarity into my thinking. Back to basics, Joseph.'

'Back to basics, ma'am.'

* * *

Cat had promised the boss that she would be on her best behaviour, and she was really making an effort, but Eric Barnes' veiled sarcasm was really getting to her. Poor old

Dave. Though he was clearly more than happy to be back at work, he seemed less than keen on being a peace-keeper in the middle of a war zone. Cat could see he was valiantly trying to hold things together, but the atmosphere in the CID room was not exactly warm and amicable.

Dave looked at them. 'Okay, guys. We've got some work to do, and as I'm office-bound, the boss has asked me to delegate.' He handed them each a sheet of paper. 'Cat, would you take a fresh look at the Blackmoor Cross incident, particularly any mention of the cellar in which Helen Brook was found.' He turned to Eric. 'And would you check the day log and see if anyone has reported anything out of the ordinary in the area of Westland Waterway.'

Cat was glad of something to do that did not involve talking to Eric, and buckled down immediately.

The accident had been one of the worst that Greenborough had ever suffered. Staring at the screen immediately took her back to the horror of that particular RTC. Even the bland "official speak" of the reports failed to hide the chaos that the lorry had caused, or the devastation to lives and families. The driver of the articulated vehicle had suffered a massive heart attack and the coroner stated that he was dead before the lorry finally came to rest. Cold comfort for the bereaved, she thought. Cat scanned a list of names but decided that wasn't what she was looking for. She exited the window, brought up another, and found herself looking at a crash investigator's report. 'Uh-oh!'

Dave looked up from his screen. 'Found something?'

'I certainly have. Listen, this is referring to the cellar area, where the DI and Sergeant Easter found Helen Brook. It talks all about her, and the location and position she was in, blah, blah.' She scrolled down the screen. 'This is it: "To the rear of the basement area there was further blood evidence. Two smears of blood, indicating that the injured party had attempted to move from one spot to another. This was at first believed to be that of the only casualty found in that sector, but later proved to be from an unknown source. DNA testing showed it to be male. No match was found to any of the other victims. (A record is on file of blood group and DNA fingerprint)." So it looks like Helen Brook might be right about that part of the story. Perhaps she's right about being followed as well.'

'Which ties in with something I've just found,' Eric added. 'A neighbour of Miss Brook reported someone hanging around in their back garden last week.'

Dave slowly stood up. 'Then I think it's time to go find the boss.'

* * *

Eric went off with a uniform to check about the intruder, and Cat was left alone in the office, wondering how things were going to pan out over the next few weeks. She loved the team like a family, but their new addition had altered the dynamic, and not for the better. She pulled a face and sighed. She'd said she'd try to make it work, but already she knew it wasn't going to be easy. She removed a sheet from her printer and scanned the data morosely.

'Okay, Cat. Either you are reading your P45, or an obituary. Which is it?'

She looked up to see Dave perching himself carefully on the edge of her desk. 'My friend, I'm sorry but I really don't feel like me anymore.'

Dave tilted his head to one side and frowned. 'So what's worrying you? Is it Eric Barnes' charismatic appearance as one of the team?'

Cat nodded, but she didn't want to offload her problems onto her old mate immediately on his return from sick leave.

'Well, for what it's worth, I happen to think he's an arsehole too.'

Cat sat back and grinned at Dave. It was so unlike Dave Harris to bad-mouth anyone that it almost made her laugh. Barnes must be a right piece of work to upset him. 'So what's he done to rattle your cage, Davey-boy?'

'Nothing in particular, he's just a brown nose. Oh yes, and I hear that he loves to belittle the DI at every available opportunity. Not that he's ever done it in my company, but you can imagine how pleased that kind of rumour makes me.'

'So? He hates women in command? Most male coppers do, if they're honest.' She threw him an apologetic smile. 'Not you, of course.'

Dave's face took on an unnaturally hard expression. 'Well, I've been around for long enough to know how tough it's been for the boss. She has had to work twice as hard as any bloke to get where she is now, and I admire her for it. Barnes has a big mouth and all that comes out of it is bigoted crap.' He paused, tilted his head to one side and asked, 'So what about you, Cat? Tell me to mind my own business if you want, but I get the feeling it goes considerably deeper.'

Cat had no intention of baring her soul, not even to her lovely Dave, but she did say, 'It's just something that got out of hand, and now the situation is beyond salvaging. Our paths crossed on a rape case, and I thought his handling of it was unforgivably insensitive.' She took a long, deep breath. 'If you really want to know, Dave, I felt disillusioned. Is he the new breed of officer coming up through the ranks?'

'I know what you mean, but if ever I feel like that I think of young PC Niall Farrow, and that restores my faith in the new ones. Eric is a one-off, I'm sure of that. Admittedly he's also intelligent, ambitious, devious, and he'll probably make superintendent long before you, but he'll never be liked by anyone, up or down the ladder.'

Cat was forced to smile. 'Thanks for that. It's nice to know I have an ally.'

'One more thing — and this should make you smile.' Dave moved closer and whispered, 'I overheard a conversation in the mess room, just prior to his leaving DI Mercer's team, and he said that he had no intention of staying in a hick town like Greenborough for long. He was just biding his time before jumping on the fast-track to the top. So just hang on in there, Cat. I bet you a year's overtime that EB will be just a bad memory in a month or so.'

Cat raised an eyebrow. She knew now that she really had to bite the bullet and rise above Eric's caustic remarks. Hard work on her part, and a good result on this case would impress the guv'nor, and Eric could bloody well fast-track out of it.

For the first time, Cat felt positive. She squeezed Dave's arm. 'Thanks for that. I feel a whole lot better. So, what's next?'

Dave patted her hand. 'Excellent. The DI and Sergeant Easter will be out in a moment, and we'll get on with finding out what this Helen Brook thing is all about.'

CHAPTER SIX

Nikki looked at her team earnestly. 'I've just had a meeting with Superintendent Woodhall. He's made it clear that peeping Toms are not CID business. It's hardly even a police matter, but he sees where we are coming from with this rather worrying confession thing. I assured him that if it were anyone else, I'd be sceptical too, but I know her and she's no flake. We have to admit that it could be some kind of delayed reaction to the trauma, and the blood could have come from anyone involved in that accident. But that doesn't feel right, and I'm admitting to you that I have a very bad feeling about this.' Actually it was more like a slimy worm squirming through her gut. 'So he's given us the go-ahead to investigate it properly. We'll take it from the top, and I want you all to be aware that Helen Brook could well be in grave danger. If someone did confess to killing a woman, in the belief that Helen was dying, he could now be very worried and very dangerous indeed.'

'So we take the threat seriously, even though it's most likely some kind of hallucination brought on by pain and being half-dead at the time?'

Eric Barnes' tone held just a hint of sarcasm, but it was enough to make Nikki bristle. She fixed him with a glacial stare. 'Do I need to repeat myself, DC Barnes? I do hope not.' She turned to Dave and her expression softened. 'Sort out who does what for me, Dave. You know what we need to check.'

Dave nodded. 'No problem, ma'am. Will you go to see Ms Brook personally? To tell her that we are formally investigating her claim?'

Nikki nodded. 'Yes, I've got a few things to tie up, then Joseph and I will give her the good news. Okay, that's all for now, so off you go.'

* * *

Helen wandered around the garden room, desperately looking for some sense of normality in her life. Everything she cherished suddenly held either emptiness, or a sinister connotation. She picked up a black onyx bowl containing a handful of shimmering white Indian moonstones. She turned them gently, watching the light catch fluorescent patches of turquoise, like trapped butterfly wings in the gemstones, and wondered what was happening to her.

She had almost screamed at Nikki. She felt terrible about it, but she couldn't help herself.

The house phone's sudden ring made her jump and her heart began to race as she waited for Andrew to pick up the extension. She looked down and saw that her hands were shaking.

'It's okay, babe. It's for me,' Andrew called down the stairs.

Relief flooded through her. She still believed that those earlier calls had been the man who was following her, checking on her, seeing if she were at home. Thank God that Andrew was there with her, and the house had new security locks fitted.

She sank down into one of the two small sofas and wondered if she should call Nikki and apologise for her rudeness. Nikki was looking out for her, and she'd repaid her by behaving like a mad woman.

As she sat in the quiet and tried to rehearse what she would say, Andrew came down the stairs. She looked up and smiled, but his face was etched with worry.

'Look, darling, please don't get upset, but I have to go into the office for an hour or two.' He was obviously pained by seeing her immediate distress, but he was still prepared to go. 'I won't be long, I promise. I'll be back by late evening. That was Teresa. She said there is a problem with one of our biggest Swiss accounts. She can't handle it alone.'

Anxiety almost choked her. 'You are going now? Oh please, Andrew. Don't leave me!'

He looked at her helplessly. 'The sooner I go, the sooner I'll get back. I wouldn't go at all if it were anything other than critical. You know that, Helen, don't you?'

If she had not been so frightened, she would have felt sorry for him. His face was a picture of misery. He was clearly torn between her and his precious bloody job.

'You promise you'll be back tonight?'

'I swear.'

It would have to do, she supposed. She could not make her feelings any more obvious. She swallowed back a sob and shrugged.

He sat down beside her and hugged her. 'I love you, Helen. It might not seem that I do, but I love you with all my heart.' He released her, kissed her on the lips, then stood up and hurried from the room. A few moments later he returned, jacket over his shoulder and his attaché case gripped tightly under his arm.

'Make sure your mobile is charged up, darling. I'll use that, then you won't have to answer the house phone, alright?' He came over and kissed her again. 'And while I'm away I want you to consider something. When this thing with Zurich is sorted, I think we should go away. Not just a holiday. I'm thinking about us going traveling for a while — six months, maybe a year? I know you've always wanted to see India, and I'd like to find some of my distant relatives in New Zealand. Now you're able to walk again, it could be the right time to do it. What do you think?'

Helen closed her eyes. 'I don't understand you, Andrew! What about all this? What about Newlands? This is what I've worked for all my life. I can't just up and walk away from it. And your bloody job! You finally got your promotion that means more to you than anything, then suddenly you want to jack it in?' She threw up her hands.

'Oh, I know it sounds stupid, Helen. What about a really long break, then? I'm sure that SKS would allow me a sabbatical, and you desperately need a holiday. We could even get married abroad. Then when you're all relaxed again, you can devote every hour you want to the clinic. It's all prepared, isn't it? You could come back with a new lease of life and give it your all.'

Helen stared at him. He looked like some overgrown schoolboy, tripping over his tongue as he made excuses for a broken window.

He glanced at the clock. 'Look, I have to go. Just promise me you'll think about it, okay? And you know I love you, don't you? Bye, sweetheart. I'll ring you later.'

As he turned to go, she held onto him. The strength of her grip was almost frightening.

'Just get home. That's all I want.'

Before his BMW had left the drive, Helen picked up the phone and dialled Nikki's number.

* * *

'He's done what!' Nikki clamped her jaw shut before she said something that might upset her friend. Andrew was dead meat. She'd made a serious error of judgement by not roasting his balls the first time around. 'That guy is something else, but I don't have to tell you that, do I?'

'Hardly.'

'Listen, why not come and stay with me tonight? I'll pick you up when I finish.'

'I appreciate the offer, Nikki, but he swore to me that he'd be back tonight. I'll give him one chance. If he's not home by eleven thirty, can I call you?'

'Of course you can, but make that eleven.' She stopped for a moment, not sure how to tell her friend what she had discovered. 'Listen, Helen, I don't want you to worry. This is actually encouraging news. One of your neighbours reported seeing someone hanging around the other night, which does rather back up your suspicion about someone watching the property.'

Helen's relief flooded down the phone line like a physical thing. 'Thank you for that, Nikki! I was starting to doubt my sanity! I know it's the last thing I need, but thank God someone else has seen him at last.'

'It's also given me a good reason to get uniform to keep an eye on you. Don't be surprised to see a police car outside, okay?'

'Oh, that's such a relief! Especially after the anonymous calls earlier. Andrew said they were business calls for him, and I know I told him to give this number to his clients, but I really don't think that's the case. I'm certain someone was on the other end, just listening to me.'

Nikki stiffened. 'Did you do 1471?'

'It registered Caller Withheld.'

'You do know that we can trace calls, don't you? If it happens again, ring us.'

'I'm giving Andrew the benefit of the doubt, Nikki, just in case I'm being paranoid. But if it happens again, I'll ring you immediately.'

'You'd better, Helen Brook, or you'll have me to deal with. While you're on the line, I was wondering about the people who come to you for treatments or classes. What are they like?'

Nikki heard a long intake of breath. 'They're mainly people in pain, I suppose, but also those who have lost their faith in allopathic medicine, or maybe have been let down by their doctors. People who hate drugs, who are stressed, people who are looking for something, maybe something more spiritual and less material than they find in their day-to-day lives. Honestly, the list is endless.'

'So, sometimes people turn to complementary medicine when all else fails?'

'Very often.'

'And if you are able to help them, do any of them become dependent on you? I mean, like . . . worship is perhaps the wrong word, but you know what I'm getting at, don't you?'

Helen's voice became stronger and more confident. She was on home ground now, talking about the vocation that she loved. 'When we are dealing with needy people, we offer them a little adage, "Never fall in love with your mother or your therapist." If you don't make your position very clear, clients can use you as a crutch. We try very hard to make sure that they don't develop an unhealthy attachment or just become too reliant on us. We like to make the client believe that healing comes from within, and their return to good health ultimately is in their own hands.'

Nikki thought hard, then said, 'Just for one moment, Helen, let's consider that you are suffering from two separate problems. The memories concerning the man who you believe was trapped with you,' she purposely omitted to tell her about the blood evidence found in the cellar, 'and someone watching or following you. It could be one of your patients following you, and nothing to do with the accident at all, just someone who has not quite caught on to the fact that he shouldn't fall for his therapist.'

Helen's voice was incredulous. 'You mean I have a stalker? I honestly can't see that. I may not be quite a Quasimodo, but when I look in the mirror, I sure don't see a supermodel looking back!'

'He might not want a supermodel, just a very attractive woman, and I can assure you, that's the category I'd put you in.'

'Thank you, but you've obviously forgotten about the limp, and . . .' As she spoke, Nikki could almost see her gently fingering the uneven purple-ish line of scarring that ran across her forehead and disappeared into her hairline.

'Battle scars are sometimes very appealing, you know.'

'Oh yes! If you happen to be starring in a Tarantino movie! But I'm a Greenborough aromatherapist, for heaven's sake!'

Nikki laughed. 'I hear what you're saying, but don't discount the fact that someone may have a major crush on you. It's not impossible. Didn't Joseph tell me something about a blog dedicated to you?'

'Oh Lord, don't remind me! A grateful client, who also happened to be a major social networking fan. He thought he needed to tell the world how I'd helped him through a difficult patch. But what about the memory? It *was* a memory, Nikki.'

'Let's go after the part we can actually do something about, i.e. the man who's watching you. If we find a connection when we catch him, then fine. If not, we'll take it from there, okay? And don't forget there will be a couple of our men with you tonight. They may even take a look around that back garden area, so don't be concerned, okay?' Nikki saw Joseph's head appear around her door. 'I've got to go now, but if anything else happens, we'll get your telephone monitored. You take care, and ring me if it gets late and you're worried.'

As Nikki replaced the phone she was overwhelmed by anger at Andrew's callousness. How can you say you love someone, then leave them when they need you most? Nikki frowned. She thought of all the times she had raced off to work, when maybe she should have spent more time with Hannah or her dad. She believed that she had done her best, but now they had both gone it didn't seem enough, and she knew that she would always live with a shadow of guilt darkening their memories.

Joseph was looking concerned. 'That's a serious face.'

She forced a smile. 'Just a maudlin moment. Take no notice. Sit down for a minute. I just need to beg a favour from uniform, then I'm all yours.'

A few moments later she replaced the handset, sat back and regarded Joseph. 'I'm worried sick about Helen. That sod of a boyfriend has left her on her own while he goes and plays with his hard drives.'

Joseph pulled a face. 'That young man really needs a lecture on priorities. Techies are a different breed. I swear they come from another planet. But maybe it's time you pointed out a few home truths, in your own inimitable style.'

'My thoughts precisely,' she growled.

Joseph scratched his head thoughtfully. 'But meanwhile, I've been thinking about Helen's snooper. I wonder if this person who is watching her has got anything to do with that article in the local paper a couple of weeks back.'

Nikki frowned, then slapped her hand against her head. 'Of course! The one on survivors! Yes! Let's suppose for a moment that Helen is right about a man being with her, and that the man really did confess to killing someone. That article may have alerted him to the fact that she hadn't dieD as he'd supposed, that she'd survived, and might be able to identify him in some way.'

'Phew!' Joseph looked concerned. 'That's one nasty supposition. I was only thinking along the lines of a stalker, or someone who idolised her.'

'Maybe, but I really don't like the timing, do you? Someone starts watching her almost immediately after a paper prints a story about her. I wonder why Helen never thought about that.'

'Got enough on her plate by the sound of it, and sometimes they do the research months before it comes out. Perhaps she just forgot.'

'Maybe, but I'd have thought she would have been inundated with mail afterwards. It was a pretty emotive article, as I remember. People are often moved to write to the survivors, you know, send their respects, share their own stories. Whatever, ring the paper and get hold of a copy of that feature. I want to refresh myself as to what exactly was said about Helen. Perhaps I should mention it to her.'

Joseph looked doubtful. 'And frighten the life out of her? You would be confirming her worst fears, and what if it's all baloney anyway?' He ran his hand through his hair. 'Why don't we take her client base to bits? You could well be right about someone having a serious crush on her.'

'Okay.' She checked her watch. 'It's late. You better get on home now, but first thing tomorrow you start hunting male bunny boilers.' She yawned. 'And before I finish, I'd better double-check that everything is in place for that squad car on Westland Waterway tonight.'

* * *

Andrew sounded odd when he rang her.

'Any more calls, babe?'

'I put the house phone directly onto answerphone, and the only calls have been clients wanting to know about the opening date for the clinic.' She knew she sounded irritable, but it was almost eight o'clock. 'Are you on your way home yet?'

'Not quite, that's why I'm ringing now. This problem with the Swiss client is a monster. I will be home, Helen,' he added hurriedly. 'And it'll be before ten thirty, but the thing is . . .'

Helen knew this particular intonation, and felt a shiver of anxiety pass swiftly across her shoulder blades.

'. . . If I can't sort it out, I may have to fly to Zurich and tackle it on site.'

'Andrew! No! Please, just this once couldn't you get someone else to do it, and put me before your job?'

'Helen, I would if I could. Believe me, no one wants this problem to disappear more than I do, but I'm afraid the buck stops with me on this one. Teresa and I designed the system in question, and we're the only ones who can sort it.'

Helen went quiet. Their long relationship had always been something of a rollercoaster. Neither was afraid to say what they meant, or to throw the crockery around if it came to it. But this time she had no wish to scream at him, or slam down the phone. Her normal explosion of emotion never arrived. Instead she was swamped by a feeling of uselessness, which gave way to a dull acquiescence. Andrew was the only person in her life who could make her white-hot angry. He was the only one she ever fought with. Sometimes she wondered how a couple who cared so deeply could fight so, then she remembered that he was also the only one who could light a fire of passion in her heart. She bit her lip, but still said nothing. When it came down to his work, she would never win, even when some nameless man was waiting in the shadows to make her his next victim.

'Helen? Are you still there?' He sounded slightly surprised, as if he too had expected the usual tirade.

Her voice sounded unrecognisably cool and she said, 'Just get home, Andrew.' She slowly lowered the receiver and placed it carefully on its rest, before bursting into tears.

* * *

Helen stood at her lounge window and saw the police car parked a few doors away. She knew that they would remain there, unless an emergency called them away. Like the new locks, it should have been a relief, but without Andrew, she felt very alone and vulnerable. The police would be watching the river walk and the front of the house, but what about the back garden, and the wilderness beyond the wall? The two officers that had searched the area earlier had found nothing of interest, certainly nothing to indicate that the garden was being used as a nocturnal lookout point for spying on her, but that meant nothing. She had seen someone there, no doubt about that, and he could come back.

She wandered into the kitchen and listlessly opened the fridge. After staring into it for a few moments, she closed it again. With every minute that passed, she felt less like eating. Perhaps she should go and stay with Nikki. That would give Andrew something to think about.

As it got later, she toyed with the idea of inviting the two police officers inside. It would be bitterly cold in the car, here they would at least be comfortable. Come on, who was she kidding? Their wellbeing had nothing to do with why she wanted them there with her. She was scared. Scared of what was outside watching her, and even more scared of what was inside, in her head. She knew that the memories had not finished with her. This could be the tip of the iceberg, and she really did not want to know any more.

She walked back into the lounge and flopped into the reclining chair that faced out towards the river. It was the not knowing that scared her most. She took a deep breath. When Andrew, *if* Andrew, came home tonight, she would talk to him about an idea that she'd had. The idea of visiting a hypnotherapist, and being regressed back to the accident, to find out what had really happened in that cellar. To find the truth. It was a slightly frightening concept, but nothing could be worse than what she was going through right now.

For the third time since darkness had fallen, she got up and walked around the apartment checking the locks and the windows, but as she gripped the handle of the conservatory door, she saw something outside on the concrete paving. It was quite tiny, but big enough to glint brightly in the security lights. Her hand moved instinctively to her ears and she gently felt the lobes. One of the diamond stud earrings that Andrew had given her after the accident was missing.

For a moment she hesitated. The thought of leaving the security of the house terrified her. Her throat constricted and she felt a tremor of fear run through her as she contemplated venturing outside into the night.

This was stupid! She was not going to give into it. With grim determination, she unlocked the door, and hurried out onto the patio.

The cold hit her like a physical blow, and as she bent forward to pick up the earring, she was thrown back through time, and into that awful cellar.

'Is someone there?'

There was a rushing sound in her ears and blackness closed in around her.

* * *

When Helen came to, she was vaguely aware of being carried, but the all-consuming feeling was of bitter, bone-numbing cold. A voice that she recognised was calling to her, his tone full of fear and compassion.

'Helen, darling! It's me. It's Andrew. What on earth . . . ?' With difficulty, he carried her into the house and still holding her, kicked the door shut with one foot, then took her upstairs to the warmth of the lounge. She felt herself being lowered very gently onto the couch. 'Don't move. I'll get the duvet. My poor darling, you're absolutely frozen!'

A moment later he was wrapping her in the thick, soft cover and lying beside her, offering his own body warmth for heat and reassurance.

After a while the shivering began to ease and she managed to sit up. 'Andrew, it was another flashback. I . . .' Before she could finish, she heard the doorbell ring. 'Who . . . ?'

'Damn! I think it's the police. There was some sort of fracas going on when I drew up.' With an exasperated sigh, he placed a finger on her lips, 'You stay here. I'll go and see what's happening.'

As Andrew went into the hall, Helen groggily stood up and followed him. She needed to know if they had actually found her stalker.

'Mr Gregory?'

She stared over his shoulder. The policeman looked impossibly young, with a haircut just a step away from baldness. 'We've picked up a man, over there.' He indicated towards the river. 'He appeared to be watching the house and he fits the description of someone that your neighbour saw hanging around here a few days ago. He's not being exactly cooperative so we may sling him in the digger for an hour or two to cool off, then we'll have a little chat with him.' He replaced the cap that had been neatly tucked under his arm as he spoke. 'We just thought you'd both like to know.'

Helen tensed. 'I need to see him. I have to talk to him!'

Andrew reached out for her. 'Hey, you're going nowhere until you've rested for a while.'

The young constable looked at them suspiciously. 'Is everything all right?'

Andrew answered. 'Helen fainted earlier. She really needs to lie down.'

Close to anger, Helen pushed away from him and stared at the policeman. 'Have you really caught him? Can I see him, please? I really do have to talk to him. It's vital that I hear his voice!'

'Sorry, Miss Brook, that's not quite how it works. And, as Mr Gregory said, you don't look too well. Why don't you just leave him with us and go inside and get some sleep. He won't be bothering you any more tonight.'

Before she could reply, there was a cry and the sound of a scuffle coming from the direction of the police car. 'Harry! Get back here and help me with this little scrote, will you?'

As the young man turned on his heels and ran towards his partner, Helen saw her chance and slipped past Andrew. Before he could grab her, she was running down the path and into the street.

'Get your fucking hands off me, pig! I know my rights! You can't touch me! I ain't doing nothing wrong! I'll have you for assault, you fucking bastard!' The boy was writhing on the floor and calling the two officers everything he could summon up from his limited vocabulary.

Helen stopped in her tracks and stared at the foul-mouthed teenager. Andrew appeared behind her, and she felt his arm around her shoulders.

Disappointment coursed through her. 'It's not him,' she whispered. 'It's the wrong voice. He's not the one.'

CHAPTER SEVEN

'Blimey, ma'am! You're in early.' The desk sergeant looked up from his screen.

Nikki nodded ruefully. 'Anything interesting happen last night, Sarge?'

'Actually, yes. A couple of my lads pulled in your peeping Tom from Westland Waterway.'

'Really?' She looked at him intently. 'And?'

'Nothing, Inspector. Just some kid trying to get his leg over with a bit of posh totty from one of those big houses. The girl's parents had barred her from seeing him, so he waited over by the river walk or in the back garden for the girl to signal to him. Apparently she'd sneak off out to the summerhouse, then he'd creep in and they'd—'

'Thank you, Sergeant, I don't think I need to know any more. Main thing is, it has absolutely nothing to do with Helen Brook?'

'Nothing whatsoever. Which is good news, isn't it?'

Nikki took a long, deep breath. 'I'm not sure. Thank you anyway. I appreciate you being there. I owe you one.'

'No trouble, DI Galena. Any time.' Before returning to his computer he raised a hand in acknowledgement to the figure walking in through the front door. 'Morning, Joseph.

I had no idea CID had alarm clocks that even worked before eight o'clock.'

'Good morning, and up yours, Jonesy.' Joseph was carrying two coffees in polystyrene cups. 'Called in to the Café des Amis on the way in. I had hoped coffee and croissants would give us a good start to the day, but seeing your expression, perhaps I should go back for a large Scotch.'

She pushed open her office door and held it back for Joseph. 'They caught the trespasser, but it's not what I thought it would be.' She told him what had happened the night before. 'Of course I'm glad she wasn't being watched, but that leaves everything else looking a bit iffy, doesn't it? Perhaps I've been too eager to believe her, maybe she *is* suffering from some sort of post-traumatic episode.'

Joseph shrugged. 'I suppose if there is no stalker, it kind of puts a different slant on things, but even so, she was genuinely scared. What we witnessed the other night was no show.'

'I do not doubt that, Joseph, but maybe we need to rethink this a bit.' She flipped off the lid of her coffee and sipped it thoughtfully. 'When I spoke to her she told me she had seen this man in other places, like the Willows and the supermarket. Well, that would have nothing to do with this randy little git and his secret bunk up in the summerhouse, would it?'

'Absolutely not.' Joseph offered her a croissant. 'Do you think there could be two different men lurking out there on the riverbank?'

'It's possible.' Before she could say more, there was a knock on her door and DI Gill Mercer walked in.

'Sorry to interrupt, guys, but I've got a problem.'

'You too! Grab a perch and reveal all.'

Joseph pulled out another chair and the detective flopped down into it.

Gill Mercer was a petite woman with dark shoulder-length hair and a ready smile, but when it came to tackling crime, she was relentless. She gave Nikki an apologetic smile. 'How are you getting on with my cast-off? I'm really sorry about that. It certainly wasn't my idea that you get lumbered, but top brass has no intention of doing what I consider to be the right thing with that one.'

'Tied hands, or so I'm told.'

'Yeah, well, there should come a time when enough is enough. He's not cut out for this job.' She shook her head. 'Actually I'm not sure what he is cut out for.'

'He's intelligent, no doubt about that, but he has a problem all right.'

'Mmm, weighed down by a chip on his shoulder the size of Flamborough Head.' She cast a glance up at the clock. 'Sorry, this is not what I wanted to ask you about. The thing is, I'm up to my neck with work right now, and the super said I might be able to offload one of my investigations on to you?'

'Sure, we can run another case in tandem. Anything in particular?' Nikki silently hoped it wouldn't be too complex and take her away from Helen. Or Stephen Cox.

'It's that body that was found in the Westland River.' Gill shook her head. 'There's something—'

'Please don't say *fishy*,' interjected Joseph.

Gill gave a short laugh. 'Odd was my word of choice. It's not quite as straightforward as I believed. Could you take it over?'

Nikki nodded. 'No problem. Pass over everything you have so far and we'll deal with it.' She paused and sipped her coffee, then added, 'Er, exactly what did you mean by *odd*?'

Gill puffed out her cheeks and drew in a long breath. 'Maybe it's nothing, but when we went to break the news to the deceased's wife, she was not there. Neither were any of the family, and they haven't been back since. A neighbour seemed to think that they all went off together in a car in the dead of night, but he reckoned the husband was with them.' She gave Nikki a puzzled look. 'We haven't had time to delve deeper and the forensics are not back yet, but the timing of their hurried departure doesn't seem to fit with how long the body may have been in the water.'

'As you say, that's odd.'

Gill stood up. 'And it's all yours. Thanks. I will return the favour, I promise.'

'You wouldn't like Eric Barnes back, would you?'

'Ah, now there I draw the line, and it's clearly time to disappear. *Au revoir, mes amis!*'

Joseph raised a hand to the retreating figure, then turned to Nikki, 'Well, that doesn't sound too taxing. Shall I get Dave to start the ball rolling?'

Nikki thought. 'I'm going to suggest that you do the initial organising, and that you use Dave and Cat on the body in the river. I'll take Eric Barnes with me on Helen's problem.'

'Is that wise, ma'am? He's not exactly tactful at the best of times, and even *we* don't really know what we are dealing with.'

'Apparently it's down to me to kick him into shape, so I can hardly farm him out to someone else, can I? And anyway, I promised Cat I'd do my best to keep them apart. She's making an effort, I can see that. So if they are on different cases, I'll be doing my bit for entente cordiale. Not that I'm looking forward to taking him to see Helen. We'll just have to pray that he's enough of a professional to keep his opinions to himself.'

Joseph pulled a face. 'Good luck with that one, ma'am. I'll keep you updated on what we find out with DI Mercer's case.'

As the door closed, her phone rang.

'Nikki?'

'Hi there, Helen, how are you doing? Sleep better, knowing that your peeping Tom has had his collar felt?'

'Hardly.' Nikki could hardly hear her. Helen sounded like someone fighting a migraine and barely coping with the sound of their own voice. 'Andrew's gone to Switzerland. He left early this morning. And as soon as he'd gone, I had another flashback.'

Nikki's heart sank. Her friend should be talking to a doctor, not a detective.

But Helen was still talking. 'I've remembered more, Nikki, a lot more. I've even remembered his name.'

'His name? Are you sure?'

'Paul. His name was Paul, and the woman he killed? She was his wife.' Helen made a small choking sound. 'I'm sorry to bother you, Nikki, but I *really* need to see you.'

Nikki thought quickly. Andrew was a selfish bastard to leave her like this. 'Look, I have to take the morning meeting here, but as soon as that is over, I'll come straight to you.'

'Can I come to the station? Frankly I'm desperate to get out of this place for an hour or so. And I'm sure you are busy, so maybe it would help you too?'

Nikki really didn't want to have to talk to Helen with all the others around, but what could she say? 'Of course. Ask for me at the front desk and I'll come down and get you.'

'Thanks, Nikki. I really appreciate it, and Nik?' There was a pause. 'You do believe me, don't you?'

Nikki bit her lip. 'Of course, I do. Now go have a long soak in the tub and I'll see you later.'

There was the sound of a long exhale of breath. 'Yes. Would ten o'clock be good for you?'

'Perfect. See you then.'

* * *

The nine o'clock squad briefing in the CID office took longer than Nikki had anticipated and then, to make matters worse, she was handed a memo asking her to go directly to see the superintendent. 'Helen will be here in five minutes,' she whispered urgently to Joseph. 'And heaven knows how long the super will take. I saw the ACC going into the lift earlier so I'm probably going to get an ear-bashing from him too.'

'Would you like me to go and see to her?' he offered.

'I think she wants to talk to me about Andrew, as well as this latest flashback. I can't let her down, not after what Andrew's done. I get the feeling I'm her only support right now.'

'Then as soon as she gets here, go tell her what has happened, and say that you'll drive over to her place as soon as you are free.'

She nodded, 'Yes, that's best. At least I'll have explained it to her face, and she'll know I'm not just putting her off.'

'I can finish off here. You get yourself downstairs and see her as soon as she arrives.'

'Ma'am?' Sheila Roberts passed her another memo. 'It's from the pathologist. He says can you ring him as ASAP. It's important.'

Nikki heart sank. 'Oh, this just gets better and better.'

Joseph raised an eyebrow. 'It never rains, huh? Go see your friend first.'

Nikki got to the bottom of the stairs just as Helen was walking through the front doors. Her face lit up when she saw Nikki, which made her feel even more of a rat than she had before. 'I am *so* sorry, Helen.' She drew her away from the desk to a quiet spot in the waiting area. 'Things have gone totally tits up here.'

'I was wrong to come when you are working. I—'

'This isn't your fault, Helen. You have a case running with us, and you have every right to be here.' She placed her hand over Helen's. 'Joseph could talk to you, or any of the others on the team, but I thought this was something you would want to discuss with me personally.'

'It is. Of course it is.' Helen looked close to tears.

'Look, it's clearly going to be a cow of a day. How about instead of me trying to escape and getting held up again, I finish early, pick up a takeaway and a bottle of wine and we make an evening of it? We can talk all night if you want.'

Helen visibly brightened. 'Oh yes, that would be lovely. And don't tie yourself to a time, just get there when you can. I really look forward to having a proper talk. I've got to offload about Andrew. He's worrying the life out of me!'

'You can bare your soul, my friend. I'll be there to listen.'

Helen leant forward and gave her a tight hug. 'Thank you, Nikki. I can't tell you how good it is to have someone to trust.' And then she stood up and walked towards the doors. 'Tonight. See you then.'

She waved and disappeared, and for some reason Nikki felt a lump forming in her throat. Helen was the kind of woman who helped everybody. She went the extra mile for her clients — fitted them in when she had no free bookings, went to their homes if they couldn't get to her. In other words, she cared. Now she herself needed help, and all she had was one overworked copper and a useless boyfriend.

As she ran up the stairs to the superintendent's office, Nikki thought that sometimes life really was a bummer.

Just as she was about to knock on the door she heard footsteps behind her and heard Joseph call her name.

'Before you get embroiled with the super, I thought you should see this.' He handed her a printout. 'I didn't think you'd get the chance to speak to the pathologist, so I rang and said you were in a meeting. It's about the body in the river, ma'am, and it makes interesting reading.'

Nikki scanned it quickly and groaned. 'Ah, so this is not going to be a simple case after all.'

''Fraid not. Someone seems to have gone to great lengths to make this look like another gang-related death. Rory Wilkinson said he was coming this way later this morning and he'll fill us in on the details when he sees us.' He turned to go. 'And good luck in there, ma'am.'

Nikki raised her eyes in exasperation. 'I can hardly wait. If it's another lecture on statistics or Home Office updates on performance indicators, I'll scream.'

'Right, I'll listen out.' Joseph grinned and ran back down the stairs.

Wishing she were somewhere else, Nikki knocked on the door and went inside.

* * *

Joseph was sitting talking to the pathologist when Nikki arrived back in the CID room. They both looked up as she entered. Things had clearly not gone smoothly.

'Bloody waste of time! I *know* we are facing amalgamation with other divisions! I know we are cutting squad numbers and uniform are going out single-crewed! Aagh!'

Professor Rory Wilkinson pulled up another chair and pointed at it. 'A good rant does wonders for the spleen, dear heart. Rest your weary body and calm your mind. Uncle Rory has a charming tale of villainous tyranny to tell you.'

Nikki found herself smiling. Their inimitable Home Office pathologist was a real one-off, and he never failed to amuse her. He was a far cry from the miserable, whisky-swilling old windbag that had preceded him. Rory was unashamedly out and proud. In fact he celebrated his good fortune in being born that way on every possible occasion. He revelled in black humour, but Nikki and her team knew it was a veneer. Rory treated each one of his "guests" in the mortuary to every care and consideration. He was also extraordinarily intelligent.

'Now that dear Joseph has provided the coffees, I will begin.' Rory pushed his wire-rimmed glasses further up his hawk-like nose and smiled benignly at them. 'The moment I saw him I suspected that our Lithuanian friend, Mr Arturas Kubilius, was not the person his identity card proclaimed him to be. Nothing about his colouring or his physiognomy was typically Eastern European. And as soon as I opened his mouth and saw some very expensive orthodontic work, I was convinced. I have checked the ID that was found on him, and Mr Kubilius is a bona fide, legal immigrant. He was a farmer's son from a village just outside Kretinga, a city in western Lithuania. He works, and probably still does, as he is certainly not the dead man in my fridge, on the land as a field worker. My frozen guest has no calluses, no broken nails and no weathered skin.' He held out his hands, palms up. 'You need any more evidence?'

Joseph grinned. 'I'd like something that says who he is, rather than who he isn't.'

'Well, as soon as his DNA profile comes back, we'll run it through the databases, and I'll let you have the results the moment I get them.'

'How did he die, Prof?' asked Nikki.

'Stabbed. A single very deep wound to the back. The blade penetrated his body, slid between the ribs, to the side of the spinal column, and pierced the arch of the aorta. Goodnight Vienna.'

Nikki frowned. 'That sounds far too precise to be a lucky strike. Would you say it was carried out by a professional hitman?'

'Someone certainly knew what they were doing, but that doesn't make them a contract killer. The killer could be trained in a dozen things that would give him a knowledge of anatomy. Doctors, surgeons, physios, vets, butchers, undertakers, oh yes, and pathologists.'

Joseph made a grunting noise. 'And not just those, there's the military too.' As a former special services operative, Joseph had first-hand knowledge of what the military taught their men in the way of killing proficiently and silently.

Nikki yawned. 'Or just possibly, that lucky stab in the dark.'

Rory nodded. 'It has been known, although I doubt it. Stab wounds are funny things. In this case the blade was very long and thin, but it was removed at a different slant to the angle of entry. I found a distorted L-shaped wound, and what does that tells us, kiddies?'

Joseph exhaled. 'He twisted it.'

'Gold star, young Joseph! Yes, he made sure that the aorta was severely damaged. He was taking no chances.'

Nikki closed her eyes, but all she saw was Helen waving to her as she crossed the entrance lobby. She knew that she should be worrying about this unidentified body, but when her friend's life was in such a state of turmoil, it was difficult to concentrate. With a great effort she dragged her mind back to the job in hand. 'So, we have a man with bogus ID on him. Did he steal it, or was it placed on him after death? And if so, why?'

Rory held up his hand. 'One pointer, if I may? He had nothing else on him of importance, and nothing personal.

No jewellery, no watch, no phone. I found only two other items in his clothing, something I think might have been an old business card that had been left in a trouser pocket when it went into the wash, and a small round piece of stone of some kind, possibly a form of agate or jasper. The kind you might pick up off the beach for good luck.'

Neither officer made the obvious comment.

'Then I would say that those items were overlooked. His own wallet, watch etc., were removed and the bogus ID put in their place,' said Joseph. 'Someone didn't want this man's real identity known.'

'I think dumping him in the river adds to that supposition. Immersion for long periods plays havoc with human flesh, and don't we all know *that* for a fact.'

Nikki grimaced. 'Okay, Joseph. As we agreed, this one is yours. Bring Dave and Cat up to speed on what you know, and find out who our mystery man is.'

'Simple as that. Oh goody.'

Nikki stood up. 'I have great faith in your powers of deduction. And right now I have a desk full of crap to deal with for the superintendent, and if the whole of Greenborough riots tonight, it can do it without me, because no way will I let Helen down again. I'm leaving at five, and that's an end to it.'

'Me too. If that's okay, ma'am? I've been summoned by my daughter to meet her in Downham Market for dinner this evening. She wants to discuss something of dire importance. Don't ask me what it is, but it probably involves me coughing up wads of money.' He grinned at her.

Nikki smiled back. Tamsin and her father had finally made peace after a very long war, and she knew that Joseph had never been happier. 'Go spend your well-earned pennies on your lovely daughter, and give her my love, won't you?'

Joseph nodded. 'Of course I will. Hopefully she'll be coming up here the weekend after next, but she's working in the Thetford Forest on some project, and she can't get away any earlier.'

'Then enjoy your dinner.'

As Nikki returned to her office she decided that no matter what Tamsin wanted to discuss, it wouldn't be nearly as draining as the conversation that she and Helen would be having that night.

CHAPTER EIGHT

She bought a bottle of Sauvignon in the local off-licence and picked up a Chinese takeaway from a restaurant near Helen's.

As she parked the car close to the side of the house, she prayed that her friend would not be too intense. She loved her to pieces but couldn't help feeling slightly uneasy about her flashbacks. She hoped she would get an opportunity to tactfully suggest that Helen saw her neurologist again. Nikki felt sure that professional help was essential to help her understand what was happening to her. And perhaps she should push her a little harder about staying at Cloud Cottage Farm until Andrew got back from his trip. Maybe a complete change of scenery, somewhere far away from the Westland Waterway would ease her fear of being watched.

She pulled the brown paper bags from the passenger footwell and locked the car. Yes, she'd ask her again. It would be company for her, and she was sure that being on Cloud Fen would help Helen chill out and relax.

Helen did not answer the door on the first ring, but Nikki knew that her damaged leg slowed her down sometimes, so she waited a while before ringing again.

When she still didn't open the door, Nikki felt a ripple of concern slide across her shoulder blades. Was she having another one of those damned attacks? Or worse than that, had Nikki underestimated just how disturbed and upset Helen really was? Had she done something really stupid? Dropping the bags on the step, she pulled out her phone and dialled Helen's home number. From her position outside the front door she could clearly hear it ringing, but after a short while the answerphone cut in.

Suddenly the evening seemed to have become several degrees colder. Nikki took a deep breath. The problem with being a copper was that you immediately thought the worst. There were still a few other scenarios to consider. Helen could have forgotten their arrangement, but Nikki didn't believe that for one moment. Helen could have fallen asleep, and that *was* a possibility. Or she could be in the bathroom and not have heard the door or the phone, which was highly improbable.

Nikki decided to try Helen's mobile. After a moment the line connected, but to her dismay she heard the distant sound of a tinny musical call tune coming from the lounge. She moved to the window and through a gap in the curtains, saw the cell phone lying on the coffee table, the coloured display panel blinking with a soft green light as it waited to be answered.

Abandoning the bags at the door, Nikki ran down the steps and around to the back of the house. The back garden was in darkness and as she rushed through the side gate she saw that the conservatory blinds had been pulled down. She never shut them of an evening, Nikki knew. She liked to look out over the pool and the garden.

Nikki's throat felt parched and her heart hammered against her ribcage. She tried the conservatory door, but it was locked and she could see the key sitting where it always sat, on the windowsill. Then she knocked on the glass, loudly enough to be heard half a mile away. 'Helen! Helen! Can you hear me?' She rattled the door handle, then stood back and looked up as a window was roughly pushed open in the flat above, and a surprised face looked out.

'Police.' She drew out her warrant card and held it up above her head. 'Have you seen Miss Brook this evening?'

The man looked confused. 'No, but I rarely do. These apartments are pretty much separate, we have no communal areas. Sorry.'

'Okay, thanks. Does anyone keep a key for her? You know, for emergencies, to water the plants or something?'

'No, she's not been here very long, so we don't know her that well. If it helps, I saw a locksmith's van out here late yesterday.'

Nikki cursed. For once in his life Andrew had actually managed to do something when he said he would, damn him. Oh well, there was nothing left for it. She told the man to go back in, and as soon as he had disappeared, she picked up a big chunk of decorative rock from the side of the pool, and smashed it into the half-glazed conservatory door.

The second hit dislodged a section of glass, leaving an uneven hole. Nikki reached into her pocket and pulled out a protective glove, hastily pulling it on before reaching inside and locating the key. Finally, slipping the key into the lock, she pushed on the shattered door, offered a silent apology to her friend for the damage she'd caused, and stepped into the darkness.

In someone's garden, a few doors away, a wind chime rang out. Other than that all was silent in the big house on Westland Waterway. Nikki stood for a moment in the darkness, trying to get her bearings. She thought that the light switches were to the left. She edged sideways, her shoes crunching in the broken glass, and ran her hand along the cold glass until her fingers encountered the rougher surface of the wall, and then the switch. She turned on the lights, and blinked a few times. The conservatory was exactly as it had been when she visited last. The plants still looked healthy and the bowls of crystals were undisturbed. Everything seemed as it should be.

The only thing that was terribly wrong was the sick feeling in the pit of her stomach.

Nikki forced her heavy feet to move carefully forward toward the wide steps that led down into the garden room. Her heart screamed at her to run inside, to shout out to her friend, but her head and her gut knew it was pointless. There was something about the total silence that told her that no living person other than her, was in that house. But of course that did not mean she was alone there.

The light from the conservatory made the big area look dim and shadowy, but Nikki did not need any more illumination to see that the folding screen had been pulled around to hide the massage table.

Without taking another step, she knew that she should have taken her friend's terrified condition a lot more seriously than she had. The cloying, coppery, metallic smell of blood hung heavy in the previously oil-scented air.

With her heart hammering insanely, Nikki moved across the room, then took a deep breath and looked around the screen.

Her cry went unheard. The only other occupant of that room could hear nothing. She never would again.

Fighting the rising nausea, Nikki staggered back from the screen, then ran clumsily up the steps to the welcome light of the conservatory. She threw open the damaged door and drew in great gulps of the cold night air, before fumbling in her bag for her phone. She knew she had to follow protocol, but all she really wanted to do was call Joseph. But she couldn't. He was miles away in Norfolk with his daughter. After dropping it twice, she finally managed to steady herself enough to be able to ring Greenborough police station.

* * *

The wind chimes still disturbed the peaceful evening with their clamour, but now they were joined by the harsh sound of sirens.

Nikki stood at the bottom of the steps with her back to the entrance to the garden room. She was upright and stony faced. Inside she felt about as cold as the light reflected in her pale eyes.

Her voice was steady. 'The scene is uncontaminated, Superintendent Woodhall. I entered, found the body of Helen Brook, and left immediately by the same route. No one has approached her since. With respect, sir, after the doctor, I want Professor Rory Wilkinson to be the first to go in. We can't afford to contaminate *anything*. This is no ordinary murder.'

The superintendent stood beside her, his eyes narrowed and his jaw set forward at an almost impossible angle. 'You are certain she's dead?'

A small bark of a laugh spilled from Nikki's lips. 'Oh yes, sir. Quite sure.'

'And the rest of the house? Did you check it?'

'Yes, sir. I rang for assistance immediately after discovering the body. Then, without going near the treatment area, I did a room-by-room check. There was no one here. Thing is, sir, there are only two entrances, and both are locked.' She allowed the implications to hang in the air.

'Is there any way this could have been a suicide?'

Nikki was forced to choke back a nervous giggle, then hung her head and sighed. 'Perhaps you'd better see her, super. Just don't let uniform in here with their size twelves. Then I think you'll understand why I don't want the world and his brother trampling all over the crime scene.'

Nikki stood aside and allowed the superintendent to pass. She had no intention of accompanying him. She would wait until Rory arrived, then she'd return to her friend's side. She waited for the senior officer's reaction. She hoped it would be dramatic in some way, to make her own horrified response seem a little more acceptable. After a while he returned to her side. She could see that his stomach was stretched taut and his chest pushed out, straining on the buttons of his uniform jacket, as he fought to breathe normally.

He swallowed hard. 'I had no idea. I think you could have warned me, Nikki.'

You had more fucking warning than I did, sir. 'Sorry, sir, I thought you knew me well enough to know that when I say something is out of the ordinary, I mean it. And now you know why I want our pathologist in there as soon as possible.'

'Damn right I do. I'll go and check on his ETA.'

It was cold comfort, but Nikki noticed that his smooth complexion looked like wet putty.

After the doctor had confirmed life extinct, she remained standing at the bottom of the stairs. No one who saw her would dare to pass. She stared at the floor and tried not to think of Helen lying there behind her. Tried not to think of how badly she had let her friend down. But she wasn't the only one. They had all let her down, especially Andrew. They had dismissed her fears as unfounded, or maybe delusional, and now she was dead. *Hey, Helen! Well, well, so you were right all along.*

A hand touched her arm and she jumped.

Rory was staring earnestly at her through his wire framed glasses. 'I'm so sorry. Are you all right?'

He's the only one who's thought to ask, she said to herself, and tears formed in her eyes.

Blinking them away, she lightly touched his hand. She nodded. 'I'm fine now. Had a bit of a wobble back there, but . . .'

He spoke gently. 'It's allowed, but in your case only once every ten years. Now, shall I go deal with this alone? Matthew will be here in five, along with a couple of SOCOs. We *can* manage.' He raised his eyebrows.

'No. I need to look at her properly. Now you're here, I'll be able to face it.' She drew herself up, straightened her shoulders and ushered him forward with a sweep of her arm.

Together they ascended the steps and moved across the room to the screen.

Rory stood at the open end of the screened off area, and for a moment did not speak. Then he stood back, bit hard on his bottom lip and stared at Nikki. 'Do you understand any of this?'

She shook her head and exhaled. 'No, none of it.'

Nikki really did not want to look at her friend's defiled body, but she knew she had to. She had to catch her friend's killer. It would never make amends, but it might ease her conscience just a little.

Helen lay on her back on her own massage table. Her body had been stripped naked and her clothes neatly placed on a chair close to the table. On top of her carefully folded sweatshirt was her wrist watch, two rings, a delicate gold chain with a small gold cross attached, and a single Indian moonstone, from her collection of crystals and minerals.

One of her own white fluffy towels had been rolled into a pad and placed under the back of her neck, raising her chin upwards. Her arms were straight alongside the body, palms up, with the hands and wrists protruding slightly over the edge of the table. The legs were chastely close together and the feet and toes gracefully pointed.

Nikki looked away for a moment, then reluctantly allowed her eyes to return to the dead woman.

Helen would have looked perfectly at peace, but for the fact that her throat had been sliced neatly from ear to ear, and because of the odd angle of the head, the wound gaped open like a second mouth. This was bad, very bad, but not nearly as terrible as what the killer had done to her body, after her heart had stopped pumping and the blood had stopped flowing.

Nikki heard her colleague whistle softly through his teeth. 'Never, in all my years in forensics, have I seen anything so mesmerizingly beautiful.'

'And at the same time . . .'

'Yes, I know. I also feel like a ghoul, or a voyeur. Look at the work!'

Nikki looked, and thought randomly of *Lydia, the Tattooed Lady*. When she was a child her father had sung the old Groucho Marx song to her to make her laugh. She wasn't laughing now. She swallowed and tried again to understand what she was looking at.

The whole torso had been painted with the most intricate design. She had no idea what it meant, but it consisted of a series of circles that began at Helen's navel and worked outwards to cover her abdomen, chest and breasts. There were scrolls, leaves, flowers, symbols and signs, all delicately painted in deep turquoise green. Part of the artwork was incisions in Helen's flesh, into which the killer had carefully inserted a variety of her semi-precious stones. Nikki saw rose quartz, amethyst and citrine glinting in the overhead light, and many others that she did not recognise. She looked at Helen's face, and felt thankful that the eyes were closed.

Not only were they closed, but covered with two round polished stones that were the deep blue colour of the night sky.

'This has to be photographed in great detail, Nikki. And I suspect . . .' He leant gently across the body and slipped a gloved finger between the slightly open lips. 'Ah yes. I can't open it any further until the rigor passes, but there is a stone in her mouth as well. Someone has spent a lot of time and effort with your friend.'

'And she should have been with me, but I was too busy with work.' Her voice cracked.

'Hey! If you're going to start beating yourself up, do it when I'm not around, will you? You are ruining the marvellous image I have of DI Nikki Galena, super cop. Detective Inspector, whoever did this had planned it down to the last brush stroke. If it hadn't happened today it would surely have happened at the next available opportunity, would not? And you couldn't watch her 24/7.'

'When you put it like that, Rory, I can hardly argue. But I still feel like shit.'

'She was your friend. As I said, it's allowed, even for super cop. Now, I see my team has arrived, so I need to get on. This is a big apartment, and I want every hair, every fibre and every tiny particle of anything at all that should not be here. I'll get my prelim report to you just as soon as I can, but this is not going to be straightforward.'

'For once, Rory, no pressure. You just do whatever you have to do. I know I can rely on you. Just look after her, will you?' Nikki gave him a rueful smile and left.

CHAPTER NINE

As Nikki unlocked the door to Cloud Fen Cottage the enormity of what she had just been through hit her. She threw her coat down and fought back the tears, but only until she reached her kitchen. With sobs racking her body she grabbed a box of tissues, and the brandy bottle from the cupboard. The rich amber liquid splashed across the table as she poured it out with shaking hands. She took a sip and coughed. There was no pleasure in that first taste of the expensive liqueur. Tonight it was purely medicinal.

She wasn't sure how long she cried for, but there was a small heap of tissues beside her when the tears gave way to sad hiccupping sighs. How could she have let her friend down so badly? Why had she not taken everything Helen said as gospel right from the very beginning? Helen had known she was in mortal danger, and Nikki had decided to play psychologist. Big mistake. Deadly mistake.

She glanced at the kitchen clock. Midnight. *Sorry, Joseph. I know it's late, but I really can't help that.* The last thing she wanted was for him to find out about Helen's death from someone else.

He answered on the third ring, listened, then said, 'Unlock the front door. I'm on my way.'

Nikki smiled sadly. She hadn't told him anything yet. She hadn't asked him to come, but he had known instinctively that she needed him. Thank God for Joseph.

She got up, took another glass from the cabinet and poured him a generous measure. She placed it next to hers and went to open the door.

* * *

Joseph grabbed a torch and sprinted along the marsh lane from his home at Knot Cottage. The moon was full and bright, but heavy clouds kept scudding across it, plunging the path into darkness. He slowed his pace. He didn't want a twisted ankle. That wouldn't help things at all.

Part of him was still on a high after a very pleasant evening with Tam. The rest was dreading what Nikki was going to tell him. From the sound of her voice, he knew exactly what that was going to be.

He stood for a moment outside Cloud Fen Farmhouse and waited for his breathing to calm. Then he knocked and went inside.

He saw the two brandy glasses, and then he saw Nikki's red eyes and the pile of tissues. 'Oh no.'

'Oh yes.'

He went over to her, squatted down on his haunches next to her chair, and took her hands in his. He looked up into those eyes, sadder than sad. 'Tell me. Tell me everything.'

And so she did. 'I'm beginning to feel like some kind of Jonah. Everyone I care about dies.'

Joseph raised an eyebrow, and saw her expression change as she realised what this implied.

'It's okay. Tamsin and I are the exception to the rule. The powers of evil have already had a bloody good go at us and failed.'

'Sorry, but sometimes I really do wonder.' She took a sip of her drink. 'I keep seeing Helen lying there, and those blue stones covering her eyes. What on earth was that all about? It was grotesque and terrible, and yet . . .'

'There was a perverted kind of beauty in it?'

'Exactly. Other than the blood and the fact that she was dead.'

Joseph inhaled. Then he tentatively said, 'I hate to say this, but because you were so close, are you going to be able to cope? It's going to be distressing beyond words. Would it maybe be better to hand this case over?'

Her face told him he'd just wasted his breath.

'You think I'd let *anyone* else deal with Helen's murder? When hell freezes over! This is our case, Joseph. I let my friend down, and the only thing I can do to make some miserable kind of amends, is to catch the bastard and give the CPS the tightest case they've ever had. I want the killer in the nastiest prison we have to offer, and serving life, with no chance of parole, until he rots.'

DI Nikki Galena was back. Joseph heaved a sigh of relief. 'Well, that's me told.'

She flashed him a sheepish smile. 'Okay, so maybe that was a little extreme, but this one's mine, until the bitter end. First thing, I'll clear it with the super, make him aware that the team is totally committed to catching Helen Brook's killer, and then we start the most efficient murder investigation we've ever mounted, okay?'

'You can count on us, Nikki, one hundred percent. But what about the body in the river? Do you think we could offload it back to Gill Mercer's team?'

'Probably not, with her present workload, but let me talk to Greg Woodhall tomorrow. We have a full complement now Dave is back. Maybe I could beg or borrow Yvonne and Niall from uniform again. And there is always DC Jessie Nightingale. She's floating since her old team got disbanded. If we can rope her in, we could handle the two cases in tandem.'

Yes, DI Nikki Galena was well and truly back. 'Okay. Now, are you going to be okay on your own tonight? My spare room is always made up.'

She rubbed her eyes. 'I'm all right now. It was the shock of finding her like that. I'll probably have nightmares for months, but the dramatics are over. I'm back on track. And I have a very important job to do, don't I?'

He frowned at her, almost fiercely. '*We* do. There's no 'I' in this team, remember?'

'True, but this one is personal.'

Again, thought Joseph, but he remained silent. 'Then I'd better get home and top up with some sleep. We are going to be flat out for the duration.'

Nikki nodded. Then she looked at him. 'Sorry, Joseph, I should have asked. What did Tamsin want that was so urgent?'

He let out a little laugh. 'I'll tell you when things have calmed down. It's actually quite funny, and it didn't cost me a penny.'

Nikki finished her drink and stood up. 'Okay, maybe you'll tell me tomorrow? But for now, thanks for coming over like that. I needed to offload, and as always, you took the brunt.'

'I'd have it no other way.' He stood up and went around to her. He gave her a hug and lightly kissed the top of her head. 'Get to bed. I won't be silly enough to say sleep. But rest anyway, we are going to be pretty busy for a while.'

As he walked home Joseph wondered how Nikki was really going to cope with her friend's murder. She valued the few friends that she had, and he knew she would be eaten up with guilt that they had not immediately believed what Helen had told them. He pulled his jacket tighter around him, and wondered what he could do to help. He'd be there for her, of course, that went without saying, but other than that? Solve the case, find the killer, what more could anyone ask of him? His mood darkened as he trudged across the moonlit fen, because if the truth be told, it wasn't just Nikki who felt a stab of conscience. They had all let Helen Brook down.

CHAPTER TEN

Nikki felt physically sick as she entered the room for the morning meeting. Having a friend as the murder victim was a new experience. It wasn't a pleasant one.

As she had expected, the superintendent had asked her if she would like to hand the case over to another team, but she had declined. She was not related or intimate with Helen, so she was quite within her rights to work on the investigation. She had noticed that Greg Woodhall seemed far from displeased at her decision. In fact there had been considerable satisfaction in his tone when he had told her to proceed. He knew better than she did that CID was in disarray. One team had been hit with some kind of virus, another was in the process of being reshaped after several retirements, and DI Mercer's team was temporarily fragmented by staff conflicts and restrictions from above.

Nikki told her team the basics, managing to hold her emotions in check.

Eric Barnes raised his hand. 'The boyfriend, ma'am? Conveniently away at the time of the murder?'

Nikki bit her lip. Eric's supercilious tone was beginning to irritate her almost as much as it did Cat Cullen. 'Yes, Detective, and I have already spoken to his company. They have confirmed that he was required to work with their Swiss clients. Unfortunately, his boss has been unable to contact him, and neither have our people. His cell phone is switched off, and he always makes his own hotel reservations. Sadly, on this occasion he omitted to tell his secretary where he was staying. So, perhaps you'd like to begin by checking out his flight, and trying to locate him for me. And DC Barnes, when you find Andrew Gregory, I want to be the one to break the news about his partner's death. Understood?'

The detective nodded unenthusiastically. 'Yes, boss.'

Joseph stood up. 'Ma'am? Can we now assume that Miss Brook's claim about the man in the accident and what he told her is a genuine route for enquiry?'

Nikki looked around the room, her gaze resting on each officer in turn. 'You will regard her claim that her life was being threatened as completely legitimate. She could hardly have done any more to prove its validity than get herself killed, could she? As to the mystery man? Yes, I believe he exists. Whether he's responsible for her death, that's down to us to find out. I have no need to tell you that we are pretty stretched, but Joseph and I are going to head up the ongoing case of the unidentified man pulled from the river, *and* the death of Helen Brook. We do have extra officers in place, so once I've set up a work rota, I do not foresee any problems. For this morning, we'll deal with getting together everything we can regarding Helen Brook, then later I'll allocate teams to work specifically on one case or the other. Cat? I want you and Dave to go over the accident reports again. And while Dave mans the office side of things, you take Niall Farrow and go and talk to everyone who was there. Every rescue worker, every witness, the safety officers who checked the building once it had been cleared, even the demolition men. I want some sort of solid corroboration of Helen's story that she was not alone in that cellar, okay?'

Her gaze roamed around the room then came to rest on her new, albeit temporary recruit, a slim blonde girl with her long hair caught back in a tidy ponytail. 'DC Nightingale, you and Yvonne check all deaths recorded on or immediately before the day of the accident that refer to married women. Helen Brook told me that the man's name was Paul and the woman he had killed was his wife. And I also want the young man that had been watching the houses along Westland Waterway questioned again. Make sure his excuse was authentic and not a cover for something else. And we will need Miss Brook's database of clients carefully checked, both at the Willows Clinic and her private clinic. And *anyone* who shows up as a possible stalker or too flaky for comfort, we pull them in and interview them.'

'What about medical ethics, ma'am? Does the Hippocratic oath extend to complementary medicine?' Cat looked dubiously at her.

'You are asking them about Helen the person, and how they felt about her. I'm sure there is a code of practice, but you are not persuading them to share the details of their haemorrhoids, or their dose of the clap. This is a murder enquiry, and I doubt that massaging toes with fragrant oil requires a great degree of confidentiality. Just because they are paying clients does not make them immune from questioning. Diplomacy, okay? So, let's make today count. Go to it and back here at four, please, hopefully with some leads.'

As the room cleared, her phone warbled at her from her jacket pocket.

'Inspector? I've got a favour to ask.' Rory sounded almost as tired as she was.

'Fire away.'

'Two things really. One, are you coming back to Westland Waterway this morning? There's something I need to talk to you about, plus a few things I need to know about Helen and this apartment. I'm sorry to say this, but other than her killer, you were most likely the last person to be in touch with her.'

Nikki shivered. She was very aware of that fact. 'Yes. As soon as I see that the team is clear on how to proceed, I'll be with you.' She paused for a moment, unsure how to ask whether her friend had been taken to the morgue.

'It's okay. She went back to my place in the early hours, if that helps.'

'You're amazing, Wilkinson. I never knew mindreading was one of your skills.'

'Heaven forbid! And you really don't want to know about my hobbies! Oh, I should warn you that we are not alone out here.'

'Press?'

'Flocks! Hordes! I'm not sure what the collective noun is for journalists? A "nastiness" maybe?'

'An "intrusion" might be appropriate.'

'Perfect! I like that. See you soon.'

* * *

Nikki drew her coat collar up to her face as she walked across the car park. A bitterly cold wind was sweeping in from the Wash, chilling everything in its path. She really did not want to go back to the Newlands clinic and the Westland Waterway.

As she flopped into her car and turned on the ignition, she shook her head and angrily growled to herself. *Time to get professional, Nikki, and start treating Helen's death like any other murder enquiry, and not some deeply meaningful crusade — even if that's exactly what it is.* This was work, her world, one she'd fought harder than most to make the grade in. She knew the names that the mess room had given her over the years. They all referred to her as a ball-breaker. She had a reputation as a tough one, and she didn't plan on losing it.

'Ma'am!' A loud rap on her window drew her sharply back from her reverie. Eric stood beside her car. 'Glad I caught you, guv. Got some news you really need to know.'

She wound down the window. Looking at those bright, ratty eyes, she found herself sincerely hoping that if there was a breakthrough, it hadn't come from him. 'Come on then, I haven't got all day.'

'Andrew Gregory never made his flight, ma'am, or any other one for that matter.'

'What?' Her mouth dropped open slightly. Then she regained her composure and said, 'So do you know where he is, then?'

'No, ma'am, but he sure as hell isn't where he said he'd be.'

'Then find him, DC Barnes. And ring me when you do. I'll be at Helen Brook's house for an hour or so, then back here.' She flipped the switch for the electric window and turned the ignition key. As she pulled out onto the main road, she cursed out loud: 'Damn you, Andrew! What the fuck are you up to?'

* * *

Nikki had been prepared for her "intrusion" of journalists, but the carpet of flowers that covered the front garden took her breath away.

The area had been duly cordoned off and an officer stood with his hands behind his back at the entrance to the drive. A WPC seemed to be permanently deployed accepting bunches of flowers and small cellophane-wrapped plants from a steady stream of men, women and children.

'It's been like this since dawn, ma'am. They say bad news travels fast, but this, well . . .' The constable spread her arms and pointed to a sea of colour that stretched from the roadway to the front door steps. 'And look at the messages.' As Nikki ignored the press cameras and surveyed the cards that accompanied the flowers, she noticed that the young woman's eyes were brimming with tears.

'What's your name, Constable?'

'Natalie Bryson, ma'am.'

'Okay, Natalie. I know this is a pretty hard call, but I want you to switch off the emotion. There's a very real chance that the killer might be somewhere in that crowd. It's well known that a murderer can be drawn back to the scene of the crime, okay? It's all about control, a massive ego-trip. So I want you to watch these people really carefully.'

The young woman's eyes had widened. 'You mean I could have taken a bunch of flowers from him? He'd have that much nerve?'

'The person who did this is capable of anything.'

Nikki scanned the messages. *"Thank you for all your help and kindness." "A beautiful woman, sadly taken from us." "With all our love, sleep peacefully, Helen." "Why take an angel?"* She felt a wave of nausea. This was her friend that all these strangers were talking about.

'Just keep your eyes open, Constable, and if anyone worries you, speak to one of the detectives immediately.'

'Yes, ma'am. Oh, but before you go in, would you have a word with that woman over there? She arrived a few minutes ago. She brought some flowers, but was asking to speak to someone in charge.'

Nikki glanced around and one woman stood out immediately. 'Tall, well dressed, wearing a long black coat and a Burberry scarf? That the one?'

Natalie nodded. 'Yes, ma'am.'

Nikki walked over to the cordon and lifted the blue-and-white striped tape. 'I'm DI Galena. Can I help you?'

'I'm so sorry to bother you at a time like this,' the woman stammered. Her voice was choked with emotion. 'But I don't quite know what to do. It's this, you see.' She handed Nikki a long, white envelope. 'My name is Duchene, Carla Duchene. Miss Brook cared for my mother. She had cancer, and for the last six months of her life, Helen helped her. Even when she was so badly hurt herself, she found time for my mother. If she couldn't get to her, or see her, she would ring and talk to her.'

Nikki wondered how many more of these touching stories would surface over the coming weeks.

'The thing is, my mother passed away recently and . . . I was bringing this for Helen. Mother wanted her to have it. Then I heard the news and now I don't know what to do.' The sob finally broke from the woman's lips.

Nikki looked at the envelope. 'Do you want me to open it?'

The woman nodded and Nikki lifted the unsealed flap. Inside was a cheque for ten thousand pounds.

She bit her lip. 'Oh dear. I see your problem. What about a charity? Maybe even the local hospice?'

Carla Duchene shook her head slowly, and wiped away a tear with a freshly ironed handkerchief. 'Mother gave plenty while she was alive. Our family is not without money, Detective Inspector. This was specifically for Helen.' For a moment or two the woman seemed lost for words. Then she looked long and hard into Nikki's eyes. 'Would you take it? Keep it for me? Maybe there will be some kind of fund set up in Helen's name. You would know about it before me. Please?'

'I'm sorry. I can't accept it, Miss . . . is it *Miss* Duchene? It would not be right. It could be misconstrued in some way, so I'm afraid I can't take it from you. But leave me your address and if I hear of something, I promise I will let you know. It's the best I can do, I'm afraid.'

Carla tore the flap from the envelope and scribbled her name and address on it. 'Thank you anyway. I'm sorry to have been a nuisance.'

Nikki stood by the cordon and watched as the tall figure moved slowly through the crowd and disappeared.

At the door to Helen's once pristine home, Nikki donned an all-in-one protective suit and pulled the hood up over her hair.

'Ah, my favourite inspector! Made it through the barrage of cameras and those cute fluffy mikes?'

'It was the flowers that surprised me.'

Rory pulled a face. 'Well, if I should happen to wrap my Citroen Dolly around a tree on the A52, please don't erect a roadside memorial with my name spelled out on a yellow registration plate and a bunch of fading plastic roses tied to it. It's just *so* tacky, darling!'

Nikki was forced to smile. 'I promise. Now, what can I do to help you here?'

Rory Wilkinson rubbed thoughtfully at his unshaven chin. 'I think I know what that body art on your friend's torso was.'

Nikki looked at him, alert.

'When Matthew, my assistant, arrived last night to help me with her, he said it was the weirdest mandala he'd ever seen. Just a throwaway comment on his part, but he was absolutely correct.'

Mandala? She'd heard that word before, and it was Helen who had mentioned it. 'It's a design to help you meditate, isn't it?'

'Yes, it's a circular visual representation that's generally used as a focal point for concentration. And Matthew says he's heard about them being used in psychotherapy.'

'Oh great! Mind you, who besides a nutter would do something like this anyway?'

'Well, you know better than I. But some killers go to a lot of trouble to point suspicion away from their clever and calculating selves, and make it look like the work of some "nutter."'

'Maybe so. But in this case?'

'Oh, definitely a nutter. But if I were you, I'd start doing some research into mandalas. I'm sure those symbols, correctly interpreted, will lead you straight to the killer.'

'Just like that!'

'Well, maybe not *quite* that easily. But why go to the trouble of doing that incredible artwork if it isn't a clue of some kind? It has to have a reason.' His tone suddenly grew serious. 'Inspector, there's one last thing I have to ask, before you run screaming from my company. Are you up to doing a walk round? As you were the last one here, apart from whoever killed Helen, I'm hoping you may spot any anomalies. I'm looking at this from a strictly forensic point of view. The slightest thing that the killer may have moved or touched could hold a print or the minutest trace of evidence in a fibre or a single hair. We've already photographed and documented the whole initial scene, now we're ready to move on to specifics. If you are up to it?'

'Of course. It's got to be done, hasn't it? Let's get it over with. Although she or her partner could have moved anything since I was here last.'

'We will eliminate them, and see what's left.'

Everything seemed as she remembered it, and after some twenty minutes of checking each room, she returned to the conservatory and slowly made her way around it for a second time. She tried to recall the place as it had been when she had sat with her friend, drinking coffee and trying to analyse her strange and frightening recall of memory. 'She never used the blinds at night, but they were closed when I found her.'

'We've taken great care there. The controls had been carefully wiped clean, but some trace might have been missed. And if it has, we will find it. I'm heading back to my eyrie shortly. I've done everything I need to here, and my little band of workers are very capable of finishing this off.'

At the conservatory steps, she was interrupted by her mobile. 'Inspector Galena?' The voice on the other end was crackly, the line breaking up and making the caller sound like staccato gun fire.

'Andrew?' She moved around the room, looking for a place with better reception. 'Andrew, is that you?'

'I've just heard the news on the radio! Nikki, please, say it's not true. Tell me what happened.'

'Andrew, where the hell are you?'

'London.' His voice cracked up again and Nikki was not sure if it was the line or his voice. 'Is she . . . ? Please, is Helen . . . ?'

Nikki took a deep breath. 'Now listen to me. You *have* to come home, immediately. I need to speak to you urgently. And you also need to know that the police are looking for you, so either get yourself to the nearest police station, or preferably come straight to Greenborough. If you are stopped on the way, get the officers to ring me directly, then they will bring you in.'

'Then it's true.'

'Yes. I'm so sorry, Andrew. Helen is dead. Would you like me to come and get you? Perhaps you shouldn't drive right now.'

There was a small sound, something like a cough, then he said, 'No. I just need to get my head round it. Then I'll come back.'

Nikki wanted to say more, but the empty howling noise told her that the phone had gone dead.

CHAPTER ELEVEN

Joseph met her in the CID office. 'Are you okay? I wish I'd gone with you,' he said to Nikki.

'I'm fine, honestly. The going back for the first time is over and done with now. And I have some news.' She told him about Andrew's call.

'But you've heard no more since?'

'No, and he was in a right state. He says he knew nothing about what happened until he caught the TV news. I've tried the number he rang on and it's switched off, so until he either gets here or makes contact again, we're stuffed.'

Joseph opened his office door and ushered her inside. 'Well, I have some good news too.' He grimaced. 'Actually there's good news and bad.'

'Let's have the good first.'

'Our Cat has confirmed that Helen had company in that cellar.'

Nikki gasped. 'Already? That's brilliant!'

'Yes, she and Dave managed to locate some of the personnel involved in the accident, and one in particular was more than informative.' Joseph looked down at Cat's report. 'Here we are, Nigel Casey, a structural engineer. He had been in the area by chance, looking for a café to grab a snack before driving back to Alford, where his company was based. Like us, he rushed to help the injured. He was the first to find two dead teenagers pinned beneath fallen masonry close to the alley. He checked that they were both beyond help, then tried to get down the alleyway. He told Cat that for some reason, maybe shock, he wasn't sure, but he had completely forgotten seeing a young man limping towards him, from the direction of the cellar that Helen had pitched into.'

'This is getting better and better!' Nikki exclaimed.

Joseph's eyes lit up. 'Even better to come. Cat asked him if he spoke to the man. And I quote his reply:

"It's strange, I think I did, I must have done, but he was walking unaided, and heading for where the emergency services were treating the minor injuries, so I kind of disregarded him. To be honest, I'd just seen those two dead kids, and I wasn't exactly oblivious to the state of the damaged buildings. It's my job, isn't it? I've seen too much one way or another. Someone only had to sneeze, and the whole lot would have come down! I did see two other helpers with a fire officer, and they were heading towards the alley. A tall, smart-looking bloke who although it was filthy in there, would still have looked good on the cover of GQ."

Joseph grinned broadly, then continued, *". . . and a good-looking woman with a determined expression, the sort you felt was well in charge of things, you know? And as soon as I saw them I knew the cavalry had arrived so I decided to get back to safety."*

Joseph laughed. 'Good description of you, don't you think?'

Nikki rolled her eyes.

Joseph read on, *"I believe the lone man to be in his thirties, very slim built, with black hair. I recall that specifically because the plaster dust adhering to it made him look quite theatrical, like a white-faced Halloween vampire. And there was blood on his trousers, across both of his shins. Other than that he seemed unhurt. I'm sure I would have spent time with him if I'd been concerned about his injuries."* And here comes the bombshell. *"If it helps, I can tell you his name."'*

Nikki's jaw dropped. 'He named him?'

'Yes, and he remembered why. Listen to this: *"It's just thinking about it all again after so long, and talking about his black, dust-covered hair. As he walked past me, he was brushing dirt and dust from his face and his clothes. As he brushed his jacket collar, I briefly saw a badge. The kind they wear in supermarkets, the ones with just their first names on. The letters were quite big. I remember now as clear as daylight. The name was Paul."*'

Nikki let out a long sigh. 'Amazing!'

Joseph nodded. 'Good, isn't it? I mean, I know it's not definitive proof that he was in the cellar, but Dave and Cat are checking out all the stores, shops and businesses in the area to try to track down this man.'

'And it all ties in. His legs were bleeding, so probably he *was* trapped, as Helen told me. He got free, saw Helen, who had probably drifted out of consciousness, thought she was dead, and got out fast. And we missed him by seconds.'

Joseph agreed, then said, 'And now for the bad news. While Dave and Cat were working their line of enquiry, Niall went out to pick up the boy from the river walk. Turns out he lives on the Carborough Estate.'

Nikki shrugged. She might have guessed that was where the rough-looking young man came from. After considerable refurbishment, the Carborough was better than it used to be, but it was still a place where you didn't walk alone after dark. 'And?'

'Niall said there is an odd feeling there at the moment.'

'Odd in what way?'

Joseph threw her an amused smile. 'He reckons it feels like suppressed anger. I think our Niall is starting to turn into another Yvonne Collins. He's suddenly developed "policeman's nose" by the bucketful.'

Nikki smiled back. 'I know what you mean. There was a time when the only two words he knew were, gung and ho. Now he's as astute as his mentor, and she takes some beating.' Yvonne and Niall were uniformed crew-mates. Yvonne was streetwise, an oracle when it came to knowing her patch, and Niall was a hero straight out of the comics, but with all the right ethics and a big heart. Together, the older woman and the younger officer made an excellent team, and Nikki trusted their judgement. 'Did he get any idea of what the problem was?'

Joseph shook his head. 'No. He said it was just very quiet, much too quiet, which was worrying enough, but then no one wanted to talk to him.'

'Maybe it's because of Archie Leonard. He is fading fast, and I know the whole family have gathered to be with him.' Nikki felt an overwhelming sadness. Over the years, she and the old villain, Archie, had crossed swords and then formed an unlikely alliance when bad things had happened in Greenborough. Archie was the patriarchal figurehead of an old-style criminal family, with his own rules and values. It was no secret that Nikki and Archie felt affection for each other, and she knew she would miss him.

'I saw young Mickey yesterday on the High Street.' While Nikki was attached to Archie, Joseph had become close to Archie's adopted grandson. As a boy, Mickey had been in some terrible fixes, and Joseph and Nikki had saved him on more than one occasion. 'He says he will ring us as soon as there is any news. He thinks it'll be days now, rather than weeks.'

'I cannot believe the old dog is still alive, but I can't imagine the Carborough without him, can you?'

'One of Archie's sons, Raymond, will carry on the family tradition, but he's not Archie and never will be. Raymond is hard as nails, whereas our old sparring partner was a gentleman — of sorts.'

Nikki leaned back against the door. 'Do you think we should be worried about this uncomfortable atmosphere?'

'We've come across it before and it didn't bode well then. Best not to ignore it. I'll make a few enquiries, and I'll ask Yvonne and Niall to see if any of their snouts have caught a whiff of something unsavoury.'

Nikki straightened up. 'Good. I'd better go and see how the team are getting on — and I have some homework to do, studying mandalas.'

Joseph grinned. 'I saw a lot of those while I was abroad.'

'If they prove too much for me, I'll hand them over to you.' Why had the killer chosen to paint this particular design on her friend's body? Nikki knew it was important. And she wanted to be the one to discover exactly what lay behind it.

CHAPTER TWELVE

Before Nikki had a chance to see the team, she was summoned to the superintendent's office. As she made her way out of the noisy CID room, she heard Sheila Robbins, her office manager, calling to her.

Sheila thrust a memo at her. 'Ma'am, you'll want to see this. Oh, and the pathologist wants another word, as soon as possible. It's about the man in the river.'

'Okay, Sheila. Ring him and ask him to give me an hour. Thank you.' She hurried towards the stairs, reading through the message from the duty sergeant. She released a small sigh of relief. Something else was going right.

Superintendent Woodhall's brow was wrinkled with concern. 'We may have an additional problem here, Nikki. Helen Brook's killing seems to have outraged the whole of Greenborough, and it's spreading fast. Look.' He handed her one of the national newspapers. 'Someone put something on Facebook and it went viral and the media picked it up.'

As she skimmed through the article she understood why her boss was so worried. 'I see what you mean. They've caught onto the fact that she survived that dreadful accident, spent a year getting her life back together, then has it torn away by some mindless murderer. Thank God they don't know the full story! I mean, what he did to her.'

'Damn right! And although we can't blame the public for taking something like this to heart, I can see it escalating into one of these national crusades.'

'And that could hamper the enquiry.'

'Easily. I've already had a request from a group of friends and clients of the Willows Clinic asking if they can hold an all-night candlelit vigil outside her house.'

'Oh great! Just what we need when we are short-staffed.'

'I've told them they will have to wait until we've released the crime scene, which could be some time But it's not going to end there, is it? The local rags will start speculating, then accusing, which reminds me, what's happening with Andrew Gregory?'

She waved the memo in the air. 'The duty sergeant has just contacted me, sir. Andrew is coming in this afternoon, voluntarily.'

'Did he live with Helen Brook?'

'Yes, but he has a small family cottage out at Fentoft Quay. He will be staying there until we release his things from the house.'

'Had they been together long?'

'Yes, sir, they became friends in their teens.'

'Means nothing though, does it? Things change, people change.'

Nikki remained silent. She wanted a very long talk with bloody Andrew before she passed comment.

Greg Woodhall paused, evidently expecting some response. Then he said, 'OK, Nikki. I just wanted you to be aware of the media's interest in this enquiry. I have to say I have a very bad feeling about it. A gathering of this sort attracts all kinds of weirdos, as well as professional troublemakers.'

'Any excuse for a punch up?'

'Even things that start out with the best of intentions can go pear-shaped if the wrong people turn up.'

Nikki was about to leave, then turned back and told the super about PC Niall Farrow's impression of the Carborough. 'We are keeping our ears open in that direction, sir, but if you should hear anything, would you keep us in the loop?'

'Of course. And I'll ask uniform to put out a few feelers for you.'

Nikki walked back down the stairs and went into her own office. She closed the door and slumped down into her chair. A candle-lit vigil? She pictured the growing sea of flowers. Ever since the passing of Princess Di, this kind of thing had become almost *de rigueur*. But here? Helen? Suddenly the whole thing seemed to be getting out of control, like an avalanche gathering momentum.

'Must phone Rory,' Nikki muttered, remembering Sheila's message. She opened her phone and found his name.

'Ah, Detective Inspector! I know how busy you are. Well, I have something for you that probably won't help to ease your frantic day.'

'Wonderful! It's continuing as it started. Okay, let me have it. I can take it.'

'I've done some work on the card that was found in the trouser pocket of your unidentified man. It is a business card as we suspected. It was produced by a great big popular printing firm. You know the one — buy five hundred cards and get a free stuffed koala.'

'I get the picture. And so . . . ?'

'Although it appeared completely washed out to the naked eye, I've traced its origin.'

'Clever boy.'

'I know. And I was going to tell you that I used exquisitely sophisticated molecular spectroscopy . . .'

'But you didn't. So what did you use?'

'A damn great standard optical magnifying glass.'

'Of course. And what did it tell you?'

'That the card is a business card from the Willows Complementary Health Clinic.'

'Helen's old clinic!'

98

'One and the same. And another thing. It's by no means certain, but that lucky stone in his pocket was not just a beach pebble. It was a polished tumble stone. A purple sage agate to be precise and it is used by crystal healers to treat disorders of the throat. I have already ascertained that your man had a thyroid disease and several associated problems in that area, so I surmise that he was looking for help from somewhere other than the NHS.'

Nikki sat in stunned silence. Could there be a connection between Helen and the man in the river?

'I think you should find out whether the Willows Clinic has a crystal healer on the staff, don't you, Inspector? Because the only other place around here where I've seen an extensive collection of rocks and crystals, is at your friend's home on the Westland Waterway.'

'I will. I'll ring right now. Thanks for that little gem.'

'Gem? Oh, very droll, Inspector. Well, better press on. I'll ring you as soon as my preliminary report on Mr Agate is ready, and obviously earlier if we get anything back from the DNA database. The same for Helen. I will be preparing you a preliminary statement so you can get a clearer picture of what happened, then when all the toxicology and lab reports come back, I'll bring you the final results.'

'Okay, we'll speak again soon.' She closed her phone and looked at the clock. It was a quarter to four, only fifteen minutes until the afternoon meeting. The Willows would have to wait until the meeting was over. Right now she needed to fill Joseph in on Rory's findings. She stared at the growing stacks of papers and scribbled memos piled on her desk and wondered when she would ever find time to get on top of it all.

Eric Barnes leaned around her door. 'Ma'am? Just been handed this. It's from uniform.'

'Put it with the rest, please.' She motioned to the tower of paperwork.

Barnes raised his eyebrows at the pile and said, 'You may want to look at this first, guv.'

'I'll decide my own priorities, thank you.' She glared at the door. Taking the hint, the detective left with a sullen expression slowly spreading over his face.

When he was out of sight, Nikki picked up the memo.

To DI Galena from WPC Bryson.

Ma'am, you asked me to mention if anyone worried me. One man has been here every day so far, he stays for over an hour but returns several times right up until late evening. He brought a bunch of flowers this morning, so I've put them to one side should you wish to check them out.

Tapping her fingers impatiently on the desk, she decided that after she had interviewed Andrew, *if* he arrived when he said he would, she and Joseph should take a drive down to the Westland Waterway and perhaps have a word with the persistent mourner. But all that would have to wait.

* * *

'Quiet! We have a lot to get through in a very short time, so find a seat and listen up. Now, Dave and Cat. Would you please tell your colleagues what you discovered this morning?' Nikki said.

Cat recounted the statement made by Nigel Casey, then concluded, 'So, with the blood evidence already on our files, it is almost certain that Helen Brook had company in that cellar, and if that's the case, there is no reason to believe that her memory is incorrect either.'

'But surely someone who had just committed murder wouldn't walk around with his name emblazoned across his chest?' asked an officer.

'Be helpful if they all did,' muttered someone else.

'Maybe it wasn't his badge.'

'Maybe he forgot he was wearing it.'

'Yeah. After all, he was probably just going about his normal daily routine. He didn't know a building was going to fall on him, did he?'

Nikki held up her hand. 'Okay, okay. Let's recap on what we actually know. Helen Brook told me that a man spoke to her. He told her he'd killed someone. Said his name was Paul and the woman he'd killed was his wife. Then, later, a man with a name badge is seen leaving that exact area. WPC Nightingale? Did you get anything on female deaths occurring at that time?'

Jessie Nightingale stood up, and not for the first time Nikki thought she looked more like a cheerleader than a detective. 'Yvonne and I could find nothing that pointed to an unnatural death, ma'am. We are still checking hospital files. There are a few men named Paul who are next of kin to women who died of various illnesses, but nothing that sounds fishy.' Still standing, she added, 'I was wondering, ma'am, why would he want to kill Helen, when she never even saw him?'

Nikki rubbed her forehead, trying to ease the headache that was slowly building. 'We don't know that, Jessie. Helen was remembering more and more fragments every day. If she'd lived, well, she might have recalled something even more damning about him. Don't forget, if what Nigel Casey says is true, our suspect walked away from that cellar and left Helen there. He had clearly extricated himself. Maybe he went to her, thought she was dead, then when he read that article in the paper about her miraculous recovery, got scared that perhaps she had seen him after all.'

'Good point, ma'am.' Jessie sat down again.

'However, we can't direct the whole investigation towards this Paul. Niall, did you speak to that young scrote who was watching the house just before the murder?'

Niall raised his hand. 'He's not involved, ma'am. He's got the best alibi going for the time when Miss Brook was killed. He was banged up in the custody suite downstairs. His posh girlfriend had been sent away to stay with her granny in the Dordogne for a week or two. He went banzai, nicked her daddy's car, and trashed it out on the marsh.'

'Right, he's out. So, did any weirdos visit her at the Willows Clinic? Cat?'

Cat thumbed through her notebook. 'I'm still checking her client list, ma'am. But they are all pretty shell-shocked. No one has a bad word for her, and lots of them seem very *dependent* on her. I guess they are scared that now she's gone, they will fall apart or their illnesses will come back.'

Nikki frowned. 'More than you would expect, in the circumstances?'

'Yes, ma'am, definitely. She seemed to have some kind of a calming influence over her patients, sorry, her clients. Even the other therapists at the Willows commented on it. Oh, and there's this guy who works there,' Cat searched through her book for the name, 'Sam Welland. He specialises in something called regression therapy. Miss Brook had asked him to help her.'

'Really? I didn't know that.'

'She wanted to be hypnotised, to go back to the accident.'

'Did she indeed?' breathed Nikki. 'And was this Sam Welland going to do it?'

'Yes, guv. She'd already arranged it for two in the afternoon, on the day after she died.'

Nikki's headache increased. 'Well, well. How very convenient that she never made the appointment. I think I'd like to talk to Mr Welland myself.' *And ask about crystals.*

'He's at the Willows, Tuesday to Friday, ma'am. 10 a.m. till 6 p.m. And I've listed some thoughts on three or four clients that seemed particularly disturbed by the death. Would you like a copy?'

'On my desk please, Cat.' *Along with all the rest.* 'And I think that will do for now.' Chairs scraped across the floor and the officers began to disperse. 'Not you, Joseph. My office in five, please. And bring some paracetamol.'

* * *

In the privacy of her room, Nikki told Joseph about the connection between the dead man, who she now thought of as "Mr Agate," and Helen Brook.

102

Joseph looked as amazed as she had. Then, after thinking for a moment, said, 'I suppose it helps us in one way, it makes him local. If he knew about or attended the Willows Clinic, whether or not it was to see Helen, he had to live or work around here. Shouldn't we be getting ourselves over there and talking to this Sam Welland character?'

'The desk sergeant has just rung to say that Andrew is downstairs. We have to speak to him first. And someone is causing uniform concern down at the Westland Waterway. I said we'd call in and check him out.' Nikki stared at her desk. The reports and memos hadn't gone away. 'I can see that this will have to get dealt with after hours.'

Joseph stood up. 'Better get moving then.'

'Get Cat to sit in on our interview with Andrew, would you? Just as an observer. She can spot a lie at forty paces. I'd like her opinion on our friend and his obsessive work schedule.'

Joseph nodded. 'Good idea. We'll meet you in the interview room.'

A few moments later Nikki was standing in front of the desk sergeant. 'Is Andrew Gregory ready yet, Sergeant?'

The custody sergeant nodded grimly. 'I've just processed him, ma'am. Did you hear that we had to escort him in? One of the national newspapers picked up on the fact that we were looking for him, and I reckon they are preparing the gibbet as we speak. Whatever happened to innocent until proven guilty? Anyway, he's in Room 3, and DS Easter and DC Cullen are down there waiting for you.'

She and Joseph had already discussed the direction the interview would take. Now Nikki had to try to forget all she knew or believed about Helen's partner, and listen to everything he had to say with impartial ears.

Joseph was leaning against the wall and stood up straight as she approached. 'He has no objections to us taping the interview, ma'am.'

'But he looks like shit,' added Cat.

They entered the room and looked around. It was basic to say the least. A wooden table and four hard chairs, all screwed firmly to the floor. Sitting on one of the chairs was Andrew, but not the Andrew she had spoken to only a matter of days ago. This was a stranger: a hollow-eyed, unkempt figure slumped forward over the table.

He hardly seemed to notice them enter. She and Joseph sat opposite him, while Cat remained standing in the background. He paid little attention as they unsealed two new tapes and placed them in the machine.

Only when Nikki spoke, did he finally look up.

Glancing at the laminated crib sheet taped to the desk, she identified herself. Although she had interviewed and cautioned thousands of cases, she knew that one error or omission could see a case flung out of court. 'I am Detective Inspector Galena, my collar number is 1255. It is,' she glanced at her watch, '16.35, on February 23, and this interview is taking place in Greenborough police station. Present with me are . . .'

Joseph added his rank, name and collar number, followed by Cat.

'Also present . . .' She looked towards Andrew. 'Could you please say your name for the tape?'

He stared back in apparent disbelief, then said, 'Andrew Michael Gregory.'

Nikki hadn't wanted a formal interview, but the super had asked her to make sure and get it taped. Nikki ached to put her arms around the man and comfort him. After all, they did have one big thing in common — the loss of Helen Brook.

She hurried through everything that had to be said, offering him a solicitor, and informing him of his rights. 'You understand that you are not being cautioned, Andrew? You are here to assist us and are free to leave at any time, should you wish to do so.'

He nodded. 'Yes, I understand.'

'Andrew. The first thing I want to tell you is that we *will* catch whoever did this.'

'When can I see Helen?'

'Just as soon as the pathologist allows. I will make sure you know immediately, don't worry about that.'

'I want to see her, Nikki. I *need* to see her.'

'I know, but certain procedures have to be followed. I promise we won't drag it out longer than we need to.

'They think I did it.' His voice was low, and without emotion.

'Who thinks you did it?'

'The papers, the people outside. You lot.'

Nikki stared hard at him. She was suddenly bitingly angry at the partner who had left his lover and best friend alone with a houseful of nightmares. Her compassion left her. His "poor me" act no longer cut any ice. 'Then tell me what the hell you were up to when Helen was getting herself killed! Where were you, Andrew? And don't tell me you were in Switzerland, because we know different.'

His eyes flew open, lights coming on in a darkened house. 'I . . . I told you when I phoned. I was in London.'

'Why?'

Andrew took a deep breath and said, 'I got to Heathrow. Just before I boarded, my clients rang me and told me to hold off the trip. They thought the work I'd done from my terminal here might have sorted the problem after all.'

'So why didn't you come home?'

He screwed up his face. 'Because they've done this to me before, Nikki — or am I supposed to call you Inspector Galena? Whatever, they've told me to back down, then suddenly it's all urgent that I get out there again. I didn't want to go back home, then put Helen through the whole damned trauma of me leaving all over again.'

'So why not ring her and explain?

'How could I? You know the dreadful state she was in. I thought it best that she believe I was abroad as planned, then if I got home early, all well and good.'

'So where did you stay?'

He shrugged. 'Some tinpot place in Victoria . . . the Brunswick, on Seymour Terrace, I think.'

'Your company didn't know this, did they? Why was that?' Joseph asked.

He hung his head. 'I get expenses while I'm away, and hell, I could just as easily have been told to catch the next available flight anyway. Why tell them and lose the cash?'

Joseph looked sceptical. 'So you hung around in some rundown hotel and waited for a call from Switzerland? Can your clients verify all this?'

There was a long pause, and Nikki felt uneasy. Then he leaned forward, and said, 'Yes, they can. But it's a big company, you will need to speak to the right person. I'll give you their name and mobile number, so you can get them direct.'

Nikki didn't see Joseph glance at her, she didn't need to. There was something very dubious about Andrew's business dealings. She let it go for the time being. They could return to it later. 'Okay, but I want the office number as well. Now, why, when the call didn't come, did you not just get home to Helen? You said yourself what a dreadful state she was in.'

Andrew seemed to wilt. He put his head in his hands.

'That was the reason why I stayed away! I hate myself for saying this, but I couldn't cope with her. I couldn't face what I thought were her fantasies. How could I have known that she was right? That someone wanted her dead?' His shoulders shook. He was crying now. 'I loved her, Nikki, with all my heart. I just hated to see her like that. She was such a strong person, so in command of her life. It was horrible seeing her so out of character, so paranoid.'

Nikki reached across the table and touched his hand. 'I'm so sorry, Andrew. She was a beautiful and brave woman, and you are not the only one who let her down. But as we can't bring her back, the best thing we can do is find whoever did this. We need you to tell us the truth about absolutely *everything*, and help us, all right?' She stared hard at him. 'For the benefit of the tape, Mr Gregory is nodding his assent. Is that correct, Andrew?'

'Yes. I will help you all I can.'

* * *

Outside, Nikki looked from Joseph to Cat. 'Your thoughts?'

Cat tilted her head to one side. 'Something decidedly dodgy about his alibi, ma'am. Lying through his teeth, I'd say.'

'Agreed,' said Joseph.

Cat shrugged. 'But I'd say his distress is kosher. He's been hit by a thunderbolt. No one could look that distraught to order.'

Joseph puffed out his cheeks. 'Well, I've seen some award-winning stuff in my time, but again, I agree. That looked genuine.'

Nikki frowned. 'I'm with you both on that. I don't want to detain him any longer than necessary, but I would just like to check out that hotel in Victoria. Then we're going to have to smuggle him out the back door and spirit him home without the media getting wind of it.'

Cat grinned. 'Leave that to me, ma'am. I'll magic him away for you.'

'Good. As soon as his alibi is checked out, go talk to the sergeant about letting him go. And Cat, make sure Andrew knows that we have to be able to contact him at all times. No disappearing off to Switzerland, or even Skegness for that matter.'

'Wilco, ma'am.' Cat turned and hurried off down the corridor.

'Next stop the Waterway?' Joseph asked.

'Mmm, but first, if you'd get Dave and Eric working on confirming everything Andrew told us. I'm praying they come up with that hotel in Victoria, and that his Swiss mates confirm what he told us. We need to know that his dodgy dealings weren't connected to Helen's death in some way.'

'On my way. I'll meet you in the car park. And I'll drive.'

CHAPTER THIRTEEN

'Which one?' Nikki looked across the ever-growing sea of sombre faces.

'There, ma'am. To the right of that big tree over on the river walk. Navy padded jacket. He's been there since dawn.' WPC Bryson looked across the road.

'And his flowers?'

The police officer picked up a small spray of three white lilies tied together with some green garden string. She passed it to Nikki. Their overpowering perfume struck her immediately. It always reminded her of funerals, and she'd seen more than her fair share of those in the past few years. She pushed the painful memories back, turned over the plain white card and read, *Death is not the extinguishing of the light, but the blowing out of the candle, because dawn has come.*

She frowned and looked across at the tall, well-built man, standing with his head bowed. He looked about thirty, possibly older. His clothes were well cared for and his dark hair was unfashionably long and wavy. 'Carefully chosen words, don't you think, Constable?'

'Beautiful, actually, ma'am. I wonder where they are from?'

'I've not heard them before. Maybe he wrote them himself.'

'No, he didn't. They are by Rabindranath Tagore.' Joseph's voice was soft. 'And you are right, Constable, they are very beautiful.'

'You never cease to amaze me, Joseph Easter. Where did you dredge that little nugget up from?'

'Actually I always thought it would be nice to have that as the inspirational thought to go on the Order of Service for my funeral.'

Nikki shook her head. 'You're a cheerful sod, aren't you? She turned back to the WPC. 'Have you spoken to him?'

'No, ma'am. I can't leave my post here.' She looked around her and shivered. 'It's spooky. Sometimes you can hear a pin drop, as if there's no one here. Then you look up and see all those eyes staring at the house.'

Nikki looked at the silent people massed in front of the house. 'Thank you, Constable. I'll go and have a quiet word. Anyone else catch your eye?'

'Not me, but my colleague asked me to mention someone he noticed on his shift.' She pulled a small piece of paper from her pocket. 'This man caused a bit of a fracas yesterday evening. Really distraught, apparently. Started screaming and yelling at us to get off our backsides and catch the killer. One of the other officers got his name and address and escorted him away. Later, PC Cooper told me he thought the man was putting on an act.'

Nikki stared at the name on the piece of paper. 'Titus Whipp? You are joking?'

'I'm afraid not, ma'am. And the address is correct. PC Cooper checked before he asked me to mention it.'

'Okay. Probably just an attention seeker, or someone with a particular dislike of the Old Bill. Still, it's worth a call.'

Nikki tucked the paper into her bag and began to make her way through the crowd, towards the man across the road.

'Hello, sir. I'm DI Galena and this is DC Joseph Easter. You look as if you knew the woman who died here.'

His eyes were dark and bovine, and the face almost pretty. He didn't answer at once. The dark eyes shone, and he said, 'Helen Brook was the nearest thing to an angel that I have ever had the privilege to meet.'

'Were you a client of Miss Brook?'

'Yes, Inspector Galena, for many years. I'm not sure how we, that is, her patients and friends will ever get over this.'

'What's your name?'

'Oliver Kirton.'

Bells rang in Nikki's head. 'Any relation to Superintendent Arthur Kirton?'

'He's my uncle, Inspector. But he was never stationed at Greenborough. How do you know him?'

'I worked out of Peterborough for a while.' Nikki had good cause to remember Arthur Kirton, or at least his bigoted attitude to women police officers, and his arrogant, condescending manner towards the lower ranks.

'It's all right, Inspector. Please don't try to find something pleasant to say about him, because I'm sure I couldn't. The man's a prick.'

Nikki raised an eyebrow. 'My officers tell me you have spent a lot of time here, Mr Kirton. Do you think that is wise?'

'Where else can I be close to her?'

The eyes were enormous, bigger than they ought to be. Nikki wondered what this man's problem was. 'Can I ask you something, Oliver?'

'Certainly, you can ask.'

'Why do you think Helen Brook affected people so deeply?'

Kirton appeared to think about this, then he raised his eyes to the grey cloudy sky. 'Because she knew how to listen. When she spoke to you, she spoke only to you. Sometimes the simplest word or gesture from Helen would leave me with a sense that I'd been privy to something profoundly spiritual. Added to the unfairness of surviving one life-threatening disaster, only to have that precious life stolen from her so cruelly.'

Nikki nodded, wondering if they were talking about the same woman. The Helen she had known certainly had a wonderful, warm, spiritual quality, and always had time for everyone. On the other hand, she had also tipped a plate of chilli con carne over Andrew's head during one of their many battles. Her fights with Andrew were sometimes nothing short of spectacular. Oliver Kirton, however, seemed to want to raise her to sainthood.

Nikki looked across to Newlands, needing to tear herself away from the intensity of his gaze. He might be eerily good-looking, but this was one creepy guy. After a polite goodbye, she thought they should perhaps check up on just how creepy he really was.

* * *

Joseph and Nikki drove directly to the Willows Clinic, hoping to get there before Sam Welland left for the evening. Helen had been a practitioner there for several years, and although she had often spoken about her colleagues, Nikki did not recall any of them individually.

Sam Welland looked every bit as shell-shocked as the rest of Greenborough. After the usual platitudes, he said, 'Yes, Helen did ask for help. I'm not sure what I expected, but she was a very good subject for hypnosis, so it could have been a very informative session.'

'What do you mean by a good subject? How would you know?' asked Nikki.

'I've hypnotised her before, Inspector. Not long after the accident. For pain relief and to help her sleep.'

Nikki frowned. 'She never said.'

It was the therapist's turn to frown. 'Did you know her? I mean personally?'

'Yes, Mr Welland, DS Easter and I were her friends.'

He sighed. 'I'm sorry. It seems there are a lot of people who are grieving her passing. She certainly touched a lot of lives.'

'More than I realised, sir. Have you been near her home recently?'

He shook his head. 'No, but I saw it on the news. It's such a shock. You never think anything like this will happen to someone you know, and I believe a lot of people actually felt they knew her, after that article in the paper a while back.'

'It seems everyone loves a good tragedy these days,' Joseph said.

His smile was very attractive. 'Oh, they always have, the guillotine being a prime example. The crowds around that were phenomenal.'

Nikki nodded. 'I suppose so. But about Helen. Can you talk about her freely?'

'Under these circumstances, of course. Normally what a client says is private. We are not required to take any oaths, but our code of practice is very clear on such matters. And I wouldn't wish to impede your investigation in any way. I want Helen's killer found as much as anyone. Please, ask away.'

'You obviously knew all about the accident, and the fact that she believed that someone was following her with the intent to harm her?'

'Yes. The purpose of our session was to see if the man really existed. She wanted to eliminate the possibility that this mystery person was a figment of her imagination. We considered that her terror could have been so great — being alone in such a traumatic situation — that she invented a friend, someone to comfort her.'

'And confess that he was a murderer?'

He grimaced. 'Ah well, that's the problem. Her mind might have allowed this figure's personality to get out of hand. She might have hallucinated, imagined things. And of course, he could have been real. In which case, we needed to know if she would be able to identify him again.'

'Knowing Helen as well as you did, did you form any impressions prior to your proposed session?'

Sam Welland took a deep breath. After a while he said softly, 'Yes, and I'm guilty of thinking she might have been suffering from some kind of post-traumatic episode. Until

I heard about her death, I believed we were going to find no more than a belated glitch in her recovery from a serious head injury.'

Nikki exhaled softly. *Yet another friend feeling the heavy weight of conscience on his shoulders. Welcome to the club.*

'And today, just before you arrived, I remembered something else.' By now, he was looking thoroughly miserable.

'Yes?'

'Helen asked us all whether we had seen anyone hanging around, someone who seemed to be watching her. We all said no.'

'And?'

Welland stared at his desk. 'I think I might have been mistaken. A couple of days before she died, I saw a man sitting on the wall outside the clinic. People often sit there, waiting for someone to come out. It wasn't unusual or suspicious, but I've just remembered that I'd seen him once before.'

'Where?'

'Helen and I had lunch together last Tuesday. We went to that coffee shop near the bridge, the one with the potted trees and tables outside?'

'Café Printemps?' said Joseph.

'That's the one. We would often sneak down there for a latte and a Danish, just for a break from our clients. Well, the same man was on the other side of the road, leaning on the railings by the river. We sat at a window table and he was out there for ages. I just know that after I'd paid, he'd gone.'

'You are sure it was the same man? Could you describe him?'

'It was the same chap, Inspector, wearing exactly the same clothes. He seemed . . . He seemed to be not much more than a vagrant. Badly dressed, shabby worn jeans, a thick, faded sweater, I forget what colour, and a really grubby jacket.'

'What sort of jacket?'

'A parka, I think, and it was a sort of dirty khaki.'

'Age?'

'I never saw his face. The jacket had a hood, and it was bitterly cold. The way he moved made me think around thirty-ish. He definitely was not a kid, but he wasn't some old wino, either.'

'And what makes you now think he was watching Helen?'

'Because it's just dawned on me that the second time I saw him, he had been sat outside the Willows for about half an hour, and he'd gone at just after midday. Helen only had one client that morning, a regular, and she always left at twelve.'

'So you think he followed her?'

'Possibly. No, probably.'

'Does the clinic have CCTV?'

'Yes, on the entrance and the fire door. I'm not sure if it goes as far as where he was sitting. Shall I check?'

'Please, and I'll take all the footage for the last month as well. Would you recognise him again, Mr Welland?'

'I'd recognise the outfit, but not the man.'

'Pity. Because he could be the man that killed her, so I doubt he'll keep that particular wardrobe for ever, do you?'

Welland sighed. 'Well, if it were me, I certainly wouldn't. I'm sorry not to be more help, Inspector. I'll get you that footage.'

'One last thing, Mr Welland. Do you have a crystal therapist here?'

'No, although we do have a selection of small crystals and stones on the counter in reception. We let our clients help themselves to them if one takes their eye. Helen did an experiment once, to prove that the body knows what the body needs. Crystals all have strong vibrations, and they work on certain ailments or particular parts of the body. She was certain that people were attracted to the right stone for whatever ailment bothered them. She was right eighty percent of the time, which I thought was pretty amazing.'

'So anyone could have picked one up at the counter?'

He nodded, looking puzzled.

Joseph glanced across at Nikki and raised an eyebrow. Nikki nodded back. She knew what Joseph was asking her.

'Sir? If we brought you a photograph of someone, would you be prepared to see if you recognised him? And before you say yes, I have to warn you that it is a post-mortem photograph of a man who had been in water for some time.'

'Oh I see. But if it's important, of course I'll take a look.'

'Thank you, sir. We'll be in touch tomorrow.'

CHAPTER FOURTEEN

Back at the station they found Cat waiting for them in the foyer. She looked worried.

'Saw you drive in, ma'am. We've hit some real snags regarding Mr Gregory's statement. I don't know what he's up to, but he's being pretty frugal with the truth.'

'About what?' Nikki pulled off her coat and they walked up the stairs to her office.

'Mainly his job and this supposed trip abroad. Everyone is so damned cagey. No one wants to talk to me or Dave.'

Nikki hung the coat on the back of the door. 'Well, did they tell him to cancel, or not?'

'He *was* due to go to Zurich, that I know, but only one woman was prepared to admit that they *may* have asked him to postpone the trip. Even getting that out of her was like getting blood from a stone.'

'Was that the person he said to speak to?'

'No, I couldn't get hold of her. The number he gave us was unreachable, and when I went through the normal channels, I was informed that she was no longer employed by the company.'

Nikki sat down heavily. 'But they *were* clients of his? Of Seymour Kramer Systems?'

'Oh yes, ma'am. And you've hit the nail right on the head there. *Were* is the operative word. They closed their account this morning, and Seymour Kramer are in uproar over it.'

'So surely that confirms it? That's why they stopped Andrew going out there.'

Cat looked at Nikki. 'Andrew Gregory went apeshit when we told him about it. You might think that's understandable, given they were his biggest client, but this was way out of all proportion, ma'am. You should have seen him. We were waiting for the sergeant to finish the paperwork, and he went berserk.'

Nikki stared at her. 'Is he all right now?'

'Dunno, guv. He demanded to be allowed to leave. He didn't wait for me to be taxi-driver, he just took off like a rat out of a trap. Anyway, I thought I'd wait around until you came back to tell you personally what happened. Oh, and ma'am, Eric checked out that place Gregory is supposed to have stayed at, and there's no hotel called the Brunswick in Victoria. Doesn't sound too good, does it?'

'So, he has no alibi for where he was at the time of Helen's death. Nice one, Andrew. You really are helping your cause no end! We'd better get him back in, Cat, and quickly. The super is not going to like this.'

'I knew you'd say that, so I've already asked uniform to get out to Fentoft Quay.'

A young officer knocked and entered. 'Sorry, ma'am, but we've just had a call from the crew we sent out to Gregory's place. He's not there, ma'am, and the place has been done over. Taken apart, by the sound of it, and Andrew Gregory's car has gone.'

'Oh shit! I should have hung on to him while I had him.' Nikki's jaw jutted out. What the hell was the stupid bastard doing? She was still sure that Andrew hadn't killed the woman he claimed to love, but she still needed answers, and there was only one way to get them.

She stood up, and with a voice as steely as her eyes, said, 'Okay, put out a call for his arrest. On suspicion of the murder of Helen Brook.'

* * *

'Got him, guv! Look. The wall is just visible to the left-hand side of the picture.'

Jessie Nightingale had been watching the footage from the Willows Clinic.

Nikki leaned over Jessie's shoulder. 'Rewind a bit.'

The film flew backwards, then they watched as the hooded figure approached the wall, and sat with his back to the camera. He was exactly as Sam Welland had described.

'What would you say was his age?'

'Hard to tell. His clothes are rubbish, but they are fairly modern. His build and way of walking are not very young, though.' Jess shrugged. 'Twenty-five plus?'

'Mmm, maybe even a little older. Look, that's Helen coming out of the building!'

'And guess who's getting up and walking after her, ma'am? She was right, wasn't she? About everything. This bloke is definitely following her.'

Nikki felt sick. Just because they had picked up that love-sick moron watching his bird's house near to Helen's home, they had chalked it up as problem solved! They should have looked further. 'Jess, if we've got the footage from the Café Printemps, would you fancy some overtime this evening?'

'They've just arrived, guv.' She pointed to a large poly-thene bag. 'And the CCTV ones taken from the town bridge as well. I've got no plans, so I'll get started, shall I?'

'Please. I want a better shot of this man. Face on. I know he has a hood, but maybe one of the cameras will give us something that the IT guys can enhance.'

'Show me committed, ma'am.' Jess undid the bag, selected a cassette and pushed it into the player. 'Don't worry, I'll find the bugger, if it kills me.'

* * *

Nikki went back to her office and sat down. She had sent Joseph out to Andrew's place to get a first-hand report of what had happened. Now all she could do was wait for his call. She sat back and closed her eyes for a few moments. It felt as if everything was suddenly escalating, getting ahead of her. There was so much to do, but it was getting late. She would need to pace herself. Tired detectives didn't work to their full capacity. As soon as Joseph was back, she would shut up shop for the night and they could start fresh in the morning.

The phone made her jump. 'Joseph? Anything to report?'

The line was crackly. 'I'd say this place has been professionally trashed, ma'am.'

'No sign of Andrew?'

'No, and it's hard to tell whether it was done before or after he got here.'

'What if he went somewhere else, not home?'

'He was here, ma'am. The jacket he wore to the station is over the back of a chair.'

'His passport?'

'No sign of it, but that could mean he already left before the heavy mob arrived, or they took it, along with him.'

Nikki winced. Andrew Gregory was either knowingly involved in something he shouldn't be, or he was in deep, deep trouble. Either way, he was probably in grave danger.'

'Okay, Joseph. Pick up every scrap of paperwork you can find there. Bank statements, credit card stuff, telephone bills, letters, anything you can lay your hands on. And bring his computer. I need to know exactly what Andrew was really doing with his amazing computer skills.'

Joseph said softly, 'Nikki? Do you think Helen's death is connected to whatever Andrew has got himself involved in?'

'I'm not convinced, but Rory Wilkinson said that all that stuff done to Helen could be a cover to make it look like a weird psycho attack.'

'When all the while it was a carefully planned execution?'

'Joseph, until we have some solid evidence, I'm ruling nothing out.' Nikki hung up the phone and shouted for Eric Barnes to come to her office.

He came in, brushing droplets of water from his overcoat. 'Just got back from interviewing Mr Titus Whipp, ma'am.'

'And?'

'One serious screwball in my opinion.'

'How so, Detective?'

'For a start, he collects stuffed birds. Has a house full of them. They give you the screaming habdabs, ma'am, all those beady eyes watching you. And the house itself is a museum. Walls covered in paintings, dusty old books lying everywhere, and, oh yes, even a human skull on his coffee table.'

'And the man himself, DC Barnes? What's his connection with Helen Brook?'

'He went to her for help about something that he prefers not to talk about. That was some time before her accident. Whatever the problem was, she helped him get over it, and I get the feeling he developed a bit of an attraction to her. He was outraged when she was injured. It seems he actually went as far as threatening the family of the lorry driver who caused the Blackmoor Cross crash. Said her blood was on their hands.'

Nikki raised her eyebrows. 'Really? Good work digging that up, Eric. So what about his feelings now? Uniform said he was abusive and aggressive outside Helen's house.'

'He's well pissed off, guv. He gave me a right ear-bashing. Said I should be out looking for her killer, rather than interfering in the lives of those that loved her.'

'He used that particular word, *love*?'

Eric Barnes nodded. 'And *adored*, and *worshipped*, all in one very long sentence.'

'Dangerous, would you say?'

'Possibly, although I suspect he's all mouth and trousers.'

Nikki was curious to know what someone named Titus Whipp looked like.

'He's forty-nine, fairly short, stocky build, receding hair, but he keeps what's left of it long and straggly. Wears Buddy Holly style glasses with thick, dark frames, and his dress sense was not present at the time of my interview, ma'am.'

Nikki wanted to smile, but didn't like to give him too much praise in one sitting. His massive ego needed no help from her to inflate itself.

'Right. Now, having spoken to him, would you consider him a possible suspect?'

Barnes shifted in his seat. After a moment's consideration, he said, 'I suppose we can't afford to disregard anyone who has a clear and present hang-up about the deceased. So, yes, I'd put him on the list, but a very long way beneath Andrew Gregory. He's the one we should be concentrating on.'

Nikki calculated that it had taken sixteen words and a fraction of a second for Eric Barnes to neatly undo a very impressive day's work. 'Thank you, Detective. Please add Whipp's details to the board. That will be all. Get yourself home now.'

Thankfully the phone rang, so she could legitimately look away and allow Barnes to leave before he could give her any more of his unwanted opinions.

'Rory?' She listened for a moment then said, 'Sure. I'm closing up here anyway. I'll meet you in twenty minutes. Give me the address and I'll be there.'

* * *

Blackstone Fen was about fifteen minutes out of Greenborough town, and Nikki was glad of the drive. Soon the sprawl of houses was left behind, and she found herself on the long straight road that led across acres of farmland to the marshes.

Rory had asked if she would meet him at a remote spot called Malford Farm. The name was familiar to her, but it wasn't until she carefully guided the big car along the bank of a wide dyke, lined with willow trees, that she realised that this was not her first trip to the place.

As she pulled into the parking area, she immediately recognised the ivy-clad Queen Anne farmhouse, and the immaculate gardens leading down to a boating lake. Rory's ancient Citroen Dolly was already there, and as she pressed the central-locking system on her car, she heard a friendly voice call out her name.

'DI Galena! How *are* you? Your superintendent conned you into manning the tombola for our garden party last summer, didn't he?'

Nikki smiled when she saw Jenny Jackson's petite form. 'For my sins. It's not my forte, to put it mildly. You'd have probably made more money if you'd employed a three-toed sloth, but you don't say no to my superintendent, especially when it comes to raising money for the local hospital.'

'I'll second that. But come on in. Professor Wilkinson's in my studio waiting for us.'

Jenny led the way through a series of corridors, then out through French windows into a floodlit courtyard. On the far side was a large barn conversion, with window panels in the roof, all finished off with a small whitewashed clock tower.

'Very nice! I didn't see this before.'

'Yes, well, you were chained to the tombola, weren't you?' Jenny's voice had a sing-song quality. She sounded as if she were about to laugh, whatever the conversation was about. 'Come on in. I'll make some coffee, and then I'll try to help you with your mandala.'

Jenny Jackson's artwork covered the walls. It was all bold photographs and mixed-media designs. Nikki looked around, amazed at the massive colourful impressions.

'This is my favourite, Inspector. What do you think?' Rory stood, hands on hips staring up at a fantastic explosion of scarlet, fiery orange and vivid green.

'Wow! What is it?'

Jenny's voice echoed from the other side of the studio. 'It's based on Kirlian photography. Computer enhanced and enlarged, but it started life showing the changes in the energy fields around a tomato plant leaf when it's cut with a knife.'

Nikki gave Rory an "Is it me?" look.

Rory laughed. 'My friend Jenny has an interesting and very colourful take on life. Luckily she also knows something about mandalas, so with your permission, I'd like to show her the design that we took from the house on Westland Waterway.' He whispered, 'Don't worry, the copies I've brought are images of the design, not forensic photographs, and I've known Jenny since university.'

Nikki smiled. 'No problem. Any help we can get is much appreciated.'

They accepted the coffee and sat down at Jenny Jackson's design bench. Rory produced a laminated sheet of paper bearing an image of the complicated green circles.

'Interesting! And by no means typical. If there is such a thing with mandalas. What do you know about them, Inspector?'

'Not a lot. A friend told me they were used as a method of concentration, in meditation. Other than that, nothing. Are they Buddhist in origin?'

'Oh no, they are universal images. They're not attached to any particular belief system, and they are used by Buddhists, Hindus, Native Americans, and yes, Christians too. Some of the most mystical designs are Celtic.'

'They don't look Christian,' said Rory.

'Ever been to Paris?'

Rory nodded emphatically. 'Many times.'

'Then you've no doubt seen the rose windows in the Notre Dame?'

His eyes widened behind his spectacles. 'They are mandalas?'

'Perfectly exquisite ones. You'll find them in churches, temples, all sorts of sacred places. The word comes from the Sanskrit, meaning circle. They are — how can I put it? Energetic spiritual doorways. Connections from us to the world about us.' Jenny stood up and went across to a long bookshelf. 'I think I've got a picture book here somewhere. It will give you an idea of how they are constructed. Ah, yes.' She withdrew a slim volume and brought it back to the desk.

Nikki and Rory looked at the pages of brightly coloured geometric forms. All made up of or within circles, they had names like Spiral Rain, Electric Harmony and Lotus Spirit.

Nikki sighed. 'I admit that these are beautiful, but it's really not my thing. I can't imagine how all these designs can mean anything. They remind me of being a kid and looking into a kaleidoscope.'

'That's exactly how you begin to understand them, Inspector. They are a primal pattern based on the circle. They emanate from the core, expand, grow, then return to the centre to begin again.

'Sorry. I'm totally lost.'

'Me too,' added Rory.

Jenny Jackson took a deep breath. 'Well, rather than try to explain sacred geometry to you two philistines, I'll tell you this. If you leave it with me, I think I can decipher it, or some of it.' She looked serious. 'But I really need to know its purpose. What is the significance of this particular design?'

Nikki thought for a moment, then said, 'Mrs Jackson, all I can tell you is that this was found at the scene of a murder.'

'Oh dear. Well, that explains the sudden visit from my friend the forensic scientist along with a detective inspector.' She looked at the paper again, this time almost suspiciously. 'Okay, I'll spend some time with this when you've gone. I can already see that there are astrological signs and some particular runic symbols that may well help your enquiry.' She looked at Nikki. 'I guess you want this yesterday?'

'I'll appreciate anything you can give me, just as soon as you can, Mrs Jackson. And please, don't show this to anyone, and don't mention that you are helping us. It is an integral part of our investigation, and a part that no one is privy to. Do you understand?'

Jenny Jackson nodded. For once the laugh had left her voice. 'For a change, I'm alone here for the next couple of days. My husband is in Ireland looking at some breeding stock for the farm, so there will be no one else here to see this. I'll ring as soon as I have something for you.'

Outside, Nikki leaned against the side of Rory's aging motor and looked at him. 'How does she know all that stuff? I'd never even heard of sacred geometry.'

'And she couldn't quote you the Road Traffic Act of 1988, dear heart.' He grinned at her over his glasses. 'Horses for courses. She studied art in all sorts of forms — tribal art, ritual stuff. She was always interested in symbolism, because she uses it in her designs.'

'Well, I can certainly use whatever she comes up with, even if I do need an interpreter to understand it.'

'Got any suspects in your sights yet?'

'Not really. We are looking at a few odd ones — a creepy client with the hots for her, and another who's determined to canonise her.' Nikki stretched. She was beginning to feel the strain. 'Which reminds me, I mustn't forget to make some enquiries about that particular man. Strangely, I knew his uncle. He was a superintendent when I worked in Peterborough, a real bastard.'

Rory's brow creased. 'What's his name?'

'Kirton, Oliver Kirton. Why?'

'Well, I'm blowed! Ollie Kirton! Must be my day for encountering old college chums. Although Ollie wasn't exactly a chum. Bit too fond of the ganja for my taste.'

Nikki slipped an arm through his. 'Rory, you are the answer to a maiden's prayer! Come sit in my car and tell me everything you know about him!'

Rory grinned. 'Perhaps we should move out of Jenny's garden? I would hate her to think we were sitting here talking about her. Pull in by the bridge just before the main road and I'll reveal all!'

Five minutes later, they were sitting in the X-Trail, the engine running to keep the heater going.

'So, he liked the weed?'

'That and anything else that was on offer. A great experimenter, our Oliver.'

'Forgive me for asking, but is he . . . ?'

Rory laughed. 'Gay? Well, not completely, but as I said before, he was a great experimenter. Sadly, the answer is no, although those haunting Byronic features gave a lot of young men restless nights, I can assure you.'

'So did he drop out of uni?' Nikki asked.

'Good Lord, no! Oliver dabbled because he was bored. He found everything so bloody easy. Nothing challenged him. He soaked up information like a sponge and sailed through his degree.'

'What does he do now?'

Rory leaned back and frowned. 'No idea. I was more than surprised when you said he was back in Greenborough. For a long while he slipped off the radar, then I heard he'd been in and out of clinics, mainly down south. Somewhere in Surrey, I think.'

'What sort of clinics?'

'Expensive ones.' Rory puffed out his cheeks, and smiled conspiratorially. 'Now you know I'm not one to gossip, but according to the grapevine, the speed finally got to him. If what I've heard is true, to say that his thought processes were disturbed would be something of an understatement. Apparently his amphetamine psychosis was virtually indistinguishable from paranoid schizophrenia.'

'Jesus! He seemed so calm when I saw him.'

'Calm? Or spaced out? Wide-eyed?'

Nikki remembered the strange eyes and that intense gaze. 'Could be.'

'Then, praise be, at least his current medication must be working.'

'What on earth would he be consulting Helen about? She was an aromatherapist, a reflexologist, not a psychologist.'

'Complementary and alternative medicine is often recommended for stress relief. Or maybe he just found the idea of a beautiful woman anointing his body with perfumed oils something of a turn-on. Why don't you ask him?'

Nikki pulled a face. 'Looks like I've got that dubious pleasure to come. Do you think he's dangerous?'

'If he's being a good boy and taking his meds, he'll be a veritable lamb. But if he's being an arsehole and either not taking them, or taking something un-prescribed, then watch out for the hallucinations, or the delusions. In fact, send someone else to do the interview, preferably someone who weighs seventeen stone and is built like a brick outhouse.'

'Well, this one is down to me, though after what you've told me, I won't go alone.'

'Sensible woman. Now I'd love to stay and gossip, but I badly need some sleep or my complexion will suffer untold damage. Plus, David is cooking paella, and I love paella! *And* I need to try to hurry up some of the reports on your friend, all before I can retire to my boudoir with small slices of cucumber on my tired eyes!'

He stepped out into the cold, pulled his coat around him and hurried towards his old Citroen. 'Catch you tomorrow!'

CHAPTER FIFTEEN

Early next morning, Nikki looked out from her office and saw heads already down. The whole team was working hard. For once there was little banter. Earnest questions were batted back and forth and telephone conversations were quietly underway. Nikki stood up and, finishing her second coffee of the day, walked over to where Jessie Nightingale was sitting.

'Last night? CCTV? Any luck?'

Jessie shook her head. 'The café's material is no better than the ones from the Willows. In fact, the clinic ones are clearer. That hood is a bummer. It masks his face very effectively. Oh, but I have seen one other thing. He has a limp. Nothing major, but he does drag his left leg.'

'Let's have a look.'

Before Jessie could press play, there was a shout from the other side of the office. 'Guv! Come and look at this. Local TV news! It's the super.'

Several officers were staring at a news update on the television. Superintendent Woodhall had finished his plea for help and the TV cameras had zoomed in on the crowd spreading down the Westland Waterway.

'Bloody hell! That has trebled from earlier today!'

An interviewer with a microphone was talking to some of the mourners. As the lens panned round the crowd, Jessie suddenly exclaimed, 'Look, ma'am! Right-hand side! Just behind that little kid with the silly fur hat! It's him! That's the bloke that was following Helen!'

Nikki ran from the office and almost fell down the stairs in her haste to get to the uniformed sergeant. 'Radio your officers at the scene of crime! There's a man there, he's wearing a parka jacket and faded blue denim jeans. He has a limp. I want him brought in now! And, Sergeant, not in front of the TV crews. Get him away from those cameras first.'

While she waited, Nikki went to find Joseph.

'Andrew Gregory's computer had been stripped of information, ma'am. IT tells me it's the most professional piece of work they have ever seen," he said.

'But they can restore it, can't they?'

Joseph looked doubtful. 'Norman reckons it would take until the next millennium. They've used a very advanced program to destroy everything on it. Some kind of super-bug, he says.'

'What on earth could Andrew have that would be sensitive enough to warrant wrecking his house, wiping his computer memory and possibly kidnapping him?'

Joseph's expression was serious. 'That's not all, ma'am. Eric Barnes has been helping me check out his finances, and Andrew Gregory has a serious amount of money. Accounts everywhere, even offshore. Eric has only scratched the surface but he's located thousands of pounds squirreled away, and all the accounts were opened quite recently.'

Nikki's mouth dropped open. 'Andrew?'

''Fraid so, ma'am. But I do have a bit of good news. Do you remember that laptop we took from Helen's house?'

Nikki nodded. 'It was hers, wasn't it?'

'It was a sort of communal one. It held a mixture of games and downloaded web stuff: e-cards, music, Helen checking on the availability of aromatherapy oils, that kind of thing. There was an encrypted file on it too, and Norman has managed to break in. It's all about something with the code name Telstar. What that is, we don't know yet, but Norman is working on it now.'

'It sounds like he might have used Helen's computer when he couldn't get back to Fentoft Quay. Maybe he didn't want certain information on his own laptop.' She whistled softly. 'Thank God we already had it in our possession! That would certainly have been wiped too.'

'No doubt of that. Oh, and I've had his computer at Seymour Kramer confiscated. One of our lads has gone to bring it back.' Joseph looked at her. 'Do you think Helen's death is tied up with all this? Like the prof said, all the weird stuff was just to throw us off track?'

'Let's see what this yob, the one who was stalking her, has to say first, shall we?'

'Have they got him yet?'

The murder room door opened. 'From the look on Niall Farrow's face, I'd say they have.'

'We have him for you, whenever you are ready, ma'am.'

'No fuss?'

'No, ma'am. Our officers had been talking to a lot of people anyway, so it didn't look suspicious. Luckily, he decided to cooperate and he was spirited away very quietly. He started to panic when I spoke to him, but Jessie soon talked him down. She was fantastic actually, really patient with him, all things considered.'

'What do you mean by that?' It was an odd comment to make.

Niall stared at her. 'You've not seen the local paper?'

'No, why?'

'I'm afraid the old story has resurrected itself. Hang on, I'll show you.' Niall walked from the room and returned a few moments later with a well-thumbed copy of the *Greenborough Standard*. 'Look, centre-page spread.'

Together, Nikki and Joseph read the article:

Three Part Tragedy.
As our town reels under the shock of the murder of
Helen Brook, our reporter, Sandy O'Neill, asks about
two other unsolved Greenborough mysteries. Who
deliberately lured Fireman Dan Moore to his death
in a blazing warehouse? And where is PC Graham
Hildred, the missing policeman who earlier in his
career risked his life rescuing a child from the River
Westland?

Joseph was angry. 'Oh shit! Not again! How many more
times will they do an article on Graham? Poor Jess! Just when
things calm down, some arsehole goes and digs it all up again.'

Niall shrugged. 'I guess they'll keep on, Sarge, until we
have an answer.'

'After all this time, that could well be never,' added Nikki.
It was an old story, but one that haunted Greenborough nick
like no other. Jessie Nightingale had been engaged to one of
the beat bobbies, PC Graham Hildred. Then one day, after
they'd had breakfast together, he had kissed her, walked out
to go to work, and disappeared. No one had seen or heard
from him since. Jess had been devastated, but had always
maintained that one day they would know the truth. She
had soldiered on bravely, but she didn't need it raked up and
thrown in her face every other month.

Nikki brought herself back to the present. 'Okay, our
stalker. What sort of man is he, Niall?'

Niall Farrow puffed out his cheeks and raised his eyebrows. 'Not what I expected. He's very jumpy, but not just
because we want to talk to him. I'd say he's twitchy, anyway,
in a fruit loop kind of way.'

Nikki looked at Joseph. 'Okay, let's see what we make
of him, shall we?'

* * *

Back in that bare room, Nikki and Joseph sat looking at a new interviewee.

This man was very different from the missing Andrew Gregory. He stammered, his eyes darted around the room, everywhere but Nikki and Joseph, and he shifted constantly in his seat.

'Your name is Paul Brant?'

He nodded furiously. He asked why they wanted to talk to him, swearing he knew nothing about Helen Brook. He refused a solicitor. 'Why do I need one? I've done nothing wrong.'

'But you did know Ms Brook, didn't you?'

'I . . . No, I didn't know her.' He bit furiously on a thumb nail. 'No.'

'Then why were you following her, Paul?'

He swallowed loudly, and rubbed his eyes with his knuckles. 'I wasn't following her.'

'We have evidence to the contrary, Paul, recorded on CCTV. We *know* you were following her.'

'Can I see my doctor, please?' He sounded close to tears.

'We have already offered you time to see the duty medical officer. Are you now saying you want to see him?'

Brant looked frightened. 'No! I need to see my own doctor, she'll understand. I can't talk to a stranger!' His eyes darted around the bare room. He looked like a trapped animal. 'And I don't want to talk to you either. I want the other woman, the nice one.'

Joseph looked at Nikki. 'I guess he means Jessie.'

Nikki nodded. 'Paul, do you mean the policewoman who spoke to you when you were brought in?'

He nodded, violently enough to induce a migraine.

'For the tape, I'm asking Detective Sergeant Easter to leave the room to see if WPC Jessie Nightingale is in the building. Thank you, Sergeant.'

Joseph left the room. Nikki wondered what this guy was on. As Niall had said, he wasn't exactly what they expected from a stalker. Although he was shabbily dressed, he didn't look like a wino or a homeless person. Rather it was as if he had given up on himself, forgotten to shave, couldn't be bothered to wash his hair. More than anything Paul Brant looked lost, and frightened.

'I don't mean to upset you, Paul. We are trying to find the person who hurt Helen, so we have to ask a lot of people a lot of questions. Do you understand?'

Brant stared at his ragged thumbnail. Almost imperceptibly, he nodded. 'Yes, I suppose so. Now can we wait for the other lady please?'

The next five minutes were spent in a silence broken only by the sound of Paul Brant chewing on his few remaining nails. Nikki was greatly relieved when the door opened and Joseph and Jessie entered and introduced themselves for the tape.

Jessie sat herself down opposite Paul and spoke softly to him.

Nikki retreated and took up a position near the door. A few moments later, and after a few suspicious glances directed at Nikki, Paul Brant began to talk.

'I wasn't following her. Well, not like you think. I needed to talk to her but I didn't have the courage. I kept trying. That's what I was doing if you saw me near her. I was trying to find the right words, and find a way of approaching her.' He stared into his lap miserably. 'You don't think I frightened her, do you?'

Nikki bit her lip. *Not much! Only terrified the shit out of her.*

Jessie assured him that Helen hadn't been frightened. Then she asked, 'What was so difficult to ask her about, Paul?'

'Would you ring my doctor? The number is in my wallet.'

'Don't you want to talk to us anymore? Only you're being really helpful.'

'I want Dr Chambers. I can't talk about what happened! Not won't — can't! She'll explain.'

Nikki noted that he was becoming excessively agitated, and decided to call a halt to the interview. 'I'll ring your doctor, Paul. You have a break and we'll talk later, okay?'

'When Dr Chambers gets here?'

'Sure.' Whenever that might be, thought Nikki, knowing the reluctance of GPs to turn out for their patients. As Joseph handed Paul over to the custody officer, Nikki added, 'And thanks, Jessie, he seems to respond well to you. Could you stick around for the next session?'

'No problem, ma'am.'

Back in her office, Nikki stared at the telephone number. It was not a Greenborough one. She recognised the code, but was not sure where it was. She keyed it in, and was surprised to hear the doctor herself answer. She introduced herself, made quite sure that Dr Chambers did indeed treat Paul Brant, then briefly described the situation.

The doctor sounded worried. 'Oh dear. I was afraid something like this would happen, Inspector. Look, I've got one more patient to see before lunch, then I'll drive over. I can make it in about an hour, is that all right?'

Nikki asked her where she was coming from.

'Oh, didn't Paul tell you? I'm based at Needham Hall Psychiatric Hospital, just outside Louth.'

Nikki replaced the receiver, and put her head in her hands. Oliver Kirton was paranoid, now she had learned that Paul Brant was receiving psychiatric care. Along with Titus Whipp, who was simply barking mad, and a boyfriend who had deep, dark secrets . . . What on earth kind of men did Helen Brook attract?

* * *

Joseph spent a few moments talking to Niall about the atmosphere the uniformed officers sensed on the streets. Nothing the younger man told him made him feel any easier. Not only was there tension among the people gathered at the Westland Waterway, the edginess in and around the Carborough Estate seemed to be slowly mounting.

Niall spoke anxiously. 'I'm still no closer to knowing what's going on out there, but whatever it is, I hope it doesn't kick off until this weird stuff about Helen Brook has gone away.'

Joseph agreed. That could be very bad for the police, very bad indeed.

Back in the CID room he went into his tiny office and closed the door. Time to try another route into the troubles on the Carborough. He pulled out his phone and found the number he wanted.

Mickey answered after two or three rings.

'Hey, Mickey! How are you doing?'

'Joe? I'm okay, and you?'

Joseph stiffened. Mickey's tone had none of its usual enthusiasm. 'Something wrong? Other than Archie?' Joseph hoped that Archie hadn't just shuffled off his mortal coil.

'Archie's not good, Joe. But you know him. He's hanging on.'

'I hear that the family has all come home to be with him.'

'Yeah, it's pretty intense around here.'

Maybe that was it. Joseph decided he had better go for broke. 'I need your help, my friend.'

'From what I hear you need more than me. This vigil thing is freaking people out. I bet you guys are run off your feet.'

'Something like that, and two murders aren't helping either. Mickey, what's going down on the estate? It feels like someone has lit a fuse and everyone is waiting for the big bang.'

For the first time since Joseph had known Mickey, he fell silent. After a moment, he lowered his voice and said, 'I can't talk about it, Joe. I dare not.'

Joseph felt his stomach tighten. 'Are you in any danger, Mickey?'

'No, no, nothing like that, but it's personal, okay? I'd tell you if I could, but . . .'

'Okay. I know the rules. But if *anything* happens and you are scared, you come to me or Nikki. Do you understand?'

'Thanks, Sergeant Joe. I won't forget.' The line went dead.

Joseph closed his phone and stared at it. Mickey was a bright, incredibly energetic teenager. As a kid he had been hyperactive, with considerable attention deficit problems, but since being adopted by Peter, Archie's youngest son, he had gone from strength to strength. After several unfortunate incidents, inside and outside the law, he had kept in touch with Joseph and they had developed a kind of special alliance. Now the boy's odd reticence to talk worried Joseph a great deal. The only thing he could have meant when he said "personal," was that something serious was happening in the Leonard family circle. Maybe it was something to do with Archie's impending demise. Perhaps there was dissension around Raymond taking the throne. He was certainly the next in line to be King of the Carborough, but he wasn't the eldest son. Joseph knew there was an older one, also called Joseph, but as far as he knew, the number one son was making an honest living as a successful businessman. As were Peter and Fran, the couple who had adopted Mickey. Joseph pulled a face. But apart from the immediate family, there were dozens of other villainous Leonards — cousins, uncles, brothers and numerous in-laws. Perhaps there *was* trouble in the camp.

CHAPTER SIXTEEN

Carolyn Chambers was nothing like Nikki had expected. She was taller than Nikki by almost a foot, an aging Amazon. Even if Dr Chambers was pushing sixty, she was exactly the sort of person Nikki would like to have with her when she interviewed Oliver Kirton. She exuded strength, but not in the physical sense. What flowed from the doctor was the fortitude of a wise woman or a high priestess.

She held out her hand. 'I do hope I've not kept you waiting, Detective Inspector. My last patient took a little longer than I had anticipated.'

Her voice was deep and calming, and her handshake firm and reassuring. Lucky patients, thought Nikki, who had come across more than her fair share of loony mental health practitioners in her time.

'Not at all. I expect you'd like a few moments alone with Mr Brant before we start the interview?'

'That would be appreciated. Thank you.'

Nikki led the way down the stairs. 'I'll have a word with the custody sergeant. He'll get Mr Brant brought to an interview room. He was pretty upset, Dr Chambers. That's why I terminated the last interview. I'm afraid he didn't take to me at all. He said it wasn't that he didn't want to talk, but he couldn't. I guessed there had been some deeply upsetting incident in his life that prevented him speaking freely.'

'You are very astute, Inspector. As soon as I've had a word with him, I'm sure he will allow me to talk on his behalf.' She gave Nikki a sympathetic smile. 'Once you hear his story, I'm sure you will understand.'

Nikki nodded. 'I hope so, or I'm afraid he could be in a lot of trouble. Ah, Sergeant Jones. This is Dr Chambers from Needham Hall Hospital. She's here to speak to Paul Brant.'

As soon as doctor and patient had been allocated a room, Nikki called Joseph and WPC Jessie Nightingale to be on hand for the second session. It wasn't long before the doctor emerged and said that Mr Brant had given his consent to her speaking on his behalf, and was happy to help them with their enquiries.

After the usual formalities, Nikki began the interview.

'We have in our possession taped evidence showing you following Helen Brook on at least three occasions, Mr Brant. You have admitted wanting to talk to her about something. Can you tell us what that was about, please?'

Paul gave his doctor a beseeching look, and nodded.

Dr Chambers sat back. She looked at the three police officers and said, 'Paul Brant has agreed that I tell you about his previous medical history, in order for you to understand why he was trying to talk to Miss Brook. You will then also appreciate why it was so difficult for him. About eighteen months ago, Paul's wife, Amy, was diagnosed with a rare form of motor neurone disease. It was rapid in its onset and, sadly, it was terminal. Initially, Paul left his job to care for her, but because of financial difficulties, he had to take part-time work, leaving his mother looking after Amy until he came home.' Carolyn Chambers looked at her patient and gently touched his hand. 'Are you all right with this, Paul?'

He nodded.

'On the day of the Blackmoor Cross accident, Paul's mother fell asleep watching the television. Amy managed to reach her medication, and took a fatal overdose. When

Paul arrived home, his mother was still asleep, and his wife was dead. He blamed himself. He convinced his mother that Amy was just sleeping, and sent her home. He then lay on the bed with his wife for a while, before pulling on his jacket and walking out.'

Nikki began to realise where this was going. She felt more than a little queasy.

'Paul was suffering from a form of dissociative amnesia. He couldn't handle what had happened, so he just blanked it out. But he walked straight into another nightmare when that building collapsed.'

Nikki closed her eyes and sighed. 'You were in that basement with Helen. You talked to her. You tried to keep her conscious, to keep her alive?'

Paul wrung his hands together and stared at Nikki. 'I thought she was dead, like Amy! I managed to get free and crawl over to her, but she wasn't breathing. I'm sure she wasn't breathing!'

'Steady, Paul. It's all right, really.' The doctor looked at Nikki. 'This is very upsetting for him. He's come to terms with his wife's death. He now knows he wasn't to blame, but this isn't easy for him.'

'I understand, Dr Chambers.' She turned to Paul Brant. 'Would you like a break? Maybe a coffee or a tea?'

'No, I want to get it over with.' He seemed a little calmer. 'It was that article in the paper. I couldn't believe my eyes! She was alive. Helen was alive! Then I started to remember all the things I'd said to her, about killing my wife.' He looked exhausted, but went on. 'I just wanted to explain, now that I was better.'

He glanced at the doctor, who added. 'Paul spent a long while as an in-patient at Needham Hall, almost six months actually. He's still an out-patient under my care. Go on, Paul.'

He sniffed, then continued. 'Yes. I thought, what if she doesn't remember what I said? Perhaps I should just let it go. But I couldn't, just in case it haunted her, upset her. I didn't want her to live believing she had been trapped in that basement with a murderer. That would be terrible!'

And it was, Paul, believe me, it was really terrible. Nikki pushed away the vision of Helen's frightened face begging her to believe her about the killer in the cellar. 'But although you followed her, with the intention of talking to her, you never actually made contact?'

'Never. Then . . .' He swallowed hard, his Adam's apple moving up and down. Tears filled his eyes. 'Then it was too late.'

'One last question, Mr Brant. Did you ever follow her to Tumby Fenside, the bird reserve?'

'Uh, yes. Yes I did. But I never went close to her. I thought I might frighten her. It's lonely out there, too lonely to accost a woman on her own. I left her walking the river path, and I went home.'

'I think that's enough now, don't you?' The doctor's voice was gentle, but it left no room for argument.

Nikki murmured her agreement. As the others left the room, she looked at Carolyn Chambers and quietly said, 'Can I have a word before you leave?'

Back in her office, Nikki closed the door and offered the doctor a seat. Leaning back in her own chair, she studied this woman, wondering how much she could safely tell her. After a moment of deliberation, she said, 'I have a problem. As you know, Paul Brant was seen following Miss Brook. We know he is — how can I put it? Not exactly stable.'

'Paul is fine, Inspector. He is improving in leaps and bounds. He is not out of control, neither is he a danger to anyone. That I promise you.'

'Forgive me, Dr Chambers, but he doesn't look in control. In fact, he doesn't look as if he's managing very well at all. Look at his clothes for a start.'

The doctor sighed. 'I know what you're thinking, Inspector, but honestly, this is just a setback. He had smartened himself up and was doing really well, until he saw that article. It knocked him sideways for quite a while, but he *was* going to deal with it. He just went about it all wrong.'

'He terrified Helen Brook, Doctor. I know, because I was her friend, and she told me so.'

Dr Chambers closed her eyes and groaned. 'Oh no, don't tell me that. He was sure she hadn't seen him, that she'd never even noticed him.'

'Oh, she knew she was being followed. We even had a car watching her house for a time. So, Dr Chambers, you actually knew what he was doing?' Nikki sounded more accusatory than she had intended.

Again Dr Chambers sighed. 'This sounds dreadful in the light of what happened to Helen Brook, but yes, he told me about the article. He told me he wanted to see her to explain about the things he had said. I didn't stop him because I believed he was doing the right thing. What I didn't know was that he would find it so difficult to make contact with her. I never dreamed he would finish up practically stalking her. I would never have allowed it to get that stupid. I did suggest he write and make an appointment, I even offered to go with him. He just said it was something that he should sort out by himself, and I honestly believed he was capable of doing it. And in his defence, I believe he would have done, had this tragedy not occurred.'

'In your professional opinion, Dr Chambers, could Paul Brant have killed Helen Brook?'

She answered immediately. 'Absolutely not. He's incapable of doing such a thing.'

'I have to tell you that he's very vague about his whereabouts at the time of the murder, which doesn't help him at all. But in my heart of hearts, I don't believe he did it. I shall be letting him go.'

The doctor gave a loud sigh of relief. But Nikki had more to say. 'However, I want your word that you will keep a close eye on that young man. And I don't want him leaving the area. My superintendent might not see this in the same light as me. If I have to bring him back in for further questioning, then I will.'

Carolyn Chambers' voice was grave. 'I understand, Inspector. I have already made one error of judgement with Paul Brant, something that I've never done before, and I won't be repeating the mistake, I assure you.' She stood up and held out her hand to Nikki. 'You are not wrong about Paul, Inspector Galena. He's not bad, he's just damaged by guilt.'

Damaged by guilt. Nikki repeated the words in her head. A strange dizziness crept over her, then she realised that Dr Chambers was still speaking. 'So, can I wait for him? I'll see he gets home safely. I know you have your job to do, but this will have put a great strain on him. I'd like to make sure he's going to be all right.'

Nikki nodded. She needed to clear her head. 'If you'd like to wait here, I'll go get the paperwork sorted, and I'll get someone to fetch you a coffee.' Before she left she turned and said, 'Paul's very lucky to have you for a doctor.'

'I beg to differ, Inspector. Luck has never had anything to do with Paul Brant.'

* * *

Joseph and the rest of the team were all in the CID room when Nikki walked in.

'Shall I get that PM photo of Mr Agate over to the Willows Clinic, ma'am?'

'Yes, but while we are all here, let's just get up to speed on where we are right now. Any news on Andrew Gregory, DC Barnes?'

'A camera caught his car heading towards the main Boston road, but that was yesterday, and he's not been seen since. His mobile has not been used either, ma'am.' Eric pulled a face. 'He's guilty as hell. Pity we ever let him go in the first place.'

Nikki gritted her teeth. She was tired, aware her fuse was short, so she went on, trying not to look at the young pillock sitting opposite her. 'Anything more on his finances?'

'Nothing to add at the moment, although we are still digging, ma'am.'

'What about this computer that was lifted from Helen's home?'

Joseph was about to answer, when his phone rang. Nikki heard him say, 'Really? Norman, would you come up to the DI's office and tell the team that? What? Right, ah, okay. See you in five.' He flipped his mobile closed.

'Guv, can we go up to IT? Norman's found something pretty important on that computer. It's too important for him to log off and walk out on the thing.'

The IT lab was on the top floor, and when the four CID officers entered they saw Norman Hebbenstall surrounded by his techno-colleagues.

Nikki felt a tremor of excitement. She badly wanted to know what Andrew Gregory was up to, and from the furore in the lab, it had to be something pretty special. 'What have you found, Norman?'

'Wouldn't I like to know, ma'am! This is the most sophisticated spyware program I have ever seen. He calls it Liberator.'

'And it's just sitting there on Helen's laptop, along with some "I love you" e-cards and downloaded Hits of the Sixties?'

'Pretty much, ma'am. It's encrypted, but the likes of us geniuses can access it easily.'

'He must have been absolutely confident that no one knew about Helen's computer.'

'That's why it's on here, ma'am, and not the main computer from his office. Charlie here has just taken a look at that, by the way. The drive has been cleaned out, completely erased. There's nothing left but its original factory settings.'

Nikki frowned. The technology had left her behind some years ago. 'So, this program? What does it do?'

There was a ripple of chatter from the techies.

'One at a time would be nice. And make it clear for a nitwit like me, please.'

Norman looked up. 'Sergeant Easter tells me that Andrew Gregory builds security programs to protect sensitive corporate data, right? Well, there's more to it than that. It appears that in this case his software program searches out security vulnerabilities, then he issues a patch and the user downloads it, ostensibly to sort the problems. And it does, but it also permits Andrew to access all the activity on the user's computer.'

Nikki threw up her hands. 'Patches? Lost already!'

Norman exhaled. 'It's keylogging at its finest. Well, the simplest way to explain it is that it's like Big Brother for the Internet. It monitors and records every keystroke made. But in this case it is very clever spyware and it leaves no evidence of its presence. It's about as good as anything I've ever seen, ma'am, and worth a fortune on the market.'

'So, this has the possibility to wreck business competitors?'

'Absolutely. My God, can you imagine what would happen to those companies' share prices?'

Nikki fought to collect her jumbled thoughts. Helen's Andrew? Toppling big businesses? This was ludicrous. He'd always been a workaholic, but some kind of super cyberthief? Surely not!

Norman went on. 'And another thing, ma'am. His work computer was erased by an outside source, not by a local operator.'

'How on earth . . . ?'

'Easy, Inspector. Send an email. Mark it urgent, put something on it that his secretary thinks is kosher, she opens it and bingo!'

'If he was so damned clever, surely he would have built in something to protect his own files?' asked Nikki.

'Oh, no doubt he did, but we are talking about messing with the big boys here. There are users out there that could get into the Pentagon, if they want to. And of course, there is also the possibility that Gregory did it himself, from his own laptop or another computer.'

'No wonder the bastard's running.' Eric Barnes' supercilious tone cut in yet again.

This time Nikki spun round and hissed, 'Detective! I'm sick to the stomach of your snide comments. If you are so damned clever, get your backside out there and bloody well find him!'

Red-faced, Barnes began to stutter a reply, then thought better of it, and left the room.

Nikki looked at Joseph. His expression said that she'd overstepped the mark. She looked at Cat, and hers said, Ace! Good for you, guv! She ignored them both.

'Okay, Norman. Thank you for all your hard work. You'd better make sure you look after this, uh, fantastic piece of kit, if that is what you might call it?'

'Don't worry about that, Inspector, I'll deal with it immediately. I'll have to notify my boss. There is a special protocol to follow in cases like this.'

Nikki returned to the murder room. She saw that Eric Barnes' desk was empty. Maybe he'd taken her literally. Then she saw Jessie Nightingale still at her computer and staring blankly at the screen.

'How late were you here last night scanning those CCTV videos, Jess?'

'Till around three o'clock, ma'am.'

'And you were back in at half seven?'

'More or less.'

'Then get yourself home and get some sleep. You can't work non-stop. This investigation has a long way to go yet.'

Jessie made a small gesture of protest, then logged off and stood up. 'Thanks. I appreciate it, guv.'

'What next, ma'am?' asked Joseph.

'We take a trip to the canteen. Then you get Cat to take that picture to the Willows while you run a background check on Paul Brant. Meanwhile, I'll try to demolish the mountain of paperwork on my desk. Oh, and if I shout for a petrol can and a box of matches, please ignore me.'

* * *

Somehow Nikki managed to work uninterrupted until early evening.

'I've brought you a hot drink.' Joseph placed the mug on her desk and sat down opposite her. 'Paul Brant seems to be whiter than white, although his breakdown was apparently something to behold. He trashed his place of work, then followed that up with a suicide attempt, hence his hospitalisation.'

'Okay. We'll put a big question mark over him for the time being, and concentrate on Andrew.' Nikki leaned back in her chair, her hands clasped behind her neck. 'Where is he? And what the devil is he up to? Hell, Joseph, we *know* him! We've had dinner with him, drunk with him, laughed with him. I just don't see it, do you?'

Joseph sounded disappointed and rather hurt. 'We *thought* we knew him. I actually liked him too. He's a total techno-brain where his beloved computer systems are concerned, but I believe he did love Helen. I guess something too big for him to handle just got in the way.' He yawned. 'Oh, and that PM photo didn't ring any bells with Sam Welland, but he said he'd ask his part-time receptionists if any of them remember a man taking the purple sage agate. Apparently they like watching people choose the crystals. It's a long shot, but one of them might just remember who took it.' He stood up and stretched. 'I thought I'd give it until about ten, but you look knackered. Why don't you get away? Take some of the advice you gave to Jessie. I'll hold the fort here.'

'Maybe I'll take you up on that, Joseph, but ring me if anything happens, okay?'

'Of course I will.'

* * *

Eric pulled down the blinds, flicked on the anglepoise lamp and switched on his laptop. The room was small and smelt of cigarettes and two-day-old pizza. It was crap accommodation by anyone's standards, but he didn't care. He wasn't about to spend his hard-earned cash on a flash apartment in this shitty little town. It was a stepping stone. Just like the job. Working with a load of carrot crunchers was a necessary evil, until he could move on — and up. His blood still boiled from the bollocking that pompous fucking bitch of a DI had dished out. What right did she have to disrespect him in front of an office full of men? Worse than the abuse, was the fact that that stupid cow, Cat Cullen, had been there. She had abso-fucking-lutely loved it. He'd seen her face, gloating at his embarrassment. Eric's jaw clamped when he thought about it. Best not think. Best just to get even. He was pretty sure he knew how to do that, and get one over on that whole fucking shower in the process.

He pulled back the wooden chair that served as seat, clothes hanger and bedside table and flopped down in front of his laptop. The narrow desk was jammed against his bed, which was fine by him. It meant he could easily access the reams of papers, memos, scribbled notes and e-mails that lay scattered across the bedspread.

You have mail showed on the screen. He took a deep breath and clicked it open.

Yes! He printed off the list of names and addresses and stared at it. All we need now is a match. He turned to his bed-top filing system and began to riffle through the papers. Finally he located the report that he was looking for. Two names matched, but one stood out. He bit his lip. So, all he had to do was tie up this new information with what was already on the PNC. But no way was he going back to the office tonight. Someone would be working late, probably the old cow herself, and he didn't want to share what he'd just discovered. He stretched and yawned. He was pretty safe until the morning. No one else had hit on this line of enquiry, and it was something of a long shot. Whatever, if the name matched, he knew it was worth a visit, and if he was right, and he was fucking sure he was, then he might just have nailed that lying bastard, Gregory. With a sigh, he pushed the papers onto the floor and flung himself onto the bed. Oh, that would be so sweet a result — *and* one up the arse for DI Galena and her precious team.

CHAPTER SEVENTEEN

Before she took the nine o'clock meeting, Nikki was called to Superintendent Woodhall's office. Moving some books from the least cluttered chair, she sat down and waited for her boss to finish a phone call.

He replaced the receiver and rubbed his brow thoughtfully. 'I've had to say yes to this vigil, Nikki. It's scheduled for tomorrow evening. I can't really see a way around it without upsetting too many people, and frankly I want it over as soon as possible, then maybe we can get the Waterway back to normal again.'

She nodded. 'I thought as much. We'll have a substantial presence there, I suppose?'

'Yes, and I've asked for volunteers from the neighbouring divisions. I want it low-key and respectful, but we can't afford to get caught out. It should go off quietly, but I don't want some gang of local yobs, or even worse, a bunch of organised rabble-rousers using it as an excuse to cause trouble. How would you feel about going? She was a friend of yours.'

Nikki frowned. It was the last thing she wanted. 'No thanks, sir. Not my scene. I'll grieve in my own way. Frankly I find this sort of thing quite bizarre. Most of the people who go won't even have met her, let alone have known her well.' She shook her head, then added, 'But thinking about it, I might go and mingle anyway. It's a good chance to observe a few people in particular.'

'Hoped you'd say that, Nikki. Take a couple of your team with you. It could be informative.' Woodhall rummaged unenthusiastically through a heap of papers, then pushed them aside and looked into her eyes. 'What's worrying you?'

'I guess it's all this stuff about Andrew Gregory, sir. I don't know him as well as I knew Helen, but, hell, we go back years! It's really hard to swallow, that someone you know, someone who's been part of your life in one way or another, is being accused of being some kind of criminal mastermind.'

'And he might have killed someone close to you?'

Nikki shook her head. 'Maybe what he's involved in got her killed, but he didn't do it, sir.'

'Then it would be nice if he'd come and talk to us, wouldn't it? Instead of bloody well doing a runner.'

'I hear what you're saying, Super, but my money is still on an outsider for Helen's death.'

He raised his eyebrows. 'But you let Paul Brant go? Now that did surprise me. He's the one she was so frightened of, the one she asked us to protect her from, for heaven's sake.'

'That's true, but she didn't know his real reason for trying to talk to her.'

'And you believe him, Nikki? Just like that? That's not like you.'

'We've confirmed about his wife dying. And we've checked with the hospital records. He was an in-patient for almost six months.'

'Maybe, but that doesn't mean he didn't kill her. If he is, or was, deranged in some way, he may well have done it. And his alibi stinks.'

'I'm aware of that, and we haven't discounted him, sir. His doctor has him on a very tight leash at present. One slip and I'll rein him in faster than the speed of light, believe me.' Nikki glanced at the ornate brass clock on the superintendent's wall, surrounded by official-looking photographs. 'I should go. I have to take the morning meeting. Will you excuse me, sir?'

Woodhall went back to ferreting through his papers, and Nikki took it as permission to leave. She had known he would be less than delighted when she let Brant go, but all things considered, it hadn't been the bollocking she had anticipated.

* * *

The meeting was over quickly. There was very little to report. As the officers moved off to their individual tasks, Nikki saw Rory Wilkinson approaching her.

He pushed an envelope towards her. 'Something new, Inspector. Helen Brook. That design?'

'Come into the office, Rory.' She led him in and gestured towards a chair. 'Has Jenny Jackson been in touch already?'

Rory shook his head. 'No, this is a forensic report on the medium used to make the design, and it's as bizarre as the rest of the case. I'd wrongly assumed the drawing material to be paint, or maybe ink, but I was wrong. The lab began the usual examinations and found it wasn't paint at all. They viewed it under the microscope, and determined its composition by infra-red analysis. Along with the chemical data, they found it to be something called malachite green.'

'I've heard of that before.' Nikki tried unsuccessfully to recall what it was.

'It's a chemical, a toxic poison actually, sometimes used as a dye, but mainly as an anti-fungal treatment for fish.'

'Fish? What, like Koi carp?'

'Exactly.'

'That's where I've seen it. When I was a child my father had carp in his pond, until a heron had a hearty breakfast one morning. He had some of it in a cupboard in his shed, used to threaten me not to even go near it.'

'It's great for fish diseases, but for humans it's pretty nasty. It shouldn't be breathed in. It's an irritant, thought to be carcinogenic. They used it extensively and very successfully in large scale fish-farming, but I believe it's been banned now in favour of something a little less toxic.'

'Why on earth . . . ?'

Rory looked utterly nonplussed. 'Search me. Sorry, but I just provide the findings. I'm afraid it's down to the good detective to fathom out the whys and the wherefores.'

A knock on the door interrupted their conversation. 'Someone down at the front desk asking for you, ma'am. A Miss Duchene?'

Rory got up and placed the envelope on her desk. 'Gotta go anyway. I'll leave you these reports, and I'll let you know what Jenny comes up with.'

She nodded, trying to remember where she knew the name from. 'I'll be down in a minute, Constable.' Oh yes, the woman who had tried to give her the cheque for Helen. *Damn! I really don't have time for this.*

The woman sat quietly in the foyer, looking at the notices pinned to the wall.

Nikki held out her hand. 'Miss Duchene? How can I help?'

'I'm very sorry to bother you, but do you have a moment or two? I really need to speak to you.' Her face was lined with worry.

Nikki immediately regretted her impatience. 'I'll see if the sergeant has a free room we can use.'

She sat down opposite Carla Duchene. 'Have you decided what to do with the money yet?'

Carla Duchene looked puzzled for a moment, then smiled. Despite her worried expression, her face was beautifully made-up and her hair looked like something from *Vogue*. The only thing marring the perfection was the sadness in her eyes, and a hint of darkness beneath them that the foundation had not managed to cover. 'Oh yes, I decided to give it to the Willows. I thought that Helen Brook would have appreciated that. After all, a lot of her work was done there.'

'I'll bet they were thrilled with ten grand!'

'We've set it up as a fund, so that those that cannot afford the treatment can still be seen.' She looked down in an almost embarrassed manner. 'Yes, they were delighted, Inspector Galena.'

'That's wonderful, a very kind gesture. But I'm sure you've not come here to tell me about that.'

Carla Duchene's face darkened. 'No. The thing is, I've joined with the Willows to organise the vigil, you know, tomorrow night?'

Nikki nodded. 'Yes, I hope to be there myself.'

'Oh good! You see, I'm not sure if I'm upsetting some-one in some way.' She delved into her handbag and retrieved a folded sheet of notepaper. 'I volunteered to pay for the flowers that we will be floating on the river. A supplier from Spalding said I can have them at cost, considering what they're for, which was very kind, of course.'

Nikki fought back her impatience. 'So, who exactly do you think you have upset?'

'Sorry, I'm getting off track. That's the problem, I don't know who. I went down to the river early this morning to meet the flower wholesaler. It was heaving with people there, terribly crowded.'

Carla Duchene was really beginning to irritate her now.

'And anyway, I must have been there for over an hour, then when I got home, I found this in my pocket.' She carefully laid the note on the table. 'It had to have been put in my pocket today, because I only picked this coat up from the cleaners yesterday.'

Nikki looked at the white paper. The words were in large, neat capitals. "CANCEL THE VIGIL. KEEP AWAY FROM THE RIVER OR SOMEONE ELSE MIGHT DIE."

Carla Duchene was still talking. 'Initially I thought someone was frightened by the number of people who would be close to the riverbank in the dark. Maybe they thought it could be dangerous, especially if there are kiddies there, and there will be, of course.'

'And now you think differently?'

Carla looked unsure of herself. 'I keep going over the wording, and now I'm wondering if there might be a more sinister message there. Cancel the vigil, or else. Am I being silly, Inspector?'

Nikki stared at the note. 'Not in the least, Miss Duchene. I'm glad you brought this in. Can I take it, please? I'd like my boss to see it.'

'Naturally. That's why I came, and to ask you what you think we should do about tomorrow night.'

'Has anyone else handled this?'

'No, only me.'

'Hold on, I'll just be a minute.' Nikki went to the front desk, retrieved an evidence bag and returned to her visitor. She carefully placed the note in the bag and sealed it. Then she turned to look at Carla. 'Did you notice whether you were jostled at any point? I know it is difficult in a crowd, but did you notice anything definite?'

Carla shook her head. 'There were an awful lot of people there, as I said. I certainly don't recall anything in particular.'

Nikki felt a shiver of concern about the warning. She was certain that's what it was. Someone with honest concerns about public safety would voice their anxieties publicly, not surreptitiously stick notes in women's pockets. 'Who at the Willows is helping with the arrangements for tomorrow?'

'Eh, Julia Abbott, the practice manager, and Sam Welland, one of the therapists. Do you think we should cancel?'

It shouldn't be damned well happening at all. Nikki looked at Carla and said, 'I think I need some advice from the superintendent. Can I ring you?'

Carla stood up to leave. 'Of course. But without being rude, the sooner the better. If we have to make alternative arrangements, we don't have much time. Naturally, we'll do whatever you advise. And, Inspector?' She looked at Nikki, almost beseeching her. 'Do you think this person means me any harm? After all, it was my pocket he put the note in.'

'I'm sure the warning is general, Miss Duchene. Someone does not want the vigil to take place. You are part of the organising team, and maybe you were easiest to accost. I would try not to worry too much. I really don't believe this is personal.'

Carla was visibly relieved. 'I hoped as much, but, well, after what happened to Helen . . . Thank you for your time. I appreciate it.'

'Would you be happy to let us take your fingerprints, to exclude them from any others on the note?'

'Of course.' She glanced at her watch, 'I have an appointment to get to, but I'll certainly come in first thing tomorrow.'

Carla Duchene left the room, leaving a trace of perfume behind. Nikki picked up the evidence bag, showed her out, and made her way quickly back upstairs to find Superintendent Greg Woodhall.

* * *

'I've reassured her that it's most likely not directed at her, but frankly I'm not too sure. What do you think, sir?'

The superintendent stared at the note and pulled a face. 'Why would anyone want to stop the vigil? And want to stop it badly enough to resort to threats.'

'Well, I wouldn't think it was the killer. According to most documented cases, he would be revelling in all the attention for what he's done.'

'Mmm. And why threaten Miss Duchene anyway?'

Nikki shrugged her shoulders. 'Perhaps it's intended to perpetuate the whole thing. Keep it boiling, make it even bigger than it is. If the media gets hold of this, the situation could get way out of hand.'

Greg Woodhall nodded. 'I see your point.'

Nikki shrugged again. 'Or it could be directed straight at Miss Duchene? Something else entirely, and they're using the vigil as a cover to get at her. She's a wealthy woman, boss. Perhaps there's another issue here.'

'Whatever, we don't stop the vigil. It goes ahead as planned, but with a whole lot more plain-clothes police officers in the crowd.'

'And Miss Duchene?'

'If she still wants to attend, we keep a very close watch on her.' The superintendent handed back the plastic envelope. 'And get this down to the lab straightaway. It may be nothing, just some crank, but then again it could be from Helen's killer, and we can't afford to miss a thing.'

Nikki picked up the plastic bag and looked again at the large, evenly spaced capital letters. 'Okay, I'll inform Miss Duchene of the decision to go ahead.'

* * *

Nikki sat with the team in the CID room. 'I'm very concerned about Helen's apartment being locked. As you know, when I arrived and found her dead, I had to break in. The place was shut up tighter than a duck's backside, and the keys were *inside*. We know that Andrew Gregory had just had the locks changed, and most of the keys have been accounted for.'

'Most?' asked Yvonne.

'Andrew has his with him, we checked that. But now he's gone missing.'

'Surely that points heavily towards Gregory being the killer, ma'am?' said Niall. 'It's nearly always someone close, isn't it?'

'You are beginning to sound like the superintendent, PC Farrow. And I'd agree with you, except that I know Andrew Gregory, and although I can't ask you to believe me without any proof, I just cannot believe he did it. He's up to his eyes in something, that's for sure, but murder Helen? I just don't buy it.'

Cat was doodling on a scrap of paper. 'Well, as we have more or less discounted her stalker, Paul Brant, what other avenues are there if it's not Andrew Gregory? The locksmith? Or a client of Helen's maybe?'

'That's where my thoughts are heading,' replied Nikki. 'Although the locksmith has been eliminated. He was from an accredited firm, we've used him on occasions, and he has a confirmed alibi for the time of the murder. It's the patients that interest me. Any more luck with the list?'

Joseph answered. 'Well, we do have a short list of special cases, all people that she treated outside the Willows Clinic. There are about six or seven that she used to see, either in their own homes or at her apartment on Westland Waterway.'

'Anyone stand out?'

'Officers have spoken to four of them. None seem anything other than deeply distressed at her death. Then there is the chap that we met at the river, uh, Oliver Kirton. We knew you would want to tackle him personally. Let's see, another one is on holiday until the weekend, and the last one is dead.'

'Kirton is next on my list, and I've been advised to take someone with me.' Nikki grinned at Niall Farrow. 'Ah yes, Niall! Someone of your physique will do nicely.'

'Is he dangerous, ma'am?'

'No idea, but an ex-university chum of his, our very own Professor Wilkinson, suggests that he may be on some kind of serious medication — or not, as the case may be.'

Niall grinned back. 'No problem, ma'am. I'll be right behind you.'

'Right *beside* me might be more useful. Now, back to the list. We have one other possibility. Andrew Gregory is somehow involved in the design of some amazing computer program which has got our whole IT department drooling uncontrollably onto their keyboards. Apparently it can bring down billion-pound businesses if a rival company gets hold of it. There is a chance that Helen Brook was murdered in order to put the fear of God into Gregory, and stop him going any further.'

Yvonne raised her hand. 'Surely a professional hitman wouldn't have used the weird method our killer used?'

'It all depends on the man who was hired to do the job. Let's face it, no one who goes around assassinating people can be regarded as normal. Maybe something there just flipped him out, and he decided to have some gruesome type of fun. Who knows? I know it's highly improbable, but not impossible.' She shivered, and tried to shake off the memory of finding Helen's body. A young detective entered the room, breaking into her thoughts.

'For you, ma'am. From Professor Wilkinson.'

'Thank you.' She took the package eagerly, ripped it open and scanned through the contents. After a moment or two, she packed the reports together and said, 'I'm going to need a bit of time to assimilate this lot. It's the initial forensic findings about Helen Brook, plus an expert's opinion on what the design on her torso may have meant. Let's meet again in an hour, then hopefully we will have something more definite to go on. Until then, continue with whatever you are working on, and Joseph, come with me. I think I may need another brain to help me make sense of all this.'

CHAPTER EIGHTEEN

It hadn't been easy, keeping what he'd discovered to himself, but now he was experiencing a delicious feeling of excitement. It had been lucky for him that those reports had arrived and taken the bitch and her sergeant away for a while. As soon as her office door had closed, Eric slipped down to the yard and commandeered a car. Now he stared down at the map book balanced across his legs and tried to concentrate. So, his precious boss wanted Andrew Gregory, did she? Then that's exactly what he'd give her, and without the help of the load of garbage that she called a team. This one was his, and his alone.

As he had hoped, two names had matched, Alex Power and Teresa Starr. And it was Teresa that really interested Eric. He'd checked up on her and found her to be a pretty low-level cog in the big wheel, something like Andrew Gregory. She was a homeworker, one of several disabled workers employed by Seymour Kramer Systems. Eric remembered that the file name on Helen and Andrew's home computer was "Telstar." It hadn't been easy finding either of them, but he had managed to locate a couple of telephone numbers on Helen Brook's computer. He traced these through a series of other numbers, to their mobile phones. It hadn't taken an Einstein to get their addresses, and calculate that the last time Gregory's car had been spotted it was heading in the direction of his workmate's home.

Tracing a finger along the lonely marsh roads and cursing the fact that the old pool car didn't have Satnav, he finally settled on the place he was looking for. Twenty minutes max, and with a bit of luck, he'd have a handcuffed Andrew Gregory in the back seat of his car. The DI could bloody well eat humble pie, and sweet little Catkin could kiss his arse!

* * *

'I still don't understand what the hell it all means.' Nikki looked from one set of drawings to the next. 'Jenny has done a very thorough job on the mandala, and I admit it seems to tell a story, but I just don't see how it fits in with Helen's murder.'

She picked up a printed list of the semi-precious stones and crystals that had been used on the body, and shook her head. 'I'm not really the right person to be trying to make sense of all this. It's too new age airy-fairy for me. But surely *you* can see something in it, Joseph? You are far more sensitive to this kind of stuff. Numerical vibrations of stones? Chakras? Astrological symbols? Oh please! I'm a bloody detective, not Mystic Meg!' Nikki looked totally exasperated.

Joseph stared at the designs and Jenny's notes. 'Come on, ma'am, it's not that bad. Let's see. Jenny has calculated that amongst other things, the mandala is made up of signs and symbols of a particular zodiac type. A Pisces to be exact. Born between 19 February and 20 March. Other signs represent runes.' He looked at Nikki's blank face and chuckled. 'Runes are an ancient form of writing, maybe Germanic or Norse in origin, but now used in the West for divining or healing.'

He picked up a couple of black and white sketches. 'It would appear that these three symbols are repeated throughout the mandala. They are called — forgive the bad pronunciation, eh, Eihwaz, which is the rune of Anger, Othila, the rune of Grief, and Ansuz, the rune of Guilt.'

Nikki raised her eyebrows. 'Well, the names passed me by, but I know what the words anger, grief and guilt mean. Even so, I think we need a witch doctor, not a detective.'

'Hang on in there, ma'am. There are also the numbers, 4, 5, 6 and 9. Jenny says if you are calculating your destiny in numerology you would be looking at a series of five, the life number, the expression number, the heart number, the Destiny number and the Fadic number. Now I know there are only four on the mandala, but she says one particular number is often repeated, i.e. heart and destiny are both 5. Jenny thinks they could be a numerological version of the killer's name.'

'Why does she think that?'

'Well, she believes that this mandala is actually a very clear description of a particular person. If we can decipher it correctly, we will arrive at a birthdate, a psychological profile and even a name.'

'You are kidding! Out of all this mumbo-jumbo?' Nikki said.

'It's not, honestly. And Jenny's obviously no flake. I'd rather like to meet her.'

'You are right, she isn't a flake. She is actually very nice, and you will meet her — but her background is in art and design, not necromancy.'

'Glad to hear it. Now let's see what she makes of the star in the middle.' Joseph had returned to the original design.

Nikki read her notes. 'Nothing in particular. She says the star has different meanings in different faiths and beliefs.'

'But she's certain that this whole thing is an artistic profile of the killer.'

Nikki sighed. 'Well, it's not Helen, that's for sure. She was a Libra — her birthday was in October. I'll get Jenny to work out her numerology numbers, but I'm damn sure they won't tally. So, who else could it be?' Nikki tentatively ran a finger over the mandala. 'I think the killer *wants* us to find the name hidden in here. It's a test, a nasty game. He's saying, are you up to solving such a cryptic problem?'

'And are we?'

Nikki pondered for a moment. 'Just because it looks like hocus-pocus doesn't mean we can't work it out like we do any other problem — logically. We'll get Jenny to continue working on it and maybe present us with something like a simplified check list.' She looked at him earnestly. 'For Helen's sake, we can do this.'

Joseph smiled. 'We can. With or without the help of Eihwaz, Othila and Ansuz.'

* * *

Eric stood silently in the yard and looked around. The bungalow had an odd feel to it. It wasn't what he had expected. It was built in a lonely, remote part of the marsh, and with the high conifer hedging and heavy gates it looked more like a compound than the home of a disabled single woman.

He parked a little way from the entrance to Teresa Starr's isolated home, and entered on foot, skirting the noisy gravel. The only car in sight was a converted people carrier with blue and white disabled stickers in the back window, which was pigging frustrating. He had banked on finding Andrew Gregory's BMW. He paused and looked around. The gravel had been pretty badly churned up, as though several vehicles had recently driven across it. Maybe he was too late. A feeling of foreboding began to suck away his euphoria. It was all too quiet.

A cold wind brushed against his cheek and he looked uneasily around the place. Way out here on the marsh, Teresa Starr had no immediate neighbours, no passing traffic and nothing to look at other than the bleak watery marshland, the deep tidal river, and a distant grey view of the Wash bank. He shivered. Eric was a city boy. He just about tolerated Greenborough, but he was most at home in glass and stone, neon lights and twenty-four hour noise. This place gave him the creeps. He felt vulnerable and exposed. Out here in the sticks his street-wise savvy was about as much use as a glass hammer.

With a great effort, he shrugged off his unease, and concentrated on the job in hand, that of getting a result — and getting one over on Cat Cullen.

The door was unlocked. Eric pushed it open and stepped inside. He saw a tidy, homely sort of room, with nothing particularly out of place. He should have felt reassured, but he didn't. His inner warning system was screaming at him that something here was terribly wrong.

He found the woman first. The sight of her bloated, beaten face caused the bile to rise in his throat. No use checking for a pulse. She was about as dead as anyone he had ever seen, and the thought of actually touching her body made him heave again. He backed out into the hall and leant against the wall, taking in great gulps of air.

Had Andrew Gregory killed her as well as his lover, Helen?

He swallowed hard, tasting the bitterness in his mouth. It had to be Gregory. If he could kill his own girlfriend, then he could most likely top a work colleague without even breaking a sweat. A small part of him was regretting his decision to go it alone, but a bigger part couldn't wait to describe this gruesome scene to the blokes in the mess room.

A curious flickering light was coming through an open door ahead of him. He moved towards it and carefully peered around the door frame, into a massive computer room. He whistled softly.

It had the works — wall-to-wall processors, monitors, printers, towers, and a vast assortment of complex peripherals. He looked around in awe, listening to the electronic hum and wondering what on earth the woman had used all this for.

He entered the room. Trashed equipment was scattered across the floor. Memory sticks, scanners, cameras and a brand new Blackberry DTEC50 lay broken and smashed. He picked his way through the mess, and found the second body.

The young man was partially concealed by a steel framed desk. Eric tried to look at the whole thing, as he had been trained to do, but his eyes were drawn to the chisel jammed into the man's throat. From the short amount of handle protruding from the flesh, there was no doubt that it had been hammered there with great force and had pierced the floor beneath him. His arms were broken, and several fingers were lying a few inches from Alex Powers' mutilated hands.

Eric backed slowly away.

In the hallway he leaned back against the wall and bent over, trying to clear his head. He should get out, switch on his mobile and bring in the troops. He stood up and ran his hands through his hair. He'd come this far, so he might as well finish the job. Gregory had clearly disposed of his two partners in crime and done a runner.

A small sound from inside the house made him draw back against the wall. He needed a weapon. He glanced around, and saw a heavy figurine on a display shelf. He sidled up to it, checked its weight and lifted it down. It would do. He thought again of radioing in. He knew he should, and he sure didn't want to finish up as the third victim, but he wanted Gregory. He wanted him badly, and he wanted to bring him in alone.

Slowly he moved forward, gripping the figurine.

The last room still unchecked had to be the bedroom. He hadn't heard the noise again, but it had come from this direction. Gritting his teeth and clamping his fingers tightly around his makeshift club, he entered the room.

'Fucking hell!'

Eric recoiled in horror, then he realised that he was looking at the man he had come after. He had his wish. He had found Andrew Gregory.

Elation coursed through him. He'd done it. No one was going to take this away from him. He'd beaten the whole damn team! Eric fought to regain his composure and took a tentative step towards the twisted shape, half leaning, half slumped against the bedroom wall.

'Christ. You really are in a mess, aren't you?' He squatted down on his haunches and stared. This was not what he had expected at all. He glanced around the room, his eyes remaining a little longer on the bloodied bed covers, and the stained ropes still attached to the uprights of the big bed's headboard. On the floor next to the bed, lying in a darkening pool of blood, was an open toolbox. Eric thought of the chisel protruding from Alex's neck. He had no idea what the hell had happened, but it obviously wasn't as simple as he'd supposed.

Gregory's condition looked as bad as the others — except that he was still breathing.

This wasn't right. It definitely wasn't how it was supposed to be. Eric could see his heroic coup sliding straight down the pan. He bit his lip. Shit! Shit! He contemplated the damaged body of Andrew Gregory. If he could just hold his nerve a little bit longer, he might yet salvage something from this mess.

He knelt closer to Andrew. 'I think we can truthfully say you have *really* upset someone, Mr Gregory.'

There was fear as well as pain in Andrew's eyes. He fought to speak, but all he could manage was a gurgling noise deep in his throat.

Well, at least he understood what was being said to him, so perhaps he would cooperate with what Eric had in mind. From his position, Gregory had little or nothing to lose.

'It's okay, I'm a policeman, Mr Gregory, and I'll get an ambulance out here as quickly as possible. As soon as you tell me that it was you who killed Helen Brook.' Eric watched the agonised expression change from relief to complete disbelief. 'Do you understand me? All I want is to hear from your own lips, that you murdered your girlfriend. A simple confession, Mr Gregory, then I call for help and we get you out of here.'

Eric waited. Surely it would take only seconds for the man to crumble? Instead, a look of intense hatred seared into him, with the slurred words, spat from between broken teeth, 'Burn in hell! Bastard! You're worse than the men that did

164

this! I never killed Helen. I loved her. I still love her, and I have to get to her!'

Eric stepped backwards and stared at Andrew Gregory. A sick feeling of shame washed over him. He had allowed his burning ambition to compromise any ethics or principles he might once have had. He staggered back, pulling his radio from his pocket. 'I'm sorry, I . . . I'm so sorry.' All he could do now was the thing he should have done minutes ago. Just get help.

He barked their position into his radio, then, noting the unnatural position of Andrew's lower body, requested the air ambulance. No way would this man survive a ride down the bumpy tracks of the marshes. If he was to survive at all, he would have to be flown out in the helicopter.

After his call, the full significance of what he had done crashed about him. He ran to the kitchen and brought back a glass of cold water and some damp towels. Still murmuring apologies, he tried to moisten the man's lips with water, but Andrew Gregory somehow found the strength to lift his broken hand, and dash the glass to the floor.

'Go burn in hell.'

CHAPTER NINETEEN

From the relative calm of her office, Nikki could hear Joseph and Dave laughing loudly. Suddenly the sound was abruptly cut short, and she spun in her chair to look. Yvonne was talking rapidly to her two colleagues and her face was grim. A moment later, she was at the office door.

'Ma'am, we've just heard that Andrew Gregory has been airlifted to Greenborough Hospital. Sounds like he's in a bad way.'

'Jesus! What happened to him? Car crash?' Nikki grabbed her coat from the back of her chair.

'It's all very vague, ma'am, but it's certainly not an RTC. It seems that Eric Barnes found him somewhere way out on the marshes. There were two dead bodies out there with him, a woman and a young man. Barnes has gone straight to the hospital. He'll meet you there.'

Nikki saw the figures of Joseph and Dave standing behind Yvonne in the doorway. She slammed her bag back down on her desk. 'What?'

'Sorry, ma'am. That's all I was told.'

Nikki's fury exploded. 'What the hell does Barnes think he's doing? Did anyone know he was out there playing lone fucking ranger?'

Joseph looked helpless. 'No, he told me he was still checking out the Seymour Kramer staff.'

'I expressly told him to ring me if he had anything, absolutely *anything*, on Andrew.' A coldness spread through her. *The bastard! He went solo, just to get his own back on me for bollocking him out! Well, if that's the case he can look forward to going back to working traffic. See what detecting bald tyres does for his ego!* Nikki lowered her voice. 'Okay, Yvonne, where was he found?'

'A place out beyond Wisdom Creek Village. Apparently it's the home of someone who worked at Seymour Kramer.'

'And who is that?'

'Miss Teresa Starr, ma'am. She's the dead woman. Uniform have got the place sealed off. Shall I go out there?'

'Yes, yes, and Joseph, you go too. Quick as possible. I have to get to the hospital. I'll ring you as soon as I've spoken to DC Barnes, and hopefully, to Andrew.'

* * *

Nikki hurried into A&E and was relieved to find that she knew the doctor in charge of the resus room from when her daughter had been in hospital. They looked at the still form of Andrew, then each other, and Nikki knew he would not make it.

Dr Lisa Campbell shook her head sadly. 'Sorry, Nikki. This is a bad one.' The doctor moved away from the trolley, leaving Andrew with two senior nurses. She took Nikki's arm. 'Let's go outside, shall we?'

As the doors closed, Lisa pulled off her mask and shook her head from side to side. 'He's too badly injured to even consider moving him upstairs to ITU. He has severe spinal injuries and huge internal damage. We have given him pain relief, but his organs are closing down and now I'm afraid all we can do is wait. What the hell happened to him? Who would do a thing like this?'

Nikki felt sick. 'It was done deliberately? I just had a call to say he'd been brought here. I have no idea how this happened.'

'Well, the poor guy's been tortured, no doubt about that.'

Nikki's heart sank. What on earth had he got himself mixed up in? 'Can I see him? Is he conscious?'

'He's heavily sedated, but he's been asking for you.' Lisa smiled sadly at Nikki. 'You know, I keep thinking that his Helen is still here, in a drawer in the mortuary refrigerator, and there's not a damned thing I can do to stop Andrew joining her.' She gave a loud sigh. 'You and I picked some really great careers, didn't we?'

'We picked the best, Lisa. It just at times like this that it feels like a really shitty mistake. Come on.' They moved back towards the resus room. 'By the way, has there been another detective here with him? A DC Barnes?'

Lisa Campbell looked worried. 'Yes, but I had to send him away. For some reason Andrew Gregory didn't want him near him. I don't know why, after all it was Barnes that got him here. He'd have died alone out on the marsh if your man hadn't called the air ambulance.'

Nikki shrugged. She had no answers. Yet.

She sat beside Andrew and waited for him to wake. She wanted to hold his hand, but the deformed fingers looked too painful to touch. Lisa's opinion was that he would be lucky to see out another hour. His vital organs were shutting down, and the best they could do was make him as comfortable as possible. Nikki needed to know who had done this, and she didn't have long.

'Andrew? It's Nikki. Can you hear me?'

He did not move.

'Andrew, please listen to me. Andrew, you must wake up.'

'I . . . Nikki?' He swallowed and blinked several times. 'Thank God! You have to help me.'

'Oh, Andrew, I'll help you all I can, but . . .' she touched his face gently, not sure how to go on.

'I'm not stupid, Nikki.' He coughed painfully then gasped out. 'I know the score. I could have let go in the night, but I held on because of Helen. What they, what they

168

did . . .' His voice was little more than a whisper. 'Listen, I need to know something.'

Nikki waited.

'Do you think I killed Helen?'

She stroked his cheek, careful not to touch any of the bruises or abrasions. 'Not for one moment, Andrew. I know you wouldn't hurt her.'

Tears formed in his eyes. 'Thank you. Now, can I ask you one last favour? This is why I'm still alive and not dead out there on the marsh.'

'Anything in my power, but please, please tell me all you can about whoever did this. I *have* to catch them. You do realise that, don't you? Just like I *have* to catch whoever killed Helen.'

'I'll tell you all I know, if you'll just take me to see Helen.' His tears flowed freely and his breathing was becoming ragged. 'I never got to see her. I was such a fool to run away, but I panicked, and now I really need to see her. Please, Nikki, can you do that for me?'

Nikki took a deep breath and stood up. 'I'll be straight back. You hang on in there.'

She found Lisa Campbell discussing Andrew's case with another doctor. 'Can I have a word, Dr Campbell? It's important.'

Lisa quickly introduced her to the consultant, then moved aside. 'What can I do?'

Nikki explained Andrew's last wish. The doctor puffed out her cheeks in concern. 'There's no guaranteeing he'll even make it down there.'

'Oh, he will. I could almost promise you that. And he's our only link to what will be a triple murder. Listen, I can page Professor Wilkinson and have Helen taken to the chapel of rest, if you would sort out this end? Please, Lisa? It's why he's still alive, the only reason he is holding on, but we both know he can't last much longer. Can we do it?'

Lisa Campbell bit her lip, then nodded. 'Yes, we can do it. But I have to tell you, the amount of morphine we'll be giving him will make him high as a kite. You'll have to sift the wheat from the chaff.'

Nikki grabbed the doctor's hands and squeezed them. 'Thank you.'

* * *

Nikki sat on a metal-frame chair and stared at the only decorated wall in the room. It was a modern depiction of a stained glass window. In the bright mix of colours and undefined shapes, she noted a white dove, a rainbow, a bridge and a waterfall surrounded by tall dark green trees under an impossibly blue sky. She felt like an intruder, but she had to be there. She had to find out what had happened. It was just a relief that Andrew had asked her to stay with him, while a worried Dr Lisa Campbell waited outside.

If Nikki thought the painting surreal, it was no less so than the scene in front of her. Two trolleys lay side by side. One supported the lifeless form of Helen, carefully and neatly dressed. The other was a tangle of drips and drains and temporarily silenced monitors, a deathbed for Andrew.

Nikki was not sure what she had expected from this strange reunion, maybe something dramatic, something Montague and Capulet. Instead, she discovered a deep sense of peace.

After a while, Andrew sighed and turned his head in her direction. 'Come and sit with us.'

Nikki pulled her chair across.

'She still looks beautiful, doesn't she, Nikki?'

'She wouldn't know how to look any other way.'

'I asked her to marry me, you know that?' There was a slight giggle in his voice.

'She told me, although I knew it was a secret. She was really happy about it.'

'She loved me, didn't she? I mean, really loved me?' The voice quavered.

Nikki wondered how long they had. 'With all her heart, Andrew.'

'But we had our moments, didn't we? Do you remember when she tipped that bowl of . . .' A rasping cough racked his body and he fought for breath. 'I'd forgotten her birthday.'

It broke her heart to do it, but Nikki knew that she had to try to focus his mind. 'Andrew, listen, we have to find out who hurt her, and who hurt you and killed your friends. Will you help me?'

He sighed, a ragged jerky sound. 'I don't want to go back there, but for her,' he looked fondly at Helen's cold body, 'I will.' He shivered and Nikki carefully drew the cover closer around him. 'It was Teresa's idea.'

Nikki almost jumped at the strength of his voice. The morphine must have really kicked in.

'And it was a bloody good one. She was a whiz, a real ace. I told her that she was probably born with a USB cable instead of an umbilical cord!' He barked out a staccato laugh. 'Alex and I were pretty bright, but by comparison . . . whatever, we decided to form a trio, and do a little moonlighting. Private work, done in SKS's time. And we started to make some serious money, Nikki! I mean serious! I was chuffed! For once in my life I could pull my weight, I could help Helen.'

'And did she know about it?'

'God, no! I said I'd got a promotion, with lots of overtime.'

'And it escalated?'

Andrew tried to move, and swore loudly. 'You could say that. We became a very valuable commodity to some very powerful companies. They wanted more and more, and we finally came up with a stunner, a really cracking piece of kit.'

'Liberator? We found it under *Telstar*, on Helen's computer.'

'How . . . ?'

'We have it, Andrew. It's safe.'

His pupils were dilated as he stared at her. 'Then don't let your IT boys play around with it. A few days before all this blew up, Teresa changed it. I always thought she was a genius, but she was a hacker too, and if she's done what I think she has, no system that you run it through is safe. It's a scavenger, it steals information. It's not a game, Nikki, it's deadly serious. I believe Teresa may have altered the patches without my knowing. Made things . . .' he groaned and closed his eyes.

'Too hot to handle?'

'Too clever. I know we don't have artificial intelligence in this kind of software yet, but if anyone could have taken us a step closer, Teresa could. Oh God, if it falls into the wrong hands!'

'Okay. I hear you and I'll make sure it's dealt with properly. I promise.'

'Destroy it, Nikki. It's already killed Teresa and Alex.' He sighed, his voice much weaker now '. . . and me, I guess.'

'Did you recognise the people who hurt you? Do you know who sent them?' Nikki asked gently.

He shuddered and swallowed hard. 'No, I'd never seen them before, but I suppose they were sent by rivals of the Swiss company we were moonlighting for. There were three men. And they used their names, so I guess they didn't expect any of us to survive.'

Nikki sat up. 'Names?'

'Yeah. They called themselves Mr Venables and Mr Fabian.' He stuttered out the next words. 'They did the hands-on work, and their boss asked the questions. They wanted Liberator.'

'And none of you told them about it?'

'They hadn't reckoned on Teresa's health problems. She died quite early on in their interrogation. Poor Alex actually didn't know where Liberator was stored, so the kid couldn't have told them even if he'd wanted to. I gathered that much at least from my night with Mr Venables and Mr Fabian.'

He began to cough again. Nikki gently wiped bloody saliva from his lips, and somehow he managed to continue. 'And I had one thing left to do before I died.' He reached out his broken hand towards Helen. 'I *had* to stay alive. Oh, Nikki, you'll never know what I went through in the darkness. I thought day would never come, and I'd never get to be with my Helen again.' His eyes filled with tears. 'But I'm here, aren't I?'

'Yes, you're here, with Helen.'

'And now, I can let go?'

Oh no, Please! You can't, not yet! 'Andrew! The man you called the boss? What did he look like?'

Andrew's eyes tried to focus. 'From a distance he looked handsome, then he turned and I saw his face was all scarred. Tall. Dark hair. Cruel eyes. Evil.'

Nikki drew in a sharp breath. *Scarred face? Surely not! Stephen Cox?* She would make guesses later. Time was running out.

'And Helen? Did they mention Helen?'

'No. I don't think they even knew about her. I begged them to tell me if they'd killed her too, but — nothing.' He turned to Nikki, his eyes suddenly clear and angry. 'But there's something you really should know. About one of your officers. The one that found me?'

'Eric Barnes?'

'That's the name he gave when he *finally* called for help.'

Nikki's jaw clamped tight, dismay quickly turning to anger, then to white-hot rage as she listened to what had happened. She bit back her disgust. She would deal with Barnes later.

'Nikki? I guess I'll never know if was my fault, but you will catch who did this to her? Get the person who killed my precious Helen?' He laid a twisted finger on his dead lover's cheek.

'Oh, I will. I promise you, Andrew.'

He murmured a reply.

'Andrew?'

He sighed again. Then he said softly, 'When Helen was injured in that crash, she told me afterwards that the most scary thing was the darkness. When she heard that man call out to her, she said it felt like a ray of sunshine bursting in.' He paused, and a bubbly cough caught in his throat. 'Then he told her what he'd done, and the light went out. I just hope she wasn't frightened of the dark this time.'

Nikki laid her hand on his. She was worried about the sudden uneven pattern of his breathing. 'She would have felt nothing, known nothing, Andrew. The doctors have assured us of that. But, listen, you try to rest, I'm going to get the doctor in to check on you.'

'Don't go, Nikki. I feel so much better knowing Helen didn't suffer.' He gave her a crooked smile. 'Funny, isn't it? How quickly it gets dark. Maybe it's my turn to offer a prayer for light.' His voice was now little more than a whisper. 'But perhaps I have no right to ask for anything. No matter how she died, or who killed her, I'm to blame. I'm guilty.'

As Nikki moved her lips to speak, she saw that his eyes were closed. She ran to the door. 'Lisa!'

A moment later, the doctor glanced at her watch, then whispered to her that he was dead.

'You won't try to resuscitate him?' Nikki asked, although knowing what the answer would be.

'His injuries were catastrophic, there would be no coming back from that.'

'Thank you.' Nikki reached for the doctor's hand and held it tightly. 'Thank you for granting his last wish.'

Lisa squeezed back. 'I need to go and make some arrangements, Nikki. Will you be alright to stay here until I get back?'

Nikki stayed. She pulled the chair closer and sat down. She spoke softly to them, made promises, and prayed she would be able to keep them. Maybe she was making promises to herself. This was how she would always remember them, side by side in the mortuary.

Was it Stephen Cox who had done this to them? Nikki felt a tightening in her chest. This time he wouldn't get away.

When Lisa returned, she had said her goodbyes. She couldn't wait to leave the chapel. The woman that closed the door and marched down the corridor was a very different person to the one who had just wiped tears from her eyes. Cold and hard, all she wanted was to get hold of Eric Barnes and place her hands tightly around his neck.

CHAPTER TWENTY

She found him waiting outside the entrance to A&E. He was slouched against a wall, kicking aimlessly at a tuft of grass that had bravely made its way through a crack in the concrete pathway. His bearing lacked its usual cockiness, and she saw him grow pale as she approached.

'Walk with me.'

They continued along the side of the hospital until they came to a service area where delivery lorries unloaded. It was empty, which suited Nikki perfectly. In a single movement, she spun round on Barnes and pushed him hard against the wall. When she spoke, her face was inches from his, and she could feel the chilly blast from her cold, cold eyes strike the man like a blow.

'Andrew Gregory is dead.' She saw Barnes swallow, but he said nothing. 'Sadly he wasted some of his last precious moments telling me about you.'

Barnes' mouth worked soundlessly.

'Now, before you utter a single word, do not, I repeat, do not insult me by trying to tell me that man lied about your actions.' She was finding it hard to keep her hands off him. She wanted to push his head into the brick wall and watch him bleed. Instead she stepped back and stared at him, saying very slowly and carefully, 'DC Barnes, can you tell me the description of a police officer's duty?'

His voice was almost inaudible. 'The protection of life and property, ma'am.'

'And did you protect Andrew Gregory?'

'*I* called the air ambulance. *I* got him out of there.' His voice gained strength. 'And it was me who found him. If I hadn't gone there he'd still be writhing in agony on the floor, or dead before anyone got to him.' Then his bravado wilted beneath her relentless gaze. 'I . . . I said I was sorry. I tried to help him, honestly.'

'Listen to me very carefully, DC Barnes. I have been told by my sergeant that you are a good detective. You are certainly bright, but your intelligence means nothing if you are an uncaring, spiteful and cruel person. If you spend all your time calculating how to get a fellow officer in the shit but come up smelling of roses yourself, then you've lost sight of your objective, and you are no damned good to me. You flatly ignored my order to keep me updated on anything concerning Andrew Gregory, because *you* wanted the kudos. Well, okay, you found him. Congratulations.' Her eyes narrowed to slits. 'When exactly did you work all this out, DC Barnes?'

'I . . . I had the numbers last night. I completed my checks this morning.'

'Then think about this, and think carefully. *If* you had told one of us immediately, we could have made the link and had an armed unit out to that godforsaken marsh last night. Your quick action could have saved three human beings from being tortured and killed. But it didn't, did it? Because you're not a team player, and you wanted the glory all for yourself.' She watched as the thought sunk in and his pale face turned completely white. 'Can you blame me for not wanting an officer like that on my team?'

Barnes hung his head.

'Well? Would you?' Her voice echoed about the yard.

'No,' he whispered.

'Louder!'

'No. I wouldn't.'

Suddenly she couldn't bear him near her. 'Okay, DC Barnes. I'm going to make a suggestion. It's up to you whether you act upon it, but if you want to keep your warrant card and go on working, I suggest you listen rather carefully.' She leant closer and spoke clearly and concisely into Barnes' ear.

She listened to his reply, and then she nodded and said, 'Okay. Now get out of my sight.'

Walking back to her car, she realised her hands were shaking and her jaw was clamped shut. It took a lot of deep breaths to calm herself. Part of her was glad that Andrew had told her about Eric's behaviour, and another part wished that the whole thing hadn't happened. She didn't enjoy coming down on an officer the way she had, but it was better to know what he was capable of. And the bottom line was that he had no place on her team. The sad thing was, the idiot was not a bad detective. It was just his attitude and his manner that was crap.

She smiled bitterly as she unlocked her car. Both she and Barnes knew that if he wanted to make a disciplinary case against her, he'd win. She had assaulted him and had only the unsubstantiated word of a dead man to accuse him with, which wasn't anywhere near enough to warrant an official warning. She was counting on the fact that Barnes really was ashamed of himself, and that he would take her advice.

As she drove back to the station, she wondered if she'd gone too far. She had wanted him to hurt. She wanted him to see the devastation that a huge ego in a small office could cause. But she'd finished up placing the responsibility for three deaths entirely on his shoulders, and that was wrong. They were all to blame. And she of all people had no right to judge anyone. Just because she still had nightmares about the past, she shouldn't wish them on others. She jammed her foot down on the accelerator. Right now, in Barnes' case, she was prepared to make an exception.

* * *

'Ma'am?' Joseph stuck his head around her door. 'Have you got time for me to update you on what we found at the crime scene out at Wisdom Creek?'

She beckoned him in and pointed to a chair. 'Sorry, Joseph. Before we discuss anything, we have to ensure that your friends in the IT department keep that damned program away from the police computer. Andrew said it must be destroyed. Apparently it's seriously dangerous and I don't think I'd be flavour of the month if I brought the PNC down, do you?'

'Don't worry, ma'am. All of Norman Hebbenstall's investigative work is done on a totally separate system, for just that reason. I was speaking to him earlier, and he's fully aware of the potential for damage of Andrew's little toy.' Joseph looked at her. 'Are you okay, Nikki? I can't imagine how awful the last few hours must have been for you.'

Nikki felt a rush of affection for him. Most people assumed that her professional position, and her cool, would allow her to sail unscathed through every adversity. Joseph knew her better. He had the courage to treat her like a human being.

She rubbed hard at her sore eyes. 'It's been horrible, absolutely horrible. You sit there, knowing a friend is dying, and yet you have to keep vigilant, detached. You have to practically grill the poor guy in his last moments, when all he wants to do is reminisce about his girlfriend and their food fights.' She exhaled loudly. 'It sucks.'

'Then I hope he managed to help in some way. Because whoever killed those people at Wisdom Creek is a sadistic bastard and an expert at cleaning up after himself.'

'Well, here's the bummer, Joseph. There were three of them. Andrew gave me two names, Fabian and Venables, *and* a damned good description of the third, the nameless one.'

Joseph's face screwed up in concentration. 'Fabian? I've heard that name before, haven't I? Wasn't he the hitman in the contract killing of that East End gangster last year?' He scratched slowly at his chin. 'Mediterranean type, something of a mystery man, apparently.'

Nikki suddenly knew who he meant. 'Which brings me to the third man. If I said tall, dark haired and with a badly scarred face, would it conjure up any thoughts?'

'Cox! Stephen Cox! But what on earth would he have to do with Andrew and his company?'

'Well, from what Andrew said it would appear that Cox has gone into the protection racket, and on a very large scale if he's using men like Fabian.'

Joseph looked pale. They wanted to get Stephen Cox behind bars more than any other criminal they had ever had to deal with. But he had hurt them both in the past and even seeing Cox again would jump start some pretty powerful emotions. For Joseph in particular.

Nikki looked at him with a mixture of compassion and excitement. 'This is our chance, Joseph. He's right in the middle of our investigation. This time we are going to get him.'

Joseph nodded. 'I'll do everything in my power to make that happen, you can rely on that.'

'I know. You don't have to tell me. But right now I have to fill you in on a rather unfortunate conversation I had earlier, with Eric Barnes.'

Joseph listened, his habitual calm expression growing angrier by the moment.

Joseph spoke through gritted teeth. 'What? Even I never had him down for such a callous bastard! The whole mess room is calling him today's super hero. Wonder what they'll think of golden boy when they hear about this?'

'They won't. Well, not from us, okay? I've given Barnes a few options to consider, and if he's got a decent bone in his body and he's the good detective that some people, you included, believed him to be, he has the chance to do the right thing. It's up to him.'

Joseph shook his head sadly. 'And you had to deal with that after everything else that happened?'

'One of those days, Joseph. I can't wait for it to end.'

'Ah, would you throw something heavy at me if I mentioned the name Oliver Kirton?'

She allowed herself to smile at her sergeant. 'No, I haven't got the energy, but I hadn't forgotten about him. I'll attend to him next, okay?'

When Joseph had left, she picked up her coat and bag, and went to find Niall Farrow. No matter how much she wanted to go home and bury herself under her duvet until she fell asleep, it was business as usual in the murder room.

* * *

Oliver Kirton had not been at home, so an hour later she was back in her office, to find a neatly typed letter from Eric Barnes. After reading it through, she opened her computer and carefully worded a reply. It wasn't easy, but it would be a damned sight easier than trying to explain what had happened to Superintendent Woodhall. Well, she knew how to explain it. The difficult bit was to do it without him hitting the roof, and taking her with him.

She got up and closed her office door. Her heart sank as her phone started to ring. It was so tempting to leave it. Hardly anyone knew she was still here, and it was very late. Even Joseph had gone on ahead, promising to get them some sort of food together.

With a sigh she returned to her desk. 'DI Nikki Galena.'

The voice on the other end was soft, full of emotion. 'I'm so glad to have caught you, Inspector. It was a shot in the dark, hoping to find you still there. It's Carolyn Chambers, Paul Brant's doctor.'

Nikki stiffened. It was too late for an informal chat, and the doctor sounded pretty upset. *Oh please don't tell me Brant's done a bunk!* The super would be apoplectic if that were the case. 'I was just off home actually. But what can I do for you, Dr Chambers?'

'It's Paul, DI Galena.'

Nikki's stomach turned over.

'I'm afraid he killed himself earlier this evening.'

180

A tiny part of Nikki was rather relieved. She had never been one hundred percent sure she had done the right thing in letting him go. Well, at least he wasn't running wild through Greenborough, terrifying more women. 'How did it happen, Doctor?'

'He hanged himself, Inspector.' She almost choked on the next words. 'I found him.'

Nikki felt the blood drain from her face. It happened in her job more often than she would have liked. You found dead people. But when it was someone you knew . . . She tried to speak, but the words stuck in her throat.

'Inspector?'

Still she could not speak.

'DI Galena? Are you still there?'

'Yes, yes. I'm so very sorry.' The hand that held the telephone receiver shook almost uncontrollably. 'Finding someone like that. It's unimaginably horrible. Are *you* all right?'

'It was only a few hours ago. I'm still trying to get my head around it. I just thought you should know immediately.'

'Thank you.' Nikki sunk back into her chair and attempted to find the right words. 'If it helps any, I do know how you feel, Doctor. I've been in the same situation myself.'

'In your line of work, I suppose you would.'

Before she had time to think, Nikki said, 'We do, but I was thinking about my friend, Helen Brook. I had taken round a Chinese meal and a bottle of wine. We were going to spend the evening together. Instead I found her murdered.'

'I'm so sorry! I didn't think. I shouldn't have been so blunt.'

'It's okay, honestly. I just wanted you to know that I understand how you feel.'

There was a sigh. 'It's the shock, isn't it? I can't get the sight out of my mind. I really let him down, didn't I?'

'Good Lord! It's not your fault, Dr Chambers. Paul Brant was a mess, poor guy, and you really did your best for him.'

'It wasn't enough though, was it? I think he truly believed that Helen Brook never knew about him watching her. Then to find out he had scared her so badly, it must have been too much for him.'

'Did he leave a note?'

'No. I suppose he didn't need to. We'd tried to talk it through. I thought he was beginning to see that her death had absolutely nothing to do with him, but it seems I was wrong there as well.' She sighed. 'Well, I'm sorry to have rung so late. You did put your neck on the block by letting him go, and I really appreciated it. At least you know he's not a threat anymore.'

'I'm still very sorry that it had to end that way. He was an innocent party really. He just got caught up in a difficult situation and inadvertently made things worse.'

'I suppose. Anyway, thank you for what you did for him. Take care.'

When the doctor had ended the call, Nikki sat in her office and thought about her reaction to the news of Paul's suicide. It had been extreme, even after the day she'd just had. She was horribly overtired, and suddenly the reality of Helen's death had caught up with her. She picked her coat off the back of the door and pulled it on. 'No more, not tonight. Time to go home.' As she closed the door, Andrew's words came back to her. "I thought he was handsome, until he turned and I saw his face was badly scarred."

Stephen Cox. Nikki gave an involuntary shiver, pulled the coat tighter around her and hurried down the corridor to the stairs.

* * *

Nikki drove directly to Knot Cottage and parked outside. Light streamed from the windows of Joseph's tiny home on the marsh, and it was the best thing she'd seen all day. He greeted her at the door with a large glass of red wine.

'Lifesaver!' Nikki took the glass and had a long, slow drink even before the door closed. 'As days go, that was one of the shittiest. And there have been far too many shitty days of late.'

Joseph took her coat and pulled out a chair at the kitchen table. 'Sit. I'll get the food.'

'Haven't you eaten?'

'I waited for you. It's a bit basic, I'm afraid, but it's hot and it's not a takeaway.'

'Whatever you cook is always perfect, Joseph, but before we eat, I have to tell you about Paul Brant.' She told him the sad story, then sat back and closed her eyes. In the quiet of the little kitchen she finally let herself relax. Knot Cottage was exactly the right place to be after the day she'd just had. Suddenly she had a memory from years ago.

She was with her young daughter, Hannah, and Martin who had owned the cottage before Joseph. They had sat around this same table and played Hannah's favourite game of Cluedo. In her head she heard Hannah call out excitedly, "Miss Scarlett in the study with a rope!" Nothing pleased the child better than to get one over on her detective mother.

"Wonderful, sweetheart, although in reality that would be highly improbable. Women don't often strangle men."

"Bad loser! Isn't she a bad loser, Martin?"

"Very bad indeed. Shame on you, Nikki!" Martin would smile his lopsided smile and say, "Time for another game?"

As they always did, thoughts of her daughter brought a lump to her throat and a terrible sadness in her heart. Such a waste! Such a terrible waste. It was something she would never truly get over.

'Penny for them? Or second thoughts, maybe not after today.'

'I was thinking about my girl, actually.' Nikki brightened. 'And talking about our girls, what did Tamsin need to see you about so urgently the other day?'

Joseph placed a bowl of delicious-smelling food in front of her. 'Thank heaven for slow cookers. Beef and vegetable casserole, and there's plenty more in the pot. Eat, and I'll tell you about my evening with Tamsin.'

Nikki smiled up at him. Thank heaven for slow cookers indeed!

Joseph sipped his wine. 'As you know, Tamsin has been going out with Niall Farrow for a while now, and the crux of it is, they are pretty serious about each other and she wants to move in with him.'

Nikki shrugged. 'How is that a problem in this day and age? Surely you are open-minded enough to let them do what they want?'

Joseph grinned. 'Not a word about this to anyone, right?'

Nikki laid her knife and fork down. 'Promise. Now tell me all.'

'Niall wants to wait.' His grin widened, 'And not because he has cold feet. Our Niall is a waiting-until-marriage kind of guy.'

Nikki sat back and shook her head. 'How refreshing! I knew I liked that lad.'

'Fine, but Tamsin isn't, and she is climbing the walls!'

Nikki laughed. 'Oh dear! The course of true love and all that.'

'And now she wants me to talk to him.' Joseph was almost beside himself. 'What do I say, for goodness sake?'

Nikki made a few unhelpful suggestions. So, finding no sensible solution to Tamsin's problem, they fell into an amicable silence while they ate.

Surprisingly, considering that most of the day her stomach had been clenched in a tight nervous knot, Nikki managed to clear her plate and have another ladleful.

She leaned back and stared vacantly at her empty plate. 'I'm dreading tomorrow and this vigil. There are so many things that could go wrong. The timing is incredibly bad.'

'But the super won't cancel it?' Joseph scratched his chin thoughtfully, then answered his own question. 'But I guess he can't really. That would cause just as many problems.'

'He wants it out of the way and a line drawn under it. Until it's over, that part of town will continue to be a nightmare.' She finished her wine, then put her hand over the top of the glass as Joseph offered another. 'Better not. I might finish up in the dyke.'

'You could walk up the lane, and pick up your car in the morning.'

She looked longingly at the bottle, but shook her head. 'No, I don't think so, thanks.'

'Sensible I guess.' Joseph pushed the cork back into the half empty bottle. 'We need to be as sharp as we can be.' He sat back down and stared at her. 'How are you holding up?'

Nikki thought for a moment. 'I'll tell you when these investigations are over. Right now, seeing Andrew in that terrible state, I just want to catch the evil bastards who think nothing of killing, maiming and torturing people.'

'*And* we also have the body in the river to worry about.'

Nikki bit her lip. 'He's connected in some way. Don't ask me how, but he's part of it.'

'If Cox is using professionals, then that single stab wound to the heart could have been pure expertise.'

'We'll get them, whatever it takes,' she whispered, almost to herself.

Joseph nodded, his eyes narrowed. 'Yes, whatever it takes.'

The moment was tense, and they both jumped when Nikki's mobile rang.

'Sorry for the late call, Inspector, but guess what? I have a name for your body, and it isn't Mr Arturas Kubilius from Lithuania.'

'Rory! You are a mind reader! We were just talking about him. Who is he?' She tapped the loudspeaker button so Joseph could hear.

'Well, I'd love to tell you that discovering his precious identity was achieved using my ingenuity and considerable guile, but I can't.' He gave a theatrical sigh. 'It turns out he's known to the police in several counties, and we already have his DNA on file. Boring!'

'And?'

'Oh yes, his name is Derek Lyle. He's from the Horncastle area, and no doubt you will discover all about him from your lovely PNC. And so to bed! Night night, both.'

'He's in the system,' Joseph murmured. 'But what did he do to get himself topped?

'Another little puzzle to be addressed tomorrow, I think. But at least we have a name, praise be.' Nikki stood up. 'Thank you for the meal, it was delicious. Now I really need to get home.'

Joseph got her coat. 'I'll see you bright and early.' He touched her arm as she moved towards the door. 'And ring me if you can't sleep or just want to talk, okay?'

Nikki squeezed his hand and felt tears forming. 'Thank you. I'll remember that.'

CHAPTER TWENTY-ONE

'Quiet!' Nikki watched as her team found chairs, then stopped talking and turned their attention to her. 'First, I have to tell you all that Paul Brant, Helen Brook's inadvertent stalker, has killed himself. He died last night.'

There was a ripple of whispered voices.

'Ma'am? Was it guilt? Did he leave a note? Did he confess to anything?' asked Dave Harris.

'No note, and although we obviously can't rule him out, I really don't believe Paul Brant was capable of killing anyone, other than himself. His doctor confirms that, although she admits she has been wrong about his state of mind on two occasions before. I think he was an unhappy victim of circumstance, not a stalker or a killer. He had been dealt some pretty rough blows, and I'm sorry he took his own life. And of course, you are all aware that Andrew Gregory died yesterday. Information received from the property where he was found, and from his extensive and eventually fatal injuries, indicates that he was tortured and left for dead by a professional assassin, or assassins. They were trying to find the whereabouts of a certain computer program, one that, thankfully, we already have under lock and key. The killers also tortured and killed the owner of the property, Teresa Starr, and a young man we believe to be named Alex Power, both employees of Seymour Kramer Systems. Professor Wilkinson has intimated that he thought the woman, Teresa Starr, although badly beaten, actually died of a massive heart attack before the men had finished with her. They then turned their attentions to the younger victim, and finally to Andrew.'

'Did he give them the information that they wanted?' Jessie Nightingale looked pale.

'No. Andrew believed that they thought he was dead, and gave up. He lasted long enough to tell us everything we wanted to know about his actual whereabouts at the time of Helen Brook's death, and about the private cyber-scam that he, Teresa and Alex were involved in.'

'So is Gregory off the suspect list?' a uniformed constable asked.

'He was never on it as far as I was concerned. But yes, he did not kill Helen. He stayed alive long enough to spend his last moments holding her hand. I was there with him, and he was certainly not acting.'

'So with our two main suspects gone, is it down to one of her patients?' Cat asked.

'It looks that way. We have practically eliminated the man in the cellar, it was not her lover, and she had no known enemies. Well, none that we know of, so that leaves her clients.'

'Or a nutter, guv.'

'Correct, or a nutter. And from the expected turnout for the vigil tonight, she obviously had plenty of friends. Which brings me neatly to the topic of the vigil. As you know, one of the organisers had a note pushed into her pocket, telling her to cancel the service, or someone else would die. Superintendent Woodhall wants us to take the threat very seriously, and apart from a very visible show of uniforms, he wants a large contingent of plain clothed officers, all wired up and mingling with the crowd. The woman who was threatened has insisted on still going, so Niall, I'm going to ask you and Jessie to keep her in close range at all times. It may not be a personal threat, but we can't risk ignoring it.'

Niall and Jess nodded. 'No problem, ma'am. We'll glue ourselves to her.'

'Do that. We have too many dead people around Greenborough for my liking.' She pushed her hands deep into her jacket pockets. 'You should also know that DC Barnes is on sick leave at present, so you detectives are one down for a while. Sorry about that, although you might like the extra overtime.' Nikki continued swiftly, allowing no time for comment. 'So, all of you, get ferreting into the backgrounds of her clients, and not just the cranks. Look at everyone, especially those who did not respond to treatment. Maybe someone was expecting too much from her and resents the fact that they are still suffering from raging beriberi or whatever. And check out the other therapists. Maybe someone was jealous of her popularity. Now, in the tradition of leaving the best until last, I have one more piece of information for you.'

All their faces were turned to her. They had seen that look before. No one spoke.

'Before he died, Andrew Gregory named two of his attackers, a Mr Fabian and a Mr Venables, and described the third, who was in charge. The description matches that of Stephen Cox.'

A murmur of shock rippled around the room.

'That's a big step up from drug dealing,' stated Dave grimly.

'If Stephen Cox is working here in Greenborough, every police officer is in danger. He is ruthless. Those of you who haven't crossed his path are fortunate. Just pray that you never do. Right now we have other things to get out of the way, like this vigil, but as soon as we get Greenborough back to normal, we will be moving heaven and earth to catch him. Is that clear?'

Everyone nodded.

'Okay, off you go, and be back at nine tonight, ready for the service at the river. And God help us all!'

* * *

Joseph tapped the name Derek Lyle into his computer and waited for a match. In a short time he had before him a potted history of a life of crime. It was mainly small time stuff. Earlier in his career, Lyle had been involved in a couple of thefts, and later he'd tried his hand at car ringing, but mostly he had been handling stolen goods. The man was a fence, nothing deep and dirty, just a cog keeping the black market wheel in motion. Joseph muttered to himself, 'Not exactly the sort of man who would attract a violent hitman. There's got to be more.'

It took a while, reading a myriad of reports and statements, but finally he arrived at it, a simple line in a record of an interview. It stated that an uncle of his had corroborated Lyle's alibi for the time of a robbery. This uncle was named as Robert Leonard, age sixty-five, of the Carborough Estate, Greenborough. A Leonard! His name was different because it came from his mother's side, but he was still a Leonard. Joseph jumped up and looked across to Nikki's office. The door was open and the room was empty. 'Where's the boss?' he called out to no one in particular.

'With the superintendent, Sarge,' called back Sheila, the office manager, 'and she's likely to be there for some time. It's a meeting with the uniformed officers about the safest way to police the vigil tonight.'

Joseph went back to his own small office. He didn't want to tell the others before Nikki, so he guessed it would have to wait for another hour or so.

His phone shrilled and he saw Mickey's name. Joseph prayed the boy was not in trouble. 'Mickey? Are you okay?'

'I'm good. Can we talk?'

'Sure. Now?'

'Meet me down by the river, on the seats next to the Fisherman's Knot car park. Know where I mean?'

'I know it.' *The spot with no camera coverage.* 'Ten minutes?'

'I'll be there.'

Joseph stared at the phone. He knew he should take someone with him, but if he did, Mickey would be off like a rat up a drainpipe. He walked over to where Cat was working.

'I'm going out for half an hour. If the boss asks where I am, tell her I'm following up a bit of street info from a snout, okay?'

'Want some company? I'm going goggle-eyed checking all these patient records.'

'No, you keep at it. It's important, now that we think Helen's killer could be connected to her business.'

Cat gave him a long-suffering smile. 'Yeah, yeah. Well, good luck with your snout.'

* * *

Mickey was there before him. Joseph flopped down next to him on the bench. The tidal river was flowing fast and looked cold and unkind. Not a nice place to end your days. 'Hello, my friend.'

'Joe.' They shook hands rather formally, then Mickey said, 'Archie sent me.'

Joseph nodded, 'Still holding the reins?'

'Until his dying breath, but I reckon that won't be long now.'

'And do the rest of the family know about this meeting?'

'They not only know, but are in agreement.'

'Even Raymond?'

'Raymond in particular.' He looked directly into Joseph's eyes. 'We want to trade.'

Joseph was mighty glad he'd done his research into the body in the river. He had a very good idea where this was going. 'Information?'

Mickey nodded gravely. Joseph could hardly believe that this self-assured teenager was the crazy youngster he had once taken under his wing.

'You wanted to know what was going down on the Carborough? I can tell you all you want to know, if you will answer one question.' For the first time, Mickey looked apprehensive. 'You don't even have to answer, Joe. Just tell me if I'm right or not.'

'Ask me the question, and I'll see what I can do.'

Mickey exhaled. 'There is a rumour on the streets that the man pulled from the river was an Eastern European. His death was like several others in recent months, a falling out between gang members, maybe over drugs, or even a row over a woman that got out of hand.'

Mickey's words were stilted and Joseph knew instantly that he had been carefully coached. He wanted to smile, but dare not. 'That's what we were led to believe, yes.'

'But that's not the case, is it?'

'No, Mickey, it isn't.'

The boy visibly relaxed and looked on the verge of letting rip with a loud whoop of delight. 'He's one of us, isn't he? He's a Leonard.'

Joseph simply nodded. It was going to be public knowledge very soon, and he felt it was a fair trade. They needed that information about the Carborough.

Mickey puffed out his cheeks and continued. 'One of the family went missing. Raymond thinks he stumbled on something he wasn't meant to, and was taken out by some serious underworld players.'

'Was his name Lyle?'

'That's right, Derek Lyle. He's not a big cheese, if you catch my drift, but *all* family are . . .'

'Sacrosanct?'

'Yeah, that's the word.'

'And that is the cause of the bad feeling on the estate?'

'The Leonards know who is behind it, and they are going to go after him. That's the reason for the scary mood on the Carborough, Joe. There's going to be a showdown. They failed once, and he has come back and hurt them. But they won't fail a second time. They are going to take out Cox and his henchmen.'

Joseph closed his eyes. Oh Christ, the vigil! What if a bloody turf war kicked off while they were all tied up at a highly emotional public meeting?

'You look pretty worried, Joe.'

'You have no idea! Did you hear about this candlelit service on the Waterway tonight?'

'For that nice lady from the clinic?'

'Yeah, and it's bound to attract a load of troublemakers, so if the Carborough erupts at the same time, we are stuffed!'

Mickey touched his arm. 'It won't. Chill out, Joe. I'll speak to Archie. He won't let the family rain on her parade.'

Joseph frowned. He wasn't sure what Mickey meant.

'That Helen woman spent some time with Archie. In fact it was Derek Lyle who drove him over to see her at that clinic. Archie said she really helped him. So don't worry, Joe, the Leonards won't cause trouble tonight, I promise.'

But Joseph *was* worried. The Leonards might be on their side for once, but Stephen Cox and his band of hitmen certainly were not. Somehow he didn't think they'd agree to an amnesty for a dead aromatherapist.

* * *

'Nikki?'

Eve Anderson was the last person Nikki was expecting to hear. She had only just returned to her office when the call came. 'Yes, it's me, how are you?'

'I'm very well, but I know how busy you must be, so I'll keep it short. Would you be free to come for dinner one evening this week?'

Nikki was on the verge of saying, 'No', when she remembered telling Helen that she couldn't make their meeting because of work. So she said, 'I'd love to, and Eve, please don't think I'm prevaricating, but I'm at the heart of a murder enquiry right now, and I don't want to let you down. Can I ring you after tomorrow and we'll set a firm date? We have a vigil taking place tonight, and it could mean trouble.'

'Then you take care of yourself. Is it the service for that young woman who was murdered?'

Even after almost two years of knowing that Eve Anderson was her birth mother, it still felt weird talking to her. Eve was a comparative stranger to her, but Nikki always felt a hint of excitement, an unaccountable feeling of affinity, whenever they spoke. 'Yes, Helen Brook. She was my friend.'

'Oh my dear, I'm so sorry. How awful for you.'

Nikki couldn't remember when someone other than Joseph and her team had been honestly concerned about her feelings. It made her want to cry. 'You're right, it is pretty awful, but I have a job to do, and I'm determined to get whoever did it.'

'Oh, I'm certain you will, Nikki. By the way, you are very welcome to bring Joseph with you for dinner. I get the feeling that the two of you don't have many secrets.'

Nikki would love to take him with her, but she knew that he would refuse. He wouldn't want to get in the way. 'I'll ask him, Eve, but I suspect he'll take a rain check.'

'Ah, yes, your Sergeant Easter is a very sensitive man, for a police officer. But I won't hold you up any longer. You look after yourself, and ring me when you can.'

'Is everything alright?' Nikki asked. There was something out of kilter in Eve's voice.

'Yes, absolutely fine, but I did want to talk to you. Actually, I am selling my house in Coningsby. It's far too big for me and I want to downsize. I might even be going abroad for a while. You might think it odd, but what I choose to do rather depends on you. Anyway, we'll talk over dinner, as soon as you are free.'

Nikki said goodbye and closed her phone, wondering what Eve had meant. Going abroad? Nikki felt let down. She'd only just found her. Was she now going to go away again? Surely not! Kathy had been her hands-on mother. Kathy was the one who had loved her, fed her, clothed her, taken her to school, cheered her on and supported her in every way possible, but Eve had given birth to her. And Nikki had discovered that she had spent the rest of her life deeply regretting having given her up. Nikki sighed. She knew all about the curve balls that life threw at you. It wasn't possible to be angry with Eve, or with her father. Neither of them had wanted to hurt anyone. The only people to have been hurt were the two of them.

'Room for a little one?'

Rory stood in her doorway, the two obligatory coffees in his hands and a bunch of reports tucked under his arm.

'Always room for you, my friend. Come on in.'

They sat together and drank the office machine's apology for coffee, while Rory sorted out his papers.

'Well, so far Helen's house has thrown up little of use. The killer was meticulous. Naturally there are hairs, fibres, all sorts of natural debris throughout. After all, the place *was* a treatment room and she massaged people there. You would expect it to be practically afloat with microscopic skin flakes, but even so, nothing showed up that directly indicates an intruder.' Rory pushed his wire-rimmed glasses up the bridge of his nose. 'However, we have isolated seven separate DNA samples, other than those matched to Helen herself, and to Andrew Gregory. So there is at least something on file. Should you pick up a suspect and he swears he's never set foot in that room, you'll be able to prove otherwise.'

'What about the conservatory blinds? It had to be the killer who closed them.'

'There was nothing visible on the control switch. I got my best examiner on that. It takes considerable expertise to lift a latent print, but again, nothing.'

'And the blood?' Nikki didn't really want to think about this. She was still getting flashbacks to a brownish-red puddle, seeping into the new yellow carpet. 'Could the killer have done all that work and not stepped in it, or got it on him?'

Rory's expression was odd, almost apologetic. 'That's why I've brought you all these reports myself. Helen's death wasn't exactly straightforward.'

Nikki stiffened. Rory could be flippant about the most serious, gruesome and morbid cases, but now he was serious and . . . sympathetic. 'Go on.'

'There's no gentle way to say this. Helen was alive when the mandala was painted onto her body.'

Nikki heard herself assuring Andrew that Helen had known nothing before she died. 'But . . .'

'I know, I know. It was wrongly assumed that she had died when her throat was lacerated, and the "artwork" done afterwards. I'm certain that's what the killer wanted us to believe. Now we have the toxicology reports back, we find evidence of a drug in her system. I made the most painstaking re-examination of her body, and found a tiny puncture wound, a needle mark.'

'So let me get this straight. She was drugged, her body painted, and then her throat was cut. Is that right? Well, at least the killer drugged her first.'

'Not exactly.'

This was going from bad to worse.

Rory looked at her grimly. 'The drug found was a muscle relaxant, the type used in surgical operations. Have you heard of curare?'

'South American Indians hunting with poisoned arrows? What exactly are you saying, Rory?'

'The drug was a skeleto-muscular relaxant belonging to the alkaloid family of organic compounds, i.e., curare-based. D-tubocurarine was administered intravenously. It induces a flaccid paralysis. I know you won't want to hear this, Nikki, but she was fully awake. She was aware of her surroundings and everything that was happening — and totally unable to move a muscle.' He exhaled loudly. 'I'm really sorry, but there is no doubt. She knew exactly what the killer was going to do, but was powerless to stop him.'

An ice-cold tremor ran down Nikki's back. This was inconceivable! What Helen must have suffered! Oh, if only she had kept that appointment! Nikki let her head fall into her hands. She rubbed her eyes, and then looked at Rory helplessly.

'Now, I didn't tell you this to send you off on another guilt trip, my friend. What I said before stands. Whoever did this was unstoppable. He would have found a way to kill her. It was all carefully prepared, and nothing was going to stop him from carrying it out, so remember that, okay?'

'If that's meant to make me feel better, it doesn't.'

'Then get over it, Detective Inspector, and catch this sadistic bastard! *That's* how you say sorry to Helen for whatever it is you mistakenly think you've done, not moping around, wailing like some lost five-year-old.'

At the harsh words, so uncharacteristic of Rory, Nikki sat upright, about to tear back into him. Then she saw him grin.

'Oooh, I've always wanted to be the strong, commanding type. I might actually get to like it!' He stared at her, daring her not to smile. 'Now, back to business. Whoever did this knew their anaesthetics. They administered just enough, at regular intervals, to keep her immobile, then, when the job was done a larger dose was given, causing a massive histamine release, followed by cardiac collapse.'

Nikki tried to think logically. 'If it was a muscle relaxant, wouldn't she have needed some sort of respiratory aid? She'd have stopped breathing, wouldn't she?'

'Not with curare. It acts at the junction between nerves and muscles and produces complete paralysis of all voluntary movement, without having any effect on consciousness. The paralysis affects the eyes, ears, toes, then the neck and limbs, and then the trunk. If allowed to wear off that happens in reverse. In extreme cases the diaphragm muscle would be the last to be affected, and then, yes, the patient would be unable to breathe.'

'And it's used in surgery?'

'Yes, as a paralysant in general anaesthesia, amongst other things. It's also used to reduce spasms and control seizures, like in tetanus. In the past it was used in conjunction with shock therapy, to reduce the incidence of vertebral fractures — one of the nastier and rarely talked about side-effects of electroconvulsive therapy.'

'Where the hell did the killer get hold of this stuff?'

'Depends on his profession, doesn't it? Easy, if you are involved in medicine or pharmaceuticals, and don't forget, the malachite green used for the body art is a chemical. This may be the work of a chemist, or a research scientist.'

Nikki shook her head. 'I can't see it. That kind of person has a scientific background, they wouldn't meddle with astrological star signs and mystical symbols. All the scientists I've ever come across look down on the esoteric in any form.'

'Perhaps that's exactly what you are meant to think. It could all be a smokescreen.'

'That's possible, I suppose.' Nikki drank the last of her coffee and stared into the empty cup. She was haunted by the picture of Helen, naked and vulnerable on that table, knowing she was going to die, and being completely helpless. She groaned. 'That poor woman.'

Rory placed his hand gently over hers. 'Just get the person who did this, and stop it happening again.'

'Again?' Nikki looked at her friend. 'Surely this is a one-off? Someone with a personal grievance against Helen?'

'I don't think you can you afford to think like that. I've only ever had one face-to-face encounter with a serial killer, and I pray it's the only one I ever have. But I remember how it escalated. Our killer started with one planned death, but he could have really enjoyed creating his little masterpiece. Who's to say he's not going to take it up as a hobby?'

CHAPTER TWENTY-TWO

Joseph put his head around Nikki's door. 'I've got news.'

'Me too, and mine isn't good,' Nikki growled.

'Ditto. Who goes first?'

Nikki puffed out her cheeks, 'You. Let's get it over with.'

Joseph told her what Mickey had said.

Nikki rested her head in her hands. 'So, just when I thought it couldn't get any worse, along comes a turf war on the Carborough!'

'But not tonight. Mickey promised to square it with the Leonard family, and I believe he will.'

'I agree, but if he starts something, they won't be able to say, 'Oh sorry, Stephen, this will have to wait until tomorrow, we have an amnesty with the police for a candlelit vigil.'

'I know, I know. Cox will undoubtedly have heard about this fiasco — and what better time to do something vicious. We have every available officer tied up tonight, and he'll know it.' Joseph let out a sigh. 'I did tell you it wasn't good news . . . And yours?'

Nikki recounted what Rory had said. 'I cannot believe that poor Helen was aware of all those terrible things that were happening to her. She must have died terrified out of her wits.'

Joseph closed his eyes. He looked to Nikki as if he were praying. After a moment or two she realised he was. She felt envious. Nikki Galena trusted nothing that wasn't based in empirical fact. But right now she would have liked something other than Butterworth's Police Law to believe in.

'And I had a call from Eve.'

Joseph opened his eyes and smiled. 'Great! How is she?'

'Mysterious. She wants me to go over for dinner so that she can talk to me about something.'

'You'll go?'

Nikki nodded. 'I'll go. I said I'd ring her tomorrow, after this vigil is over. And she invited you as well.'

'Kind of her. Please say I appreciate it, but—'

'I know. I told her you'd most likely take a rain check. I know you pretty well, don't I, Joseph Easter?'

He raised his hands. 'I guess you do.' He looked at his watch. 'But right now, shouldn't we be getting to grips with Oliver Kirton?'

She nodded. 'Will you come with me this time? As back-up?'

'Actually I can't wait to get another look at this guy. He's something of an enigma, isn't he?'

Nikki stood up and took her coat off the hook. 'Okay, let's go grill the enigmatic Oliver!'

* * *

Nikki and Joseph stood on the path in front of Oliver Kirton's home. She had tried to call on him once before, and although he had been out, she had been taken aback by the Gothic exterior of the building. From the impression Rory Wilkinson had given her of the man, she had expected something seedy, even temporary. She certainly hadn't expected an expensive Victorian townhouse.

'Very nice, ma'am, in an Addams Family sort of way. Did you say the family had money?' Joseph looked up at the thick stone window sills and high gables. 'Does he live here alone?'

'I believe he lives alone, but I've had mixed reports about the family. His ghastly uncle, Superintendent Kirton, always gave the impression of being loaded, but as for Oliver, his contemporaries seem to think that most of his inheritance went up his nose.'

'Well, this place certainly wouldn't come cheap.' Joseph rang the bell, took a polite step back from the door and whispered, 'I think I hear Lurch approaching.'

Oliver Kirton's dark eyes still had that strange haunted look. With Rory's information under her belt, Nikki could well appreciate that he had set many a young student's heart aflutter.

'May we speak to you, Mr Kirton?'

The man stood back and with an almost theatrical bow, ushered them into his home. 'Please come in.' He led them down a long hallway where numerous ancestors gazed at them severely from their portraits, as they walked along the thick carpet.

He opened two glass-panelled doors that led into a large and rather cold room.

'My aunt's place, before you ask. She's in Guatemala, or somewhere tropical like that, saving a rainforest. I'm house-sitting until she returns — *if* she returns.' He raised his eyebrows. 'Her missions, or should I say her crusades, are legendary. I doubt I'll see her before next Christmas, if then.' He stared at them in a slightly vacant manner. 'A drink of some kind?'

'No, sir. Thank you.' Nikki sat where he had indicated, in a deep and incredibly uncomfortable armchair. Joseph wisely chose to stand. 'We need to know a little more about your relationship with Miss Helen Brook. Did you ever go to her house on the Westland Waterway for a treatment?'

'Yes, once or twice, although I generally saw her at the Willows.' Kirton draped himself languidly against an ornately carved fireplace. 'Why?'

'We need to identify and eliminate any evidence found there. Would you consent to providing a DNA sample, sir?'

'Of course. Anything to help.'

Nikki was bothered by his vagueness. 'Thank you.' She indicated to Joseph, who was beginning to tear open a testing kit. 'DS Easter here can do it straightaway, or you can have it done in the medical room at the station, whatever you prefer. There's nothing to worry about, it's simply a sterile swab wiped across the inside of your cheek, no more than that.'

Oliver Kirton shrugged. 'Here is fine.'

A moment or two later, as Joseph was filling in the form attached to the DNA kit, and sealing the bag, Nikki continued to question Oliver Kirton.

'If I may ask, what was your reason for visiting Helen?'

The man raised his eyebrows in a delicate arch. 'Migraine actually. And a sleep disorder.' He took a deep breath and said, 'I'm sure you already know that in my misspent youth I had a problem with, ah, over-indulgence. Heroin, cocaine, alcohol, amphetamines, barbiturates, you name it, I tried it. Sadly, such abuse does leave the old body in somewhat of a mess as one ages.' He smiled sardonically. 'I'm sure my dear old friend Rory Wilkinson has filled you in on all the gory details.'

Nikki shrugged. 'He mentioned you were at university together. Actually he said you were quite brilliant, sir.'

'Said that, did he? Well, he was no slouch himself. Some of his work fell not far short of remarkable.'

'What did you study, Mr Kirton?'

He paused, and a wistful look came over his handsome face. 'I studied archaeology at Cambridge, then I went to the States, to the University of Colorado at Boulder, studying the Palaeolithic Age at their Institute of Arctic and Alpine research.' He sighed. 'I suppose I had my moments of brilliance, Inspector, times when I managed without any little helpers. The studying was easy, far too easy. I have a brain like a sponge. It's life that I find so bloody difficult to handle. One little upset, and bingo, I crumble.'

'Are you clean at present?'

'At present, yes. I have been for some while. The last clinic was awfully good. But tomorrow? Who knows? I'm an addict, Detective Inspector Galena. Brilliant, but an addict nevertheless.'

'And Helen helped you?'

'More than you'll ever know, Inspector.' He drew himself straighter. 'That is why I'm so worried. I'm not sure how I will cope without her.'

'Is there no one else at the Willows who would see you?'

'I have made an appointment to go there, but Helen was very special. I feel that I have lost more than just an understanding therapist. It frightens me.'

Nikki looked at the tall, enigmatic figure and wondered if anything would really frighten Oliver Kirton. His act was good, but she doubted that he was telling them the truth. She wondered why he was lying.

* * *

On the other side of town, outside a rambling, down-at-heel cottage in a lane that led towards the fen, Yvonne Collins and Jessie Nightingale tossed a coin for who was going to take the lead interviewing Titus Whipp.

'Detectives should always go first,' said Yvonne smugly.

Jessie tried flattery. 'But you have *so* much more experience than me, Vonnie.'

They had read Eric Barnes' initial report and both were wishing they could have shifted this particular call onto the sergeant.

Yvonne sighed and opened the car door. 'Okay, let's get this over with. And I warn you, if I catch even the slightest glimpse of a stuffed dead bird, you are on your own.'

Titus Whipp answered the bell almost immediately. Both women were treated to a ghastly leer.

Yvonne took one look over his shoulder, and decided that the interview was going to take place right there on the doorstep. No way was she going inside a museum packed full of dead animals.

'Come in, do!' They were treated to the smell of unwashed clothes and musty rooms long closed off from fresh air and sunlight.

'It's all right, sir. We just have a few questions for you. We won't take long.'

'Then please, come in and sit down.'

Jessie frowned and glanced at her colleague. Eric Barnes had said that Titus Whipp was rude, aggressive, and unhelpful. The change of attitude must be due to the fact that they were women. Not only that, but they were attractive too.

'No, we're fine, sir. Now, can you tell us whether you ever went to Helen Brook's treatment room at Westland Waterway?'

The man brushed long straggly hair from his neck, and stared at them. He was obviously annoyed by their reluctance to enter his home.

'Yes, once. I was booked in at the Willows, but her car was in for a service so she saw me at her home.'

Yvonne shuddered. How could Helen have actually shared a room with this man? Let alone touch his grubby body. 'May we ask why you were seeing her, sir?

'No, you may not. I am hardly likely to discuss my medical problems out here on my doorstep, am I? In fact, I have no intention of discussing my private business anywhere.'

'Fine, sir. But I'm afraid we are going to have to ask you to call into the station as soon as possible. We need a DNA sample from you.'

'And why would you want that? I can refuse you know.'

'Everyone who has been to Helen's home needs to be tested in order to eliminate them from our enquiries.' Yvonne was impressed that Jessie even managed a smile.

Titus Whipp looked suspiciously at them. 'Or place the suspect at the scene of the crime. Am I right?'

'Naturally we are looking for the person who murdered Helen Brook, sir. You'd expect no less from us, surely? After all, it was you, sir, was it not, who threatened the family of the lorry driver who caused the Blackmoor Cross accident? If you felt that strongly about her being injured, I would think you would be distraught at her death.'

Whipp looked down, breathing heavily. Yvonne saw that his hands were balled into tight fists. 'Yes, it was me. Perhaps it's time you two got on with your jobs.' He began to shut the door. 'I'll give you your damned sample, but in my own time, all right?'

The door closed with a rush of stale air.

'That went well.'

'Didn't it just.' They walked back to the car. 'Did you see those dead birds in the hall behind him?'

'It was the badger that got me! Those beady eyes and those yellow teeth!'

'The badger's? Or Titus Whipp's?'

'Not much difference!' Jessie slammed the car door, and they both began to laugh.

'Frankly, if there's got to be another interview with Road Kill Man, Joseph or the DI can have it. What a nightmare!' She turned the key in the ignition. 'Where next?'

'The Willows. DI Galena wants to know if any of the staff or organisers of tonight's vigil have been threatened again, and we have to be discreet. No frightening the shits out of anyone.'

'Okay, no problem, Vonnie.' Jessie flipped her indicator and turned left. 'I wonder what Mr Whipp's medical problem was anyway?'

'Oh please! Pass me the sick bag!'

CHAPTER TWENTY-THREE

All leave at Greenborough police station had been cancelled. Uniformed officers hung around in groups, talking quietly as they awaited their instructions for that night. The atmosphere was subdued, quite unlike the usual organised chaos that preceded any operation requiring a mass police presence on the streets. On this occasion, no one knew exactly what to expect.

In her office, Nikki read through the latest report to land on her desk — Professor Wilkinson's prelim on the late Andrew Gregory. It made sickening reading, and the letter attached made it no easier to bear.

Detective Inspector. Just to let you know that, as previously discussed, Mr Gregory died at the hands of one or maybe two, professional killers, men skilled in the art of torture. The worrying thing to my mind is that in his case, the serious damage, the terrible internal injuries and the broken bones, were all inflicted with bare hands. (This included the manipulation of spinal vertebrae allowing the intervertebral disc to press on the spinal cord, causing paralysis of the legs and dysfunction of the bladder.) I believe the tools found in the bedroom at the crime scene were simply trappings intended to frighten the victim. None of them were used to inflict any of the mortal wounds. The person or persons who tortured

Mr Gregory had a high degree of anatomical knowledge, especially as regards the positioning of vital internal organs and nerve centres. I do not know how the victim managed to live through the night and into the next day. His need to be reunited with his loved one must have been exceptionally strong to override his appalling injuries.

Now, my dear colleague, I know I'm not the detective here, but humour me, if you will. I am certain these men were hired by people with an awful lot at stake, and a small fortune to spend. Killing and maiming like that does not come cheap, and I swear you won't find any boot camp in this country with such specialist skills in their instruction manual. I have only ever seen this kind of thing once before, and that was in Asia. I know these men were unsuccessful this time, but I'm sure they could count their failures on one hand. Miss Starr had a long-term illness which caused her to suffer a massive heart attack after a relatively short beating. The younger man, Alex Power, was extensively beaten and tortured prior to being strangled. The chisel was hammered through the neck post-mortem. Why, I have no idea. (Maybe anger at not finding out what they wanted to know?)

In Andrew's case, I suspect the killers were unprepared to find a man they probably had down as just some computer geek. They hadn't reckoned on his strong will to stay alive. Proves even hired assassins can't win them all. Thank God. Good luck tracking down this delightful pair, although frankly, I doubt you will ever trace them. Sorry, Rory.

Nikki closed the file. This would have to wait until after tonight.

'Nikki?' The superintendent was standing in her doorway.

'Come on in, sir. Are we all geared up and ready to go?'

'Almost, although I've made one change of plan.' He sank slowly onto a chair. 'Under the circumstances, I have asked the organisers of the vigil to bring forward the flower float to midnight instead of dawn. It should lessen the amount of people hanging around all night.'

'Good move, sir. Hopefully once the flowers have been dealt with, a lot of the crowd will go home.'

'That's the plan. Although the officers already down there say it's been building up all afternoon. Apparently it looks like a mini rock festival.'

'But a lot quieter, I hope.' Nikki noticed her boss looked unusually drawn. 'Has intelligence tracked anything planned for tonight? Hecklers? Yobs out for a punch up?'

'Nothing obvious. No social media chatter asking the usual troublemakers to meet up here.' Superintendent Woodhall stretched his shoulders and shook his head. 'But I still don't like it.'

'Is it that warning note, sir?'

'I really don't know. I just feel very uncomfortable about the whole thing.' He stood up and took a deep breath, 'Still, we can only be vigilant and deal with things as they arise. Let's hope I'm wrong, huh? Thirty minutes, and we meet outside for a final briefing, okay?'

Nikki nodded. 'I just need a few minutes with my team, and we'll be there.' As the super made his way down the corridor, Nikki went to the murder room where her group was waiting for her.

'Before we all muster, anything we should know from the Willows Clinic? Yvonne? Jessie?'

'They've not received any form of warning, ma'am. We asked if anyone had objected to the gathering on the grounds of public safety. That seemed the best way to ask the question without causing alarm.'

'But no one had heard anything, ma'am,' added Yvonne. 'The only extra piece of info we have is that one of the part-time receptionists remembered the man who picked up the piece of purple agate. She confirmed that he was the driver for an elderly man who was a patient of Helen Brook's.'

Nikki nibbled thoughtfully on her lip. 'Then our other murder victim has no direct connection with Helen. That is something of a relief. Okay, well, back to tonight's threat, let's pray it's just some irate resident who doesn't like the idea of his front garden being filled with candle stubs and Mars bar wrappers.' She gave them what she hoped was a reassuring look. 'I'm sure it will all go off fine. It is a vigil after all, not a protest rally.'

'Does it have some sort of programme, ma'am?' Niall Farrow asked.

'Yes. At seven o'clock the candles will be lit, then the vicar from the local United Reform Church is going to lead a short service and open the book of condolence. After that a group of local people, some of her friends at the Willows in particular, are going to say a few words about Helen, you know, their recollections and memories of her. Then the crowd will gather along the Waterway side of the riverbank for a silent prayer vigil. Superintendent Woodhall has brought forward the flower float to midnight. Hopefully there will only be a faithful few who remain and stick it out in the cold until dawn. It's hard to believe, but it looks as though most of this has been caused by some web site that was operating long before she died. Some well-meaning ex-client of hers decided that she was some kind of miracle worker. He wrote a blog about how marvellous she was, and invited half the country to post their own experiences on the site. Naturally, it went viral when she was killed, and then the media caught on. Hence this goddamned freak show tonight.'

Niall Farrow raised his hand. 'Do we know if Miss Duchene is still going to attend?'

'I spoke to her an hour ago. She will be there, and I have said that you and DC Jessie Nightingale will stay close to her. She was very relieved to hear that, and Niall, she's pretty spooked by that note. She just doesn't believe she should be frightened off doing what she wants to do.'

'Quite right, ma'am. Jessie and I will keep an eye on her, don't worry.'

'Okay. Any questions?' She looked around the room.

Cat stood up. 'Ma'am? What about through traffic? Westland Waterway is a busy road.'

'When we go down to the assembly point the super will fill us in on whatever detour Traffic has set up. They've certainly got something in place. So, if you're all ready? Let's go join the troops.'

* * *

Superintendent Woodhall stood on the steps and addressed the officers massed in the yard.

'I want this dealt with tactfully and discreetly. Most of the people attending the vigil are doing it with the best of intentions, to pay tribute to a beautiful woman who had already suffered more than most, a person who cared for others and was needlessly killed. They are there because they are outraged by the injustice of it. What I don't want is for them to turn their anger on us. It's early days regarding the enquiry, so they won't be baying for blood yet, but keep your behaviour exemplary, okay?'

There was a murmur of agreement.

'So, having said all that, we *have* had a threat telling us to cancel the whole shebang. We have chosen to ignore it, so keep your eyes open and if there is the slightest hint of trouble of any kind, quash it as speedily and as tactfully as you can. And, every minute that you are there, bear in mind that the man standing next to you could be Helen Brook's killer.'

There were a few muttered comments, a shuffling of heavy boots.

'Right, before we leave, you must know that there is a massive media presence down there — TV, radio, journalists, the lot. They will be watching us like hawks, looking for the slightest indiscretion, so don't give them any excuse, and that's an order. The road is closed off from Milton Avenue to Wordsworth Crescent and a diversion is in place that misses the riverbank completely. The green at the back of the town hall has been opened for free parking, to ease the expected congestion. And that is about all I can tell you. CID, you will mingle and keep your ears open for anything suspicious, any talk of violence, any indications of individuals stirring up trouble, anyone acting oddly. Uniform, do what you are supposed to do and keep the peace. Just make sure this remains a vigil from start to finish. Lastly, and very importantly, remember the threat to Miss Duchene. We have designated officers looking out for her, but please, all of you, be on your guard.' He took a deep breath. 'Right. Time to go and join our colleagues at the river. Good luck all of you. Let's move out.'

* * *

Nikki had expected a massive turnout, but she was not prepared for what they found on the banks of the River Westland.

Despite the cold east wind, the road, the river path and every available square foot of space was packed full of people. Nikki gazed out across a sea of faces — men, women and children, babies, the very elderly, and the disabled. She saw Joseph's jaw drop and heard him mutter, 'My life! If something kicks off, we are in deep shit!'

Cat pushed her hands deep into her coat pockets and shivered. 'Touch wood, they all look very calm, in fact, have you ever seen so many people in one spot and heard so little noise?'

'Only at the Cenotaph, during the two minutes' silence.'

'Exactly. It's creepy.'

Niall and Jessie stood a little apart from the others. Niall looked at his watch, then turned to Nikki and asked, 'Ma'am? How on earth are we going to locate Miss Duchene in this lot?'

'I've told her to be at the corner of Wordsworth Crescent at ten to seven. Meet her there and stay close to her. Keep in touch, okay?'

Niall and Jessie moved off through the crowd.

'I see what the super meant about it looking more like a rock festival. Look over there.' Nikki pointed towards a small grassy space that was normally used for riverside picnics. A mass of brightly coloured one-person tents covered the ground like an eruption of giant mushrooms. People milled amongst them carrying sleeping bags and folding chairs, along with the ubiquitous bunches of flowers and cards.

'Lord! If Helen could see all of this, she'd be horrified.'

'She was hardly the ostentatious type, was she?'

'Oh, no way! She was quiet, unassuming, and about as far from this kind of thing as you could get. She even hated the way they praised her on that web site.'

'Do you think the public will change their opinion of her when we release the details about Andrew Gregory's misdeeds?'

'That depends entirely on how the papers deal with it. If they intimate that Helen might have known about his crooked dealings, then mud sticks, no matter how much you try to prove otherwise. Then again, if they get wind of the last farewell in the chapel of rest, well, everyone loves a romantic drama, so who knows?'

Joseph leaned back against a rough brick wall. 'Speaking of Andrew Gregory, ma'am, I meant to tell you, I had a message from a mate of mine who works in the Met. He's come across the infamous Mr Fabian before. Apparently he used to work for a foreign criminal organisation, a Mafia-type group. He decamped about a year ago. No one knows where he lives or anything about him, other than that he seems to be Italian. His name, and that of Mr Venables, have cropped up pretty regularly over the last eight or nine years, all in connection with disappearances, violence or killings. Thing is, they don't seem to exist. Interpol told my friend that they are hunting ghosts.'

Nikki gave a small laugh. 'So Rory would make a good detective after all.'

'Ma'am?'

'Nothing. Thanks for checking, Joseph. Well, we'd better get ourselves into this crowd. It's almost seven. Look, if we get separated, I'll try to keep close to the house, near the vicar and the book of condolence. You never know, the murderer might get off on signing his name in the book.'

* * *

Jessie spotted Carla Duchene first. 'Bit overdressed, don't you think?'

Niall raised his eyebrows. 'I think she looks very chic, in a mature kind of way.' He grinned and gave Jessie a comically deprecating look. 'There's no harm in looking your best, is there?'

They made their way towards her, Jessie muttering, 'Thanks a bunch. I wonder what *she'd* look like in Gore-Tex and sensible shoes. Over to you for the introductions.'

Niall stepped forward and held out his hand. 'Miss Duchene? I'm PC Niall Farrow, and this is DC Jessica Nightingale.' Jessie hated it when people gave her full name. 'Now, are you quite sure you still wish to attend? It's not too late to change your mind. We are happy to escort you back home if you like.'

Carla Duchene bit her lip. 'To be honest with you, Officer, I'm terrified. But I'm damned if I will be frightened off by some stupid threat.' She looked fearfully at the crowd. 'There are far more people here than we ever dreamed. And look at all the press! The national press! And even the BBC! It's simply amazing.'

'It's not just Greenborough. Thanks to some website, the whole country has taken her death to heart, Miss Duchene.' Jessie was feeling the weight of her responsibility for keeping this woman safe. 'Look, no one would think any less of you if you avoided this. You've paid for the flowers for the float, and helped organise it all, surely that's enough?'

'What are you saying exactly, DC Nightingale? That I really should not be here?' Carla Duchene looked even more concerned.

Jessie really did not want to frighten her further, but felt she deserved to be aware of the truth. 'No, of course not. It's just that, well, we hope the threat wasn't serious, but watching you for several hours in this huge crowd could be difficult. I just don't want you to think we're being flippant.'

A man shoved Niall as he hurried into the opening service. Niall glowered at him. 'See what we mean? Jessie's right, miss. We take all threats seriously, and unless we handcuff ourselves together, we could very easily lose sight of you.'

Carla hung her head and shook it slightly. Then she brought it up and looked at them defiantly. 'No. I owe it to Helen, for my mother's sake. I'll be fine, honestly. Now, we should go. Do your best, that's all I ask. And I'll try to keep close.'

* * *

Cat Cullen slipped in between a small group of damp-eyed teenage girls clutching flickering candle lamps, and eased her way through the crowd towards her boss. This really was something else! 'All going pretty well so far, ma'am.'

Nikki nodded. 'Very orderly, especially the queue for signing the book. Seen anyone acting oddly?'

'No, but that foul man, Titus Whipp, is here. Yvonne Collins is keeping a close eye on him.'

'But he's behaving himself?'

'At present, guv. But I think if he even looks at Yvonne funny, he'll find himself marched out of the area.' She gave a short laugh, then said, 'The sarge is pretty jumpy tonight. It's not like him at all.'

'Joseph? I hadn't noticed. Any idea why?'

Cat shrugged. 'None at all. It's just so out of character. I mean, he's never gung-ho like some of the guys, but he's always up for a rumble. He did say he'd got bad vibes about this, but who hasn't?' She looked towards the makeshift podium that had been erected in Helen's driveway. 'Who's that? About to say his bit?'

Her boss smiled grimly. 'Oliver Kirton. I thought he would have something to say.'

They took a few steps closer to the front of the crowd and Cat stared at the tall, dark man on the rostrum. 'Damn! He's well fit! Why didn't I get to interview him?'

'Because he's not what he appears. And according to Prof Wilkinson, you wouldn't want to meet him when his medication has worn off.'

Cat puffed out her cheeks and rolled her eyes, 'Oh, I'd be willing to take that chance. What a looker!'

Nikki grinned. 'DC Cullen! That leer is hardly profes-sional.' Then she held up her hand. 'Hold on. I want to hear this.'

Kirton had taken the microphone. Unlike the speakers before him, he had no notes. He stood in silence and stared around him. Then his eyes rested on a large picture of Helen Brook, a blow-up of one the local paper had run. It was taken before her accident, and she had a particularly haunting smile on her elfin face. He began to speak, and all that could be heard was the gentle hushing sound of the wind.

'There has been little light in my miserable life. I have done nothing to be proud of. I considered suicide, but then I am a coward, and despite myself I did not want my family to suffer. Then, light walked into my life, in the form of the beautiful woman that we are mourning here tonight. But now that light has been extinguished.'

He gazed at the picture of Helen Brook and spoke into the night:

'I had a dream, which was not all a dream.
The bright sun was extinguished, and the stars did wander dar-
kling in the eternal space,
Rayless, and pathless, and the icy earth,
Swung blind and blackening in the moonless air;
Morn came and went — and came, and brought no day,
And men forgot their passions in the dread
Of this their desolation; and all hearts
Were chilled into a selfish prayer for light.'

He took a long breath. 'But light will never come again. Someone stole it. There is now only darkness.'

He handed the microphone back to one of the organisers and stepped down from the rostrum.

* * *

Cat swallowed. The silence persisted.

Then someone started clapping, and soon was joined by others, until the street echoed with thunderous applause. Cat looked around, but Oliver Kirton had disappeared and DI

Galena was staring at the podium muttering under her breath. 'Thank you very bloody much, *Dr* Kirton. Just what we did *not* need! For God's sake get someone else up there to say their bit.' She turned, and said to Cat, 'This is not good. All we need is a gap before the next mourner and some big mouth will be asking what the police are doing to catch the bastard who stole the light! Then all hell could break loose. The one thing we don't need right now, is audience participation on this kind of scale.'

Before Cat could answer, the DI's phone rang. Cat watched her boss's face. Evidently the call was not making her feel any happier. She flipped the mobile closed and said, 'There's trouble down near Milton Avenue. Joseph's gone to see what it's about. Uniform are there too. You stay here, Cat, and I'll go find Joseph. We need to keep a lid on whatever is kicking off.'

Before Cat could even agree, her boss had been swallowed up by the seething mass of people. She was left wondering exactly what had driven the gorgeous Oliver Kirton to deliver such a powerful speech. Heartfelt loss and emotion? Or was he trying to ignite a fire?

* * *

In the heart of the gathering, a single soul stared distraught at the hordes of people around them. It shouldn't be like this. This was a travesty. All the work, all the planning, all the time spent on those very specific and important designs, and the final act, the taking of Helen Brook, all reduced to this circus. The eyes stared around in horror. This should not be happening. It had all gone horribly wrong! The people here, the fools who worshipped her, were now carrying candles and arms full of flowers ready to be floated down the river. Hideous! And the police were making it worse. They were crawling all over the place, with sad faces and kind words for the stupid rabble that increased with every hour. And the television crews, and the prying, insensitive media! Someone must pay for this. Someone *would* pay.

What could be done? Maybe there was a way to make use of this awful debacle. Forget the reason why these fools are congregating, and simply see the crowd as a seething mass of unstable matter. Then it could certainly be used to advantage. What was the old saying? Change that which can be changed.

* * *

'It's just a group of yobs, as far as we can tell, ma'am.' Joseph brushed earth from his jacket sleeve, the remains of a plant wrenched from someone's garden and used as a missile. 'Uniform has contained it. Heaven help us when it's chucking out time at the pubs. You look really worried. Is it something to do with that Kirton bloke and his bloody speech to the nation?'

'The atmosphere has changed since his blasted outpouring.'

'Yes, I've noticed that, damn it. But it was dramatic, wasn't it? I wonder why he chose that particular poem of Byron's? *Darkness* was all about the end of the world, man turning on man. Maybe it was deliberate.' Joseph raised an eyebrow. 'But Oliver Kirton does have a lot of charisma, I'll give him that.'

'Yeah, like a sodding Svengali. Until Oliver chucked in his tuppence worth, it was really peaceful. Now there's an undercurrent.'

'And the last thing we need is a hyped-up crowd of this size.'

'On the banks of a tidal river! In the dark!'

Joseph's radio crackled into life. 'Sergeant Easter. WPS Yvonne Collins is near the bridge and has reported that the white male she was keeping an eye on is causing a disturbance. Could you attend? Over.'

'Roger. Show me on my way. Over and out.' Joseph looked at Nikki. 'Bloody Titus Whipp! Are you coming, ma'am?'

'No, I should get back to Cat. I'll check on Niall and Jessie too, see how they are coping with their guard duty.'

Joseph loped off towards the bridge, and Nikki began to make her way back to Helen's house. Her progress was slow. The queue to sign the book was three deep and over two hundred metres long. Then there was the main candle-bearing throng, milling around in the road and along the river walk. As she moved through the wall of coats and jackets, hats and scarves, she heard singing. Calming, at least. It sounded like a cross between a hymn and some country music. Suddenly it was drowned out by shouts.

Nikki stiffened and immediately headed towards the source of the noise. About six houses down from Newlands, was a group of young men carrying badly-painted, hand-made banners. They were chanting something about "fakes" and "phonies." Nikki reported her position, and pitched in and confronted the apparent ring-leader. Within seconds she was surrounded by a group of youths yelling obscenities at her.

She knew back-up would arrive soon, but things were fast becoming ugly. Someone grabbed her from behind, and swinging round, Nikki was treated to a blast of beery breath and a thug with a head like a badly peeled potato. He shoved his broken nose into her face.

'Filth!' Saliva hit her cheek. Two other men were holding her arms behind her back, and she was powerless to move away.

'Let me go!' Nikki aimed a flying backwards kick. There was a howl of pain and one arm was released. Whipping around, she managed to throw the second man off balance. She leapt back, ready to take on whoever was coming for her. Where the hell was uniform?

Potato-head was moving forward again. 'Filth!'

She took a step back and tried to call for urgent assistance, but her radio was snatched from her grasp. The side of her head suddenly felt as if it had exploded. Her jaw cracked shut, filling her mouth with blood as her teeth caught her tongue. Jagged spears of light flashed behind her eyes. There was a rushing, roaring noise, and she pitched forward.

'Ma'am!'

The voice sounded muffled amid the roaring, but someone had managed to catch her before she hit the concrete. They half-carried her away from the fight.

'Eric?'

'Jesus, ma'am! You took one hell of a swipe from that placard. Are you okay, or should I get the medics?'

Nikki shook her head, then wished she hadn't. 'Oh, shit!' She leant for a moment against a thick wooden fence, taking deep breaths and touching the lump on the side of her head. 'No, I'm okay. Thanks to you. What on earth are you doing here? And what about that bunch of yobs?'

'Don't worry, uniform have sorted them out. I was looking for you, ma'am. And it *is* all leave cancelled, although I know that didn't actually apply to me.' Eric Barnes looked different. He seemed subdued, serious. 'Are you sure you don't want the ambulance guys to check you over?'

'No, I'll be all right in a minute.' She'd suffered worse.

'Come round here, ma'am.' DC Barnes led her into a small cul-de-sac containing a few private houses and a small nursing home. 'It's a bit quieter, and you can sit here.' He placed her handbag beside her on a low wall. 'I found this, but your radio was pulverised under some scrote's boot.'

Nikki carefully lowered herself down onto the stone lintel and breathed a sigh of relief. 'A placard, did you say? It felt more like a steel beam.'

'Well, a bit of chipboard nailed to a chunk of four-by-four is more like it. Nasty.' Eric Barnes sat down next to her. 'You look a bit better.'

'Apart from a bitten tongue and a bruise the size of a coconut, I'm great.' She winced as she touched it again. 'So why were you looking for me?'

The young detective looked down at his trainers. 'To apologise. Wholeheartedly. And before you ask, when I return from my supposed sick leave, I will be taking your advice. Moving on is fine by me. I was a prat. A callous, unthinking prat, and now I keep seeing Andrew Gregory's face.' He shuddered. 'Thing is, I did try to tell him. I tried to say sorry, but he wouldn't have any of it. He told me to burn in hell. If you'd seen the hate in his eyes. I'm having nightmares about it. So . . .'

Nikki held her head and tried to concentrate. This was more than she had expected of him. 'I know, Eric. We can't undo some things. Can't go back and have another shot. We just have to learn from them and move on.'

He looked thoroughly miserable. 'I thought, well, I can't just leave and have you thinking I don't give a shit, because I do. I . . . Well, I've always had problems with women who're in control. I know it's no excuse, but I didn't have a good childhood. My mother and my sister . . . Anyhow, it's no excuse, but I get really angry.' He stared at the ground. 'And before someone else tells you, I have said some terrible things about you, you know. I just couldn't help myself.'

Nikki looked at the young detective. 'You *have* to lose that attitude, Eric. You could make it to the top if you wanted to, but only if you ditch the past and start to trust your new team. Women are here to stay, Detective. Like it or not, we aren't going away.' She gave him a half-smile. 'And I'm not your mother!'

'No, you're not. She was a sadist. And I can't believe I'm saying this, but you are okay.' He stood up. 'I've got to go, ma'am. Thank you for listening. Will you be all right now?'

'Yeah, fine. I'll just sit here for a minute or two, then I'd better find the others. And, DC Barnes? I appreciate your help back there. Thank you.'

Nikki stared after him as he rounded the corner and joined the crush of mourners. She wondered just how much courage that had taken. She had firmly believed that he would hate her for asking him to request a transfer. Perhaps Andrew Gregory's courage had brought the boy to his senses. She hoped the breakthrough would last, but she wasn't totally convinced. Eric's new team was bound to have at least one woman detective in it, maybe even another Cat Cullen, if that were possible. It would be interesting to see how he coped in the job long-term.

She looked at her watch and tried to calculate how long it had been since she left Cat. Not long probably. The fight had most likely only lasted a few moments, and although her conversation with Eric Barnes had been pretty intense, it could not have taken more than fifteen minutes. Whatever, she had better get back before she was missed.

Steadying herself against the wall, she took a few tentative steps. She knew she was going to have the granddaddy of all headaches. A dull thud was already pulsating between her temples. She sat back down for a moment, then took a deep breath and walked to the end of the close, where she halted to survey the scene on the Waterway.

Thank God, it seemed to have returned to its original mood. The crowd were now singing along with three young women on the rostrum. It was a fair rendition of Robbie Williams' *Angels*.

She looked over towards the river and saw the outline of Yvonne Collins, silhouetted in front of a large portable light, passing out armfuls of flowers from a huge pile of cardboard boxes. The critical point seemed to have passed.

Nikki couldn't see Cat, but guessed she would still be at the house. She pulled out her mobile to ring her, then pushed it back into her pocket. It would be hard to hear with all the singing, and she could be there by the time Cat had answered the call.

Gathering herself together, she began to walk towards Newlands. Although she kept close to the garden fences and walls, she was still jostled and pushed, which did little for her aching head. She would be glad to get this bloody night over. A hot drink and some paracetamol seemed like the Holy Grail right now.

Two young couples, arms draped about each other and trying unsuccessfully to walk four abreast, drew level with her. At the same time someone hurried up behind her, nudging her into their path. She felt a sharp stinging pain at the top of her leg, and cursed to herself. A wasp? A bee sting? What the hell now?

More people were surrounding her, someone was calling frantically for a missing child, and others were hurrying to get to the river before the flowers were all scattered.

Nikki let the crowd flow past her. Something was wrong with her. She turned around. She needed to get back to the wall, and sit down again. Perhaps she should have let Eric get the medics after all.

Nausea overcame her, and her head began to swim. She reached helplessly for a gatepost, and then, with a small whimper, pitched into darkness.

* * *

Cat pushed her way through the crowds on the Westland Waterway, searching for her boss. The size of the crowd was beginning to frighten her. Finding a single woman would be almost impossible. She pulled out her phone. 'Sarge? It's Cat.'

Joseph's voice was crackly. 'I can hardly hear you, Cat. Can you speak up?'

'Have you got the boss with you?' she shouted.

'Sorry. I haven't seen her for a while. I thought she was with you. Try her mobile.'

'I have. There's no reply.'

Joseph faded, then came back, 'She's probably trying to sort one of these stupid spats of trouble.'

'I suppose, but it is much quieter now that the flowers have been floated. Can you tell her to ring me if you see her, Sarge?'

There was another crackle and the line went dead. Cat closed her phone and looked around again. She couldn't believe so many people wanted to linger. She drew her jacket closer around her and shivered. It was one bloody long night. And where the hell was DI Galena?

'DC Cullen! Got a minute?' Jessie was kneeling down beside a young woman wearing a thick imitation fur jacket and high boots. She was sitting on the kerb, looking dazed and pale. 'One too many alcopops in the Pink Crocodile, I think. And her mates have deserted her.'

'What can I do? Get a paramedic to look her over?'

'Sorry, no, it's not this. I can cope here. It's the superintendent. He's looking for DI Galena.'

Cat felt a trickle of concern run down her backbone and she absent-mindedly rubbed at the scar on her face. 'I can't find her either, and her phone is not picking up.'

'Have you left a message on voicemail?'

'It's not responding, Jessie. I'm really worried about her. No one's seen her for over an hour.' Cat looked around at the surreal scene of candles and arc lights, darkness and shadows. 'Where is the super? I think I'd better have a word with him.'

'On the bridge.'

As Cat made her way to where she could see Superintendent Woodhall and several other officers gathered, she had a sudden flash of memory. That threat. *Someone else may die.* She quickened her pace. It was time someone pulled the plug on this powder keg. They'd had their service, their candles, songs and flowers of remembrance. Trouble had been sporadic and easily contained, but enough was enough. It was time to call it a day before someone got hurt — if they hadn't already.

Fear gripped her gut and twisted it hard. She broke into a run.

CHAPTER TWENTY-FOUR

It was not so much an awakening as a slow drift in and out of consciousness. One moment she seemed to be waking up — she could see shadows and hear muffled noises — only to slip away again before awareness fully returned.

Finally her head began to clear, and this time she fought to stay awake. The room lurched and spun, but she fought the desire to close her eyes, and slowly everything settled. The pain in her head was indescribable, but she pushed back the waves of nausea and hung on grimly. She had to be in hospital. Where else would they have taken her? But why couldn't she see anything? It was night, maybe she was in a side ward and the door was shut. That was probably it.

Nikki swallowed hard and tried not to be sick. There should be a bell somewhere. The nurses would want to know she was awake. And water. More than anything she wanted a drink of cold water. Groggily she turned and reached out for her bedside locker. Her hand touched something cold. The water carafe? Then with a choking cry she drew her hand back. What she had felt was a stone wall.

Fear slipped with her into that dark place. If she was not in hospital, where the hell was she? Awareness began to return, and with it, the full horror of her situation.

She moaned softly in the darkness. She had to get herself together. She needed to get away from wherever this was. Then two people filled her thoughts, Joseph, her dearest friend, and Eve, her mother. She saw their faces, and felt their anguish. In her time she'd told enough desperate families that one of their loved ones was missing. She knew exactly the dreadful uncertainty that they would suffer, and she could not put them through that. No matter what had happened to her, or who had taken her, she had to get away, and fast.

* * *

'CCTV! Are there any cameras along the Westland Waterway?' Superintendent Woodhall demanded.

'There's one camera at the town end, just by the traffic lights, and one at the far end by the playing field. Nothing near where the vigil took place, sir.'

'And was she seen on either of them?'

Dave looked grey. 'We're checking now. But it's going to take a while, with all those people coming and going, sir. Oh, and we think there might be one in the grounds of the nursing home in the cul-de-sac. We've sent someone out to check.'

'Sergeant! Get hold of all the media who were present. I want every picture, every downloaded photo, every memory card, every roll of film and every bit of recorded footage. Someone must have caught her on camera.'

Jessie entered the room, her face as drawn as Dave's. 'We've got the remains of her radio, sir.' She held up a plastic bag. 'Deliberately smashed to bits, by the look of it.'

'Are the boards in place outside Newlands, asking for information?'

The uniformed sergeant looked exhausted. 'Yes, sir, and at both ends of the Waterway. And we are doing a house to house. Under the circumstances, we decided not to wait for daylight.'

'Quite right. Keep me posted on everything as it comes in, okay.' Woodhall turned and beckoned to Joseph. 'You, Sergeant Easter, and DC Cullen, come to my office.'

* * *

Joseph leant against the wall and tried to keep a hold on his emotions. How could he have even let Nikki out of his sight? They knew what a volatile situation it was, and yet he'd gone dancing off trying to keep the peace, when uniform could have done the job just as well. He knew he would never forgive himself for this. He looked around miserably. Cat was slouched in the only spare chair and Greg Woodhall was leaning heavily forwards, his elbows planted amid his files, reports and scattered memo pads. Every man and woman on the station was overcome by shock and disbelief, and the superintendent seemed to be no exception.

'Joseph? Should we notify her mother, Eve Anderson?'

'I don't want her to see it on the news. No matter how much we try to keep this under wraps, it will get out, if it hasn't already.'

'I agree. Would it be better coming from someone she knows?'

Joseph nodded. 'I'll do it after this meeting.' He had no idea what he would say. All his training, all the wisdom gained during years of travel, suddenly meant nothing. How would he tell a mother that the child she had just found again after years of being separated had been abducted? For that's what this was. Someone had taken Nikki, and it was his fault.

The superintendent was staring at him. 'No time for self-recrimination, Joseph. I know exactly what you are thinking, and no one could have kept watch in that crowd.' He paused, then gave Joseph a rueful smile. 'And don't forget, we are talking about Nikki Galena here. Do you honestly think she would have meekly stuck by your side when there was work to be done? Get real, lad, and get your detective's hat on and concentrate. Now, the first question I have to ask is, do we think Nikki has been taken by Helen Brook's killer?' He stared intently at Joseph.

With a wrench, Joseph pulled himself together. Woodhall was right. He could beat himself up later. Right now he needed to find one of the few people in the world that he truly cared about. 'I would think there is little doubt about that, sir.'

Cat clenched her teeth and added. 'I agree, sir, although we cannot rule Stephen Cox out of the equation. He is in the area, and he hates the police.'

'Let's look at Brook's killer first. Where are we with the suspects?'

Joseph said, 'Most people had fingered Andrew Gregory as the main suspect, but he is now dead. Helen's stalker, Paul Brant, is also dead. We are left with a small group of her clients, two in particular — Titus Whipp, a known trouble-maker and a real oddball, and Oliver Kirton, a well-educated, well-off PhD, with a long-term drink and drug problem.'

'One that has left him seriously psychologically disturbed,' added Cat.

'Although his condition is controlled with medication, or so we are led to believe,' Joseph said.

Greg Woodhall pulled at his shirt collar and looked uncomfortable. 'You do know we are talking about the nephew of Superintendent Arthur Kirton, don't you?'

'We had heard, but it makes no difference, does it? If he's a suspect, he's a suspect.' Joseph sounded more than a little irritated.

'I could not agree more, Joseph. I just wanted you be aware, that's all.'

'Thank you. We are aware. Other than that, we are still interviewing all the other patients who ever visited Helen Brook at her home. Because of the business of the locked room, it has to be someone she was happy to invite in, or someone who knew the place really well.'

'I want every one of them interviewed tonight. And I suggest you search both Whipp's and Kirton's homes. I'll organise the warrants.' He ran a hand through his thick greying hair.

'Now, all the other teams have volunteered to work overtime to help you. We have still got our work cut out to find the killer of the body in the river, as well as the evil bastards who tortured and killed those poor souls out on the fen, so I can't give them to you officially. But I don't have to tell you how crucial these first hours are in finding Nikki. Forget the budget for once, and use every officer we have. Just get her back.'

There was a lump in Joseph's throat as he opened the door to leave. Then he saw Jessie Nightingale running towards him. 'Sarge! The nursing home on the corner of Westland and Milton? The CCTV has picked up the guv'nor! PC Farrow is bringing it in now.'

In ten minutes they were staring at the footage.

'Who's that with her?' The superintendent leant closer to the screen.

'Jesus! It's Eric Barnes! What the hell was he doing at the vigil?' Cat's eyes were wide with amazement. 'I thought he was on sick leave.'

'He was,' added Joseph solemnly, 'On the DI's instruction. And there is no love lost between him and the inspector.' He looked at the grainy footage and frowned. 'But that looks as if he's hit her! Or is he helping her? No, he's supporting her! See the way he's gripping her, she can hardly stand!'

Woodhall's lips were a tight white line. 'I'm passing no judgement at this point, but I want that young man brought in, now. Whatever happened out there, DC Barnes seems to be the last person to have seen before she vanished. So go find him! Fast!'

* * *

Nikki lay in the darkness and tried to remember what had happened. The last thing she could be sure of was the vigil, Oliver Kirton's eulogy, and then some sort of scuffle. She had a vague memory of an ugly face pressed close to hers, mouthing the word, *filth*, then after that, nothing. She also had some impression that Eric Barnes had been there. That had to be some sort of dream or drug-induced fantasy, because she knew the stroppy young detective had been nowhere near the vigil. She almost smiled. It had to be a dream, because she seemed to remember him apologising to her. Hell would freeze over before he'd do that.

But this was not helping anything. What mattered now was to get out and get free. She took a deep breath and tried to keep calm. A while ago she had tried to stand, but to her horror, her legs had acted like unset jelly, and she had slipped clumsily to the floor. It had taken her a very long time to haul herself back onto the bed.

And it was a bed, a real one, with a quilt and a pillow. Apart from that, without being able to physically do a recce of the room, she knew little else. Except for the fact that, wherever she was, it was a long way from Greenborough town.

She recognised the salty, ozone smell of the marshes. She could also hear seabirds crying, and the constant sound of rushing water. There was no other sound at all, and she knew she was somewhere quite remote, which would make finding her very difficult indeed.

She had lived on the marsh almost all her life, but there were still parts of this lonely fenland that she had never even seen.

She drew in a deep breath and tried not to panic. Sadly, the very nature of her job meant that she was acutely aware of the seriousness of her position. She knew that she had most likely been abducted by Helen's killer. She had one advantage. She was stronger than Helen had been. She was trained to fell the heaviest adversary, and fit enough to run like a greyhound — if she got the chance.

She rubbed her aching head. Right now she felt about as strong as Superman in a kryptonite cage. She needed to try to rest and regain her strength, but she had no idea how much time there was. She needed to get her legs working. Then at least she could explore her prison.

Holding her head with one hand, she levered herself upright, determinedly fighting back the nausea that still came with every movement. Her feet touched the floor, but — nothing. No feeling, and no strength. She swore loudly, then screamed out, 'I'm damned if you'll beat me! No way are you going to fuck up my life! Do you hear me? Not now I've got it back!'

The shout certainly didn't help her legs, but it made her feel a whole lot more alive. She sank back on the bed. It was true. She suddenly realised that, after years of wallowing in guilt over Hannah, she had found a way to be happy again. She liked her life!

A feeling something akin to elation welled up in her. She suddenly thought of Rory Wilkinson. She saw his intelligent face, the shrewd grey eyes peering at her earnestly through his wire-rimmed glasses, and heard his words: "The killer really knows his stuff regarding anaesthesia." She swallowed hard and rubbed at her legs, willing sensation to return. Right now she didn't want to remember what he'd told her about how Helen died. She rubbed harder. One thing was for bloody certain, she was not going the same way.

'So you want to be a detective, Rory Wilkinson? Well, if anyone can help me now, it's going to be you. And before I finish up on your poxy dissecting table, get your finger out and solve the riddle of that sodding mandala!'

* * *

And Rory Wilkinson was doing exactly that. He was on his way to Jenny Jackson's home, coaxing every ounce of speed that he could from his aging Citroen. Jenny had called him earlier, asking if he could get her the personal details of all Helen Brook's clients and close associates. She thought that she might take them one by one, and see if any of them fitted the picture that she had built up from the mandala.

Rory had cleared it with the police, so he was taking them to her personally. He was glad of the distraction. He didn't have many friends — his job saw to that — but he was fond of Nikki, and he was damned if he was going to lose her.

230

It was three in the morning and Jenny looked tired. Her face, normally carefully made-up, was bare. After hearing the news about Nikki, she had cancelled all her commitments, and had offered to help the police in any way she could, full-time.

They sat together at Jenny's large drafting table and stared at sheet after sheet of sketches and notes.

Despite the lines beneath them, Rory noticed that her eyes still gleamed with enthusiasm for the task that she had set herself.

'I'm certain that at least, I can reduce this list down to a few likely suspects. If I have their birth details, their names, and any other salient information about them, I can check them against the mandala, and see what we're left with.'

Rory looked at the lengthy list of names. 'Rather you than me, dear heart. There must be fifty names here.'

Jenny gave him a weary smile. 'Then I'd better get to work, hadn't I? By the way, what did you say was the medium that was used on the body?'

'Malachite Green, a chemical. It's a dye used in the health care of fish.'

'Mmm, I thought that's what you said. I'm wondering if it's actually a key factor here. In colour healing, green is used in connection with the circulatory system, the abdominal region, and glands, especially the endocrine gland. But then it's also used to reduce hypersensitivity to food additives and half a dozen other things as well.'

Rory peered at a page full of runes. 'I'm sure it is important. What does green mean historically? Apart from Robin Hood's dreadful taste in couture?'

'It denotes life, spring, hope, and envy, as far as I can remember. But this isn't a true green, is it? It's more turquoise. A blue-green mix.'

'And that means?'

Jenny left the table and pulled a paperback book from a shelf. After flicking swiftly through a few pages, she took a deep breath and said, 'It's supposed to stimulate the highest level of talent and creativity in art.'

'Ah, so it may have been chosen as an aid to produce this masterpiece of a mandala, rather than a reference to the artist?'

'It looks that way, doesn't it?' She pushed the book back into place and searched among the colourful spines for another. 'Let's just check out malachite. Uh, where is it? Oh yes, here we are. It's a calming stone. In ancient times it was thought to have the power to strengthen teeth, aid those with poor eyesight, and warm a cold heart.'

'Well, you wouldn't get any colder than the bastard who did this. Where does it come from?'

'The main sources are Zaire, Zambia, Zimbabwe, and Siberia and the Urals, I think — hang on, there's something here about it bringing up old pain and traumas, and bringing suppressed feelings into the open. I wonder if that means anything?'

'It could be something to think about after we find a candidate for the birth signs and the numerological information.'

Jenny nodded. 'Yes, you're right. I'll make a note of all that but go back to basics, starting with the star sign for Pisces. Leave it with me, Rory. I promise I'll ring you the minute I find anything worth following up.'

'Okay, and if you need any other information, Sergeant Joseph Easter said to give you his mobile number and he'll try to help you.' He passed her a scrap of paper with the number on it. 'Don't get up, I'll see myself out.' He gave her arm a squeeze. 'Good luck, Jenny, and although I don't want to put pressure on you, finding Nikki could be down to you making sense of that bloody awful tattoo.'

* * *

In Greenborough police station, Cat Cullen was poring over the CCTV and media footage that was just beginning to come in. She had told herself that she didn't have time to be upset by her boss's abduction. She would turn herself into a human robot and do whatever it took to find her. From the moment she couldn't raise the guv'nor on her mobile, she had known something was terribly wrong. Now all she wanted to do was work.

Joseph had set up a rota so that the whole team wouldn't be shattered after the long day and then the evening spent at the vigil, but Cat could not switch off. Not with Nikki missing. Right now, all she could think about was what had happened to Helen Brook, and what might happen to the boss if they didn't find her in time. She had already ascertained that Eric Barnes had left the guv'nor sitting on the wall by the nursing home, and walked off into the throng at the end of the road. She had also seen the DI take a few tentative steps alone, then sit back down again. From that point on, there was nothing. Either the tape had malfunctioned or the camera had been tampered with. Whatever, there was a break of about five minutes before the street became visible again, and by then, the wall was empty.

'Got another one here, Cat.' Jamie, a young detective who was helping them out, passed her a still photo. It was black and white and grainy, and showed Nikki Galena staring hard at someone, and looking seriously pissed off. 'What's upset her, Cat?'

Cat looked at it and passed it back. 'That was when we were listening to that Kirton guy doing his Hamlet bit. She thought he was about to incite a riot. But we've got that timed already, mate, we need something from later.'

'How about this?' He passed her another print.

Cat's face wrinkled into a frown. 'This must be the fight that uniform were called to. Some idiots protesting against complementary medicine. You can just see the banners.' She peered closer. 'Yes! That's definitely the back of the DI's coat, and that arm around her, the person helping her move away. Do you recognise him?'

Jamie tilted his head to one side. 'DC Eric Barnes for sure. That designer leather jacket is a dead giveaway.'

'Any more in this series?'

Jamie shook his head. 'No. It's a one-off.'

'Bugger! Still, it proves that Barnes really was helping her. I've run that CCTV from the nursing home a dozen times, frame by frame, and I have to admit, it really doesn't look as if he's threatening her.'

'And he did leave her alone and walk away. He even waved when he reached the main road.'

Cat sighed and picked up another sheaf of pictures. 'Why was he there at all? That's what I'd like to know.'

Jessie Nightingale placed a cup of coffee on Cat's desk, then sat down opposite her. 'Bit more caffeine. It helps.'

'Thanks.' Cat managed a weak smile, and looked at Jessie's pale, tired face. 'You should go home and take a break.'

Jessie stared back belligerently. 'Like hell! I'll sleep when we have the boss safely back in her office, ranting at everybody.' She let out a long sigh. 'Sorry, it's just that this has brought back that time with my Graham. It was like this when he first disappeared.'

'Of course! I'm so sorry, Jess. This must be purgatory for you.'

'It's not good. It would have been our anniversary tomorrow, which doesn't help.'

Cat shook her head. 'I still can't believe we found nothing. I mean the case was never closed, and I know there's a team over at Fenchester who still spend time each week checking for new updates or information.' She leaned across and touched the detective's hand. 'They'll never give up on him, Jess.'

'And neither will I, but this isn't helping the boss, is it?'

Cat noticed a tear in Jess's eye, and decided that she was right. 'Okay, let's press on with the photo evidence.'

'How close are we to pinpointing the last time she was seen?'

Cat rubbed her forehead. 'A member of the public caught her on a mobile phone camera. Look, here, this is the last sighting so far.' She passed Jessie the small device and pressed play. Jessie stared at the jerky and slightly out-of-focus pictures. The intended subject was a teenage girl holding a candle and a wilting bunch of flowers, but in the background, walking slowly down a side road, was Nikki Galena.

'That's not her normal walk, is it? She looks dazed.'

'From what we've pieced together from witnesses to a minor fight earlier, she took a blow to the head, but someone rescued her and led her away from the youths involved.'

'Eric Barnes.'

Cat nodded.

'Can I have another look at the CCTV footage?'

'Be my guest. It's still in the machine.'

Jessie and Cat sat in front of the screen and forced themselves to concentrate. They watched it through, then let it run on to the point after the break to where the road was empty. Five minutes after the boss had left. They stared at the flickering screen, then Jessie gasped. 'Maybe the boss didn't leave at all! Cat, look at this!'

Cat looked closer.

'There! Look, on the other side of that low wall, what's that?' Cat took the remote and ran the video back, stopping it several times, freezing the scene. 'I'd say it was a hand, wouldn't you?'

'Exactly. But all that shrubbery along the edge of the nursing home is making it difficult to be sure.'

Cat's eager face was reflected in the silver light from the television screen. 'Run the tape further on.'

'Hold on, I'll forward it now.' Jessie moved closer and together they scrutinised every inch of the footage.

'There! There is movement behind the bushes. Look!'

'Got it! God! That dark shape. I think it's dragging something away from the wall and into the nursing home grounds!'

'Jess, go get the super. I've got some more CCTV from the nursing home here, but it's angled from the front door out into the car park. We haven't checked it yet. I'll set it up. Maybe if we synchronise the timing with this one, we'll see more.'

Jessie returned with the superintendent. Cat had already got the footage ready.

'Nothing clear, sir, but there is something. Look across the parking bays to that clump of trees. Is that a vehicle parked in the shadows there?'

'I think so, Detective, but it's well out of sight of the cameras. Get over to the nursing home and check the grounds.' He spun around. 'DC Cullen, take DC Harris and a couple of uniforms and sweep that whole area from the wall by the road to the car park. Ask if anyone usually parks there at night, and check for tyre tracks. Go!'

Cat grabbed her jacket, yelled for Dave Harris, and ran from the room.

* * *

Thirty minutes later, as she continued to trawl through the images, Jessie received a call from Dave. Apparently there were distinct signs of something or someone having been dragged through the overgrown shrubbery. He had cordoned off the area and asked the SOCOs to check it for evidence. Cat had discovered that the shadowy spot where the vehicle had been parked was not even a designated parking bay, but the overgrown base of a tool shed, long since gone. No one used it, especially at night. However, Cat had been told that one resident, an elderly man who kept very late hours, had mentioned to the warden that someone had parked a car there for at least two hours the night before. Sadly he had no interest in cars, so all he could tell them was that it was a dark coloured four-by-four. Dave asked Jessie to check with the list of Helen Brook's clients and see who owned four-wheel drives.

With fingers that flew she brought up the details of client after client on her computer screen. At least seven had that kind of vehicle, nothing unusual in the wild, marshy, fenland farming area. She printed off the names, and when she realised that Oliver Kirton's name was one of them, warning bells began to ring.

'What's the matter, Jess?' She looked up to see Joseph's hollow eyes looking at her across her desk.

'Have you been interviewing Oliver Kirton, Sarge?'

'More like he's been interviewing me, the pompous git. I've just come up for air and a strong coffee before I go back in. Why?'

Jessie told him about what she had seen on the CCTV, and the mysterious vehicle parked close by. 'Does he have an alibi for where he was after he gave his speech last night, Sarge?'

'Home alone, grieving, so he says. Are there any tyre tracks at the nursing home?'

'SOCOs are checking that now.'

'Well, I think I'll get uniform to pop round to Kirton's garage and make a note of what kind of tyres he has, just in case.' Joseph smiled at her. 'Good work spotting that hand, Jess. This must be hell for you, having been through it all before.'

Jessie swallowed hard. 'Every morning when I wake up, it comes back to me in a flood of pain and heartache.' She fought back tears. 'I just want to know if Graham is still alive. I feel certain that he is, but . . .'

Joseph walked around the desk and put his arm around her. 'Hang on in there, Jess. You'll have your answers one day, I'm certain.'

She smiled back. 'Fingers crossed, huh?'

'You will, I just know it.'

A WPC stuck her head around the door. 'Everyone wanted in the murder room in twenty minutes. The super's called an emergency meeting.'

'Don't like the sound of that, do you?'

Jessie shrugged. 'Probably just an update on what the search parties have found at the suspects' houses. I hope.'

'Mmm. I just hope it's not more bad news. I've had enough of that to last a bloody lifetime.'

CHAPTER TWENTY-FIVE

Superintendent Woodhall prowled up and down the room like a caged bear. 'I don't think I have to reiterate that DI Galena is in grave danger, and so far we have sod all to go on.' He pounded a clenched fist onto a desk as he passed. 'So, here is the state of play right now. Titus Whipp has been allowed to go home. His house contained nothing of interest, unless you are a taxidermist, and he has a solid alibi for his whereabouts at the time when we believe Nikki Galena was abducted. He was cooling off in a cell downstairs, after mouthing off at two of our officers at the vigil. Oliver Kirton's house is also clean, and although his alibi is unsubstantiated, we have got nothing concrete to hold him on. There were no identifying tyre marks out at the nursing home, so we can't use that. The best we can do is let him go, but watch him like a hawk.'

He continued to pace back and forth. 'We have to assume that Nikki's abductor is also Helen Brook's killer. So to find DI Galena, we need to use every scrap of information we have regarding Helen's murder. I want you to go over all the original statements made by Miss Brook's clients, friends and work colleagues. Look at everything again. Anything odd, chase it up, talk to them again. Ask the questions you failed to ask before, the ones you were frightened to ask. Take their houses to pieces, from attic to basement. Check every outbuilding, every caravan, every coal shed and every barn. I want to know everything about the people around Helen Brook, because one of them has taken our comrade, and I want her back. Alive!' He flopped into a chair. All energy seemed to have drained out of him. 'DI Gill Mercer and DS Easter are temporarily in charge, so take everything to them.'

Joseph nodded soberly. 'Sir? Do we think it was the same person who put the warning note in that woman organiser's pocket? Was the threat a real one, and DI Galena the intended victim all along?'

'I think so, don't you, Sergeant?'

Joseph thought that Greg Woodhall's voice had suddenly lost its power. The enormity of the situation had hit even the superintendent.

'I do, sir. And believing that, I'll see if the lab can get anything else from that note.'

'Okay, do that. So, all of you, get on with it. We'll meet again at four this afternoon, unless we have a breakthrough.' He stood up. 'And I pray that we do.'

* * *

'Do you really think that DI Galena was the intended mark, Joseph?' Gill Mercer was sitting in Nikki's chair.

Joseph nodded. 'She had to be. I mean, look at the coincidence factor if it wasn't her. We uncover a warning note telling us to stop the vigil, we refuse, and our DI disappears.' He threw up his hands. 'Plus, she was a friend of Helen Brook. She had to be the intended target.'

Gill Mercer's face was a mask of concentration. 'Why not the woman who received the note in the first place? Why not her?'

'She was there on the night, and no one laid a finger on her.'

Gill tipped her head on one side, 'Because they couldn't, could they? You said that Niall and Jessie were practically super-glued to her arse all evening.'

Joseph was unconvinced. 'You mean the killer couldn't get to his intended target, so he took Nikki instead?'

'Maybe. What do we know about the woman?'

'Nikki told me that her mother had been under Helen Brook's care until her death a short while ago. She left a cheque for a considerable sum of money to Helen but, well, she was murdered before Miss Duchene could deliver it. She finished up giving it to the Willows Clinic. The family appears to be pretty well off.'

'Do you know anything personal about her? Like why someone might want to hurt her?'

'Not really, other than the fact that she's apparently loaded.' He ran his hand through his hair. 'I think I'd better get Jessie and Niall. If they were with her all evening they must have talked about something.' He stuck his head out of the door and called to the two officers.

'Carla Duchene. Can you tell us about her? What happened at the vigil?' Joseph looked at Jessie and saw that the old spark was back in her eyes. 'You stayed with her all evening. What did you talk about?'

Jessie shrugged. 'She said nothing about herself. It was mainly about the vigil and the people who had organised it. She was gobsmacked at the size of the turnout.' Jessie thought for a moment then added, 'She told us how much her mother had admired Helen Brook. The old lady gave up on regular doctors when they said her cancer was terminal. Apparently she put all her trust in Helen, and was at least positive and comfortable in her last months. One of the therapists from the clinic stood with us for at least half an hour, but she didn't even seem happy talking to him. Frankly, I don't think she was in the mood for idle chat. She was nervous and jumpy all evening. That note had really got to her.'

'But she stayed to the bitter end?' DI Gill Mercer asked.

'No, ma'am. It got too much for her. Niall and I took her home just before eleven o'clock.'

Niall nodded. 'She wanted to stay, but the crowds were so much bigger than she had anticipated. As Jessie said, they finally got to her.'

'So you drove her home?'

'Not exactly, ma'am. We escorted her back to her car, then followed her, just to make sure she was safely indoors.'

'Where does she live?'

'Oh, not far from the Waterway, ma'am. Glebe Avenue. Very posh drum. We were back at the vigil in less than fifteen minutes. Then Niall helped Yvonne with dishing out the flowers and I got stuck in with the public relations.'

Gill Mercer was silent for a while. Then she said, 'Has anyone spoken to her about Nikki's disappearance?'

Niall nodded. 'I did, ma'am. I rang her myself. I didn't want her frightened by seeing it on the news or in the morning paper.'

'How did she take it?'

'She was pretty shaken, guv. Kept saying that she knew that note was not a hoax.'

'And what about keeping an eye on her? I suppose, with everything else going down, she's been left out in the cold.'

Joseph frowned. 'That's a valid point, and rather worrying. All available manpower is being used to search for the DI.'

Gill took a long, deep breath. 'Ring her, Sergeant. Now, please.'

Joseph didn't like where the inspector's thoughts were heading. 'I'll get her number.'

Niall flipped open his pocket book. 'I've got it, Sarge. Here.'

The phone rang on for an eternity, then a recorded voice spoke. "I'm sorry there is no one here to take your call. Please leave your name and number and we'll get back to you."

'Answerphone,' Joseph muttered.

'Hang up.'

He put the phone down and looked at Gill enquiringly.

'Get round there, Joseph. Take Niall. He knows where she lives. Ring me immediately you know she's safe.'

The two men stood up and hurried from the room.

* * *

Gill Mercer and Jessie left the office and joined Cat in the murder room.

'While we are waiting for Sergeant Easter to ring in, the two of you check out everything you can about Carla Duchene, especially regarding anyone who may benefit if she dies.'

Cat drew in a breath. 'Do we believe she's in danger too, ma'am?'

'Anything's possible. Have we heard from Eric Barnes yet?'

'No, ma'am. He's not at home and his mobile is on voicemail. DC Jamie Dean has left messages everywhere.'

DI Mercer rubbed her hand across her forehead. 'Jesus! This is one enormous cock-up, isn't it? It's bad enough when anyone goes missing, but when it's one of your own . . . Oh shit! I'm sorry, Jessie. Me and my big gob! You've been in this very situation for the last year, haven't you?'

The younger detective sighed. Then she smiled. 'Well, that should be a lesson to everyone. I haven't given up on Graham, so we certainly are not going to give up on the boss. We'll find her, I know we will.'

While the two women trawled through the files, Gill Mercer returned to Nikki's office and sat behind her desk. It seemed appropriate somehow. It was Nikki's investigation, so it should be conducted from her office. She looked around the plain, business-like room, and Nikki Galena's things. She examined the photos: a teenager, an elderly man wearing military ribbons, and a dog-eared old photo of a group of what looked like RAF types, all with glasses in their hands, raised in salute. Other than an unnaturally healthy houseplant, the room was bare of knick-knacks — no clutter. She stared at the plant. 'Bet you wouldn't dare to even drop a leaf, let alone die.' There was nothing here that would help her find her colleague. Even the mountain of paperwork on the desk was orderly, and apart from a small pile of memo notes, the surface was clean. Gill didn't even like to put her coffee mug down, so she held it to her chest.

The noise of her phone almost made her drop it.

Joseph's voice was full of emotion. 'DI Mercer? Looks like you were right! Miss Duchene didn't answer the door, and as her Peugeot is still in the drive, I effected an entrance. She's not here, ma'am.'

'Any signs of a struggle?'

'None, but her mobile phone is still on the kitchen table, along with her handbag and purse. Nothing touched, nothing stolen. Bed not slept in.'

'Okay. I'll tell the super and get the SOCOs over there immediately. Close off the scene, Joseph, and you and Dave get back ASAP.'

'Roger.'

Gill snapped her phone shut. This was going from bad to worse. She stood up and pushed the chair back just as the desk phone rang.

It was the desk sergeant. 'DI Mercer? I've got Eric Barnes on the line, ma'am. Can I put him through to you?'

'Yes, yes,' she said impatiently. 'DC Barnes?'

'Ma'am, I've just heard the news! What's happening?'

'Where the hell are you?'

'On my way to my brother's in Nottinghamshire, ma'am. I heard it on the radio. DI Galena? Is she really missing?'

'Damn right she is. And you were probably the last person to see her!'

'Oh shit! I'll turn round, ma'am. I'm on my way back.' The line went dead.

Gill threw the receiver back into the cradle and, cursing under her breath, strode out to find Superintendent Woodhall. 'And put your fucking foot down, sonny boy, because I just can't wait to talk to you.'

* * *

'The name Duchene rings bells somehow.' Cat frowned and looked hopefully across the desk at Jessie. 'Any thoughts?'

'Nope. Can't say it does, and I've certainly never seen her before all this happened.'

Someone on the far side of the room called out, 'Did you say Duchene?'

Both women looked up. The owner of the deep, rasping voice was a uniformed officer on loan from Spalding. He raised his eyebrows and smiled apologetically. 'Sorry to butt in, but I know of an Esther Duchene, if that helps.'

Jessie sat back in her chair. 'That would be this woman's mother. She died quite recently.'

'I know, and so does any local who likes wildlife — birds in particular.'

'She's famous?' asked Cat.

The constable walked over to them. 'Could say that. She was one of the best ornithological photographers of her time — well, any time really, although she's probably better known for her work on conservation. It was down to her that the Flaxton Mere nature reserve was saved. Owls and herons were her speciality. Oh yes, and she wasn't only a renowned photographer. She was the granddaughter of some Victorian adventurer. Made a fortune out in Africa, I think.'

Cat put a hand to her temple. 'Of course! That's it! There was a programme about her on TV not so long ago.'

'And there was a big write-up in the local papers after she died,' added the constable.

Cat nodded to him. 'Thanks for that. I'm not sure how it helps, but it means there may have been some serious dosh in that will of hers.'

She turned back to Jessie. 'And if it all went to her daughter, Carla?'

Jess tapped in a few words on her keyboard. After waiting a moment she looked up from the monitor and said, 'Mmm, it certainly looks that way. I've got a potted bio here on Google. Esther was widowed quite young and she had two children, Carla and Jonathan. The boy was killed in an accident when he was ten, so that just leaves Carla.'

'Who is probably a seriously rich woman now.'

'A seriously rich, *missing* woman.' Jessie shivered. 'God! Do you think Helen's murder and the guv's disappearance is all some sort of smokescreen for actually getting to Carla Duchene and her money?'

Cat frowned. 'A bit extreme, but I suppose it's possible. Let's get some concrete evidence about Carla Duchene's finances before we go to the DI. I'll check out the family solicitor, you keep digging up anything you can on Carla herself, okay?'

'I'm already on it, but hell, I don't like this one little bit.'

* * *

Gill Mercer looked around her colleague's office and wondered if she had made a mistake by trying to work there. Without Nikki's huge presence, the room seemed sepulchral, almost sinister. Gill shivered and began leafing through a pile of Nikki's reports. She smiled ruefully as she stared at the fastidiously prepared notes. Nikki's handwriting was clear and neat. Gill wondered if she got it from her RAF father.

'Hello, who's this guy?' She was reading through the record of Nikki's meeting with Dr Sam Welland from the Willows Clinic. 'A hypnotist, huh?' She recalled his name being mentioned as having worked on the vigil committee with Carla Duchene. Her brow furrowed. Maybe he'd know where the Duchene woman was. She turned back a page and scribbled down his number. Worth a try, she muttered to herself.

Sam Welland answered almost immediately. 'No, sorry, Inspector, I haven't seen her since the vigil. Actually I was going to ring her after we heard about your DI Galena going missing. Dreadful business that. Poor Carla was terrified after she received that awful note, but it seems that she wasn't the intended target after all, was she?'

Gill did not answer. 'Do you know Miss Duchene well?'

'Hardly at all. Don't think I spoke two words to her until she gave us that donation from her mother, and then offered to pay for the flowers for the float, of course.'

'And her mother? You knew her, surely? She was a patient at your clinic, wasn't she?'

'Oh yes! She was Helen Brook's client but we saw her regularly. Now *she* was a wonderful woman, a really lovely lady. I say, Inspector, is there a problem? I mean . . . is Carla missing as well?'

Gill Mercer's response was guarded. 'We just want to talk to her, Dr Welland. As she wasn't at home, we are checking around, that's all. If you hear from her I'd be grateful if you'd contact me.' She gave him the number, then added, 'Is it doctor or mister? I just had the name Sam Welland on my memo.'

'It is doctor, Inspector. I was fully qualified before I decided to go the complementary route.'

'Oh, and for the record, Doctor, what sort of car do you drive?'

He sounded perplexed. 'Oh, eh, a Landrover Discovery. I know it's hardly an ecological statement, but if you saw where I live, right out on the marsh, you'd understand. Why do you ask?'

'Just eliminating tyre tracks, sir. Please don't worry yourself, and thanks for your time.'

She carefully replaced the handset. Another four-by-four. Perhaps she'd add him to her list of suspects. After all, he knew Helen Brook, Carla Duchene *and* Nikki Galena. Something about the conversation bothered her slightly. Something about his way of referring to Carla, compared with his obvious fondness for her mother. It really didn't sound as if he liked her very much. Now, why would that be, she wondered, especially after the woman had landed him with a load of cash? Maybe she should go visit the hypnotist. She would like to see if his eyes said anything different to his lips.

* * *

246

Not too many miles away from the station, Nikki fought to stay awake. She was scared that if she slept, her captor would slip into the darkened room and administer another dose of whatever insidious drug she'd been given in order to get her here. She was still weak as a kitten, and although a tiny amount of feeling had returned to her legs, they still refused to support her. She felt drained, but her life could depend on keeping her eyes open. Desperate to keep her mind active, she made herself recite the names of her fellow trainees from police training school. Then she went on to schoolfriends, classmates and friends in general. Then she came to Helen Brook and changed the subject. Okay, countries this time, A to Z. Argentina, Austria, Angola, Australia, Andorra, Africa, Afghanistan. Somewhere between Nepal and Norway, she fell asleep.

* * *

Something akin to fear had arisen in the Fenland police station. The officers went about their business, but there was a hint of desperation in their actions. Voices were either too loud or little more than a whisper. Most of the time a stunned silence prevailed. They grabbed a little sleep as and when they could, but most were either too hyped up or too worried to rest.

'I think you should know that I have had a memo from higher up. They want me to keep Oliver Kirton's involvement strictly to ourselves.' The superintendent was still pacing, and Gill Mercer began to wonder how long it would be before the underlay showed through Nikki's office carpet. Then she realised what he had just said.

'Well, that's bloody ridiculous! Uncle doesn't want anything nasty rubbing off on him, I suppose.'

'Frankly I have to agree with you, being one of the few higher-ranking officers without a funny handshake and a weird apron. And the more this goes on, the more I wish I'd kept him in the slammer.'

Gill Mercer massaged her temples. 'Well, close surveillance has been set up for all of them, sir. Oliver Kirton, Titus

Whipp, and now Dr Sam Welland and one or two other former patients of Helen Brook.' Her face became even grimmer. 'We've also seen fit to add one or two villains to the list, those who might not wish DI Galena well.'

'I should think there's quite a few of those, Gill. Nikki's reputation for getting convictions is pretty impressive.'

'You can say that again, boss. But there are only one or two really nasty pieces of work that would actually go so far as to want her dead. Stephen Cox for sure. Maybe someone has taken advantage of the mayhem surrounding Helen Brook's death in order to get at Nikki. Not probable, I know, but . . .'

'Yes, I know, leave no stone unturned.'

'More like any port in a storm actually, sir.'

The superintendent laid a file on the desk and pushed it toward her. 'And now we have another problem. The DNA results from Helen Brook's treatment room.' He jerked an accusing finger towards the folder. 'We have nowhere to go with them either. There was nothing at all on her body and nothing in the close vicinity either. The killer was meticulous.'

There was little Gill could say. They had been relying on forensics to give them something, no matter how small. She looked gloomily through the glass panel into the outer office. She saw Joseph's tall form moving across the CID room towards his own office. Gill stood up and said, 'I've just seen DS Easter arrive, so if that's all, I'd better get back out there, see if we have any leads on the Duchene woman.'

'Wait.' Glen Woodhall frowned hard. 'I want another word with Kirton. Get uniform to pick him up again. Any excuse, just get him back in.'

'Sure, sir, I'll do it now.' As she closed the door, she saw Woodhall still striding back and forth across the empty office.

* * *

'Carla Duchene's got a big, beautiful house, ma'am. The elegant sort, you know, the kind of people who have taste as well as money.'

'But nothing stolen, nothing disturbed?'

'It's like the Marie Celeste, ma'am. She's vanished into the air.'

'Well, that would indicate that she knew whoever came calling, and either went with him voluntarily, or was stunned and quietly removed. Did the neighbours see anything?'

Joseph shook his head. 'Not that kind of road, I'm afraid. It's all detached houses with lots of trees and high walls. They'd not see a Pickford's lorry unless they happened to be standing at the bottom of her driveway.'

'And what about her telephones? Any unusual calls?'

'No. The last call on her landline was Dave Harris informing her about the DI, and the mobile hadn't rung since the night before.' He leant back against the wall. 'I brought back her address book, ma'am, and took the most used numbers from her mobile's call log. One of the team is ringing round now, just in case there's a logical reason for her disappearance.'

'Did she keep a diary, Joseph?'

'Not as such, but she wrote all her appointments on a big calendar in the kitchen. There was nothing listed for today.'

Gill's anxiety shifted up a gear. There was little doubt that they now had two missing women, and one murderer still walking the streets of Greenborough.

'Okay, Joseph. Nothing more you can do there, so I'd like you to check up on someone for me. I was going to do it myself but I need to finish going through Nikki's reports. I want you to talk to a colleague of Helen Brook. His name is Welland, and he's a hypnotist at the Willows Clinic. I get the feeling he wasn't a great fan of Carla Duchene, and I'd like to know why.'

'Fine. Shall I phone him first?'

Gill smiled darkly. 'I think not, Sergeant. Try the element of surprise.'

CHAPTER TWENTY-SIX

In the murder room, Gill Mercer walked from desk to desk, staring at the monitor screens, the untidy piles of reports and hastily scribbled notes. As she walked she looked into the tired eyes of Nikki's team. Their haggard faces all showed strain and anxiety. It was as if every officer believed it was their personal duty to find something that would lead them to their missing colleague.

Worst of all, everyone now knew that Helen Brook had been conscious and restrained while the murderer worked on her, fully aware that she was about to die.

'Has anyone heard from Eric Barnes yet?'

There was a series of negative replies. Where the hell had he got to? From what he had said earlier, she had believed him to be little more than an hour away, and that was ages ago.

Jessie held up a receiver. 'Ma'am! It's the desk sergeant. Bad news, I'm afraid.'

'Sergeant? What's the problem?'

'Sorry, DI Mercer, but I've just heard that the surveillance car outside Oliver Kirton's house . . . Eh, it seems that they've lost him.'

'What? How the bloody hell did that happen?'

'He tricked them, ma'am. A visitor called, a man who arrived by car, stayed for about ten minutes, then left — or so our officers thought. Turns out he swapped places with Kirton. Kirton wore the man's coat and hat and took his car. When they got your call to bring him back in, they found a stranger in the house, and Kirton gone.'

'Did they get the license number? And the make of car?'

'We've already found it, ma'am. But Kirton was nowhere to be seen. I've put out a call to bring him in as soon as he's spotted. I don't think he'll get too far, ma'am.'

Gill was seething. 'I wish I shared your optimism, Sergeant. Have you got the other man?'

'Yes, I've sent a car for him. He's an old friend of Kirton's. Seems Kirton rang him and fed him some cock-and-bull sob story about mistaken identity and how he desperately needed to go out to meet someone. Life and death, he said, and swore he'd be back in an hour or two. We are still watching the house, just in case he actually meant it.'

'Let me know the moment there's any news on him.' Gill almost threw the receiver back at Jessie. 'Damned incompetents! For God's sake! Kirton is a fucking murder suspect, not some petty criminal. The super is really going to love this!'

Before she could move, the phone rang again. 'Sorry, ma'am, for you again. It's Professor Rory Wilkinson this time.'

She gritted her teeth. 'Have you got anything for us, Rory?'

The forensic scientist sounded edgy. 'I'm not sure, but maybe. Is it all right if I bring a friend of mine in to see you? She's been helping us with the mandala design. She thinks she's on to something.'

'Then for God's sake get her here! Time is not on our side right now.'

'On our way. Be with you in fifteen.' The line went dead. Gill felt a frisson of excitement. Maybe this would be it, the one piece of information that would set the ball rolling. Meantime, she needed to break the news about Kirton to

Superintendent Woodhall, and she was not looking forward to that one little bit.

* * *

Half an hour later, in Nikki's office, Rory and Gill stared down at a mass of diagrams and notes, and listened intently to Jenny Jackson.

'So I thought, this is just too weird! But it has to be! I have checked every single patient on Miss Brook's client list, and *everything* on this mandala,' she stabbed her finger on the original design, 'is relevant to just one person! The birthdate, all the astrological and numerological numbers, Life, Destiny, Expression and Fadic, every one of them is personal to one woman. And that particular person is dead! So that was when I rang Rory, because I really do not understand.'

Rory took a deep breath. 'And I phoned you, DI Mercer. I'm afraid we were wrong when we believed that the mandala represented the killer. Now we know what the design is all about, obviously the killer was leaving us a coded clue to who he was really after — and pointing us clearly in the direction of the Duchene family.'

Gill stared at the complicated design. 'So all this adds up to just one person?'

Jenny nodded. 'Esther Duchene, born 1 March 1937, a Pisces. It even explains the central star, Esther, from the Persian for star.'

'Carla Duchene's mother.' Gill's mind was spinning, but Jenny was still talking.

'The Runic signs refer to anger, grief and guilt, which could be associated with the emotions felt after a bereavement, and most of the minerals and crystals used have healing properties pertaining to the areas affected by her particular type of cancer. The others, and the malachite, are found in the Congo. Through my work as an artist I know a bit about Esther, and I know that along with her predecessors, she spent a lot of time in Africa. There is absolutely no doubt that this is a personal chart for Esther Duchene.'

Rory looked intently at Gill Mercer, raised an eyebrow and said, 'Much as I don't wish to try to teach my grandmother to suck eggs, dear Inspector, don't you think maybe we'd better go pick her daughter up?'

'You don't know, do you?'

Rory frowned. 'Know what?'

'I'm afraid your discovery came an hour or so too late. Carla Duchene is also missing.'

'Oh shit!'

'Exactly.' She looked apologetically at Jenny Jackson. 'I'm really sorry, but I have to go and report all this to the super. Can you stay around for a while? He will want a word with you. I'm not sure I'll be able to explain all this stuff as well as you did.'

Jenny nodded. 'No problem, Inspector.'

'Damn it! I really thought we were one step ahead of him.' Rory ran a hand through his hair. 'Still, I suppose if we find Carla Duchene, we also find Nikki?'

'Let's hope so. My added worry is that we also have a missing suspect.'

'And you think he may have taken both women? Who is he?'

'Oliver Kirton, he's a—'

'Ollie! You *are* kidding, aren't you? Ah, I see you're not. Well, I hope for everyone's sake that it's not dear Oliver, because if he's messing with his medication, he could be seriously off his head, and very dangerous.'

Gill froze. 'You know him?'

'University. Strange man. Long story.'

'Could he have been capable of concocting that mandala?'

'He studied ancient tribes for a long while, but in an academic way. If he invented that design, he did it as a huge joke.'

'But he could have done it?'

Rory gave a little shrug. 'There's nothing that Oliver could not do if he set his mind to it. Except stay clean for any length of time, that is.'

'And he *had* been in Helen's flat for treatment sessions, so he could have stolen a key! Oh God, this is looking really bad.'

Gill left the office and almost ran to the murder room. 'Okay, all of you! Listen up! I want to know everything there is to know about Carla and Esther Duchene, and I want it fast.' She looked at the mass of worried faces and added almost gently, 'And I know I don't have to remind you of this, but DI Galena's life depends on it.'

She stopped for a moment at the door of the superintendent's room before entering. Something was worrying her, but she was damned if she knew what it was. Oh hell! It'd have to wait. The super needed to know what Rory and his friend had discovered, and what Rory had said about Oliver Kirton.

* * *

Nikki awoke, and for a moment wondered where she was. Then reality crashed in on her, and she began to shiver. How long had she been asleep? She had lost precious time. Suddenly she saw the elfin features of Helen Brook. Her eyes looked down sadly and her arms were held out in front of her, palms upwards. "You promised to help me." Somehow this calmed Nikki. Yes, she had promised, and she always kept her promises. Somehow she had to find a way out of this terrible situation and catch Helen's killer.

She knew that they were hunting for her. Any moment they could be here — Joseph, Cat, Dave, Jessie, Niall, Yvonne, Greg Woodhall, Rory. They *would* find her, but would they be in time? She imagined them, all rushing through the door to save her.

Nikki gathered herself together and gritted her teeth. Sentimental thoughts would not help her now. What she needed was her competent and logical detective's brain. She had to find out who had taken her, and who had killed her friend. And to do that, she had to get out of this bloody place, wherever it was.

Nikki eased herself into a sitting position, started to massage her numb legs and forced herself to think of what she knew best, her police training. First, try to evaluate your situation. Okay, well, she wasn't restrained in any way, good so far. What worked and what didn't? She tested her arms, neck and legs. Two out of three was better than nothing, but the legs were a problem. She had to have been given some kind of epidural, but surely that should have worn off by now? It was hard to tell because she had no idea how long she had been incarcerated. When her eyes had got used to the darkness, shadows had appeared and she knew that she was in some sort of windowless basement room. It wasn't a cellar, because it wasn't freezing cold and it didn't smell musty or bad. Nikki screwed up her nose. In fact, there was something about the smell of the place that was vaguely familiar. She had always had a heightened sense of smell, a trait that she recently found out was inherited from her mother. So where the hell was she? She could still hear the distinct sounds of seabirds outside, and somewhere some way away, the muffled hum of an engine. So, legs or no legs, she needed to do a recce of the room, and to do that she had to get off the bed.

Her head was still hammering after the incident at the vigil, but her memory was gradually clearing. She now remembered that she had waded in to a group of yobs and got clobbered with a placard, and then, strangely, Eric Barnes had helped her. Right now she wished she had let him call for the medics. She would certainly not be lying on a tatty old bed massaging her dead legs.

Oh well, here goes nothing. Nikki moved her legs over the edge of the bed, positioned them directly in front of her, then, hanging onto the mattress, pushed off.

She crashed to the floor, jarring her spine and making her aching head feel like lightning had struck her. 'Well, that went well,' she muttered aloud. She sat and gathered her breath, then tipped onto her side and began dragging herself across the room.

The bed had been set against one wall, so by the time she reached the opposite wall she reckoned the room to be about fifteen feet long. Now she needed a door. She pulled herself around the perimeter of the room, and found it.

Excellent! Now, if only . . . she froze. There was a noise. It was different to the sounds she had been hearing, and it was coming from within the building. Her parched throat almost closed. She was listening to footsteps. They were soft, deliberate, unhurried.

Nikki was certain that whoever was out there would hear her heart beating, and she tried to calm it. There was no way she would be able to get back onto the bed, so she stayed where she was, leaning back against the door, and prayed that whoever was on the other side didn't want to enter.

The noises changed. The feet moved away, then returned, but there was another noise now, a grunting, groaning sound, followed by a sort of scraping and shushing.

She became aware of a draught of cool air underneath the ill-fitting door, and then there was a bang and the jingling, metallic sound of keys. The outer door had been closed and locked.

Nikki exhaled, breathed deeply and tried to make sense of what she had just heard. Someone had opened an outer door, gone in, then retraced their footsteps and returned dragging something heavy across the floor before leaving. She nibbled anxiously on her bottom lip. What was it that had been dragged into the room? What — or *who*? Nikki let out a slow breath. Maybe she was no longer alone.

* * *

'Ma'am! I've spoken to the Duchene family solicitor. Esther Duchene left a fortune to her daughter, but most of it is tied up in trusts and funds and property abroad. He said it's so complicated it will probably take years to sort out.' Cat glanced at her pocket book. 'And Carla is well off in her own right. Her father left her a tidy bequest that she came into when she was twenty-five.'

'But she's been living at home with Mummy?' Gill looked somewhat bemused.

'Only since Esther became ill. The solicitor said she worked abroad prior to her mother's diagnosis.'

'Abroad where? And doing what?'

'Africa. She worked for some charity organisation out there.'

Jessie looked across from her desk and frowned. 'An aid worker! Blimey! Appearances can really be deceptive! She sure didn't give that impression, did she, Niall?'

Niall Farrow shook his head. 'No way! She didn't look as if she'd done a day's work in her life, apart from maybe as something like a fashion editor.'

Cat shrugged. 'Well, that's what he said. And she didn't have to have been striding barefoot across the desert with a water container balanced on her head.'

'Okay, cut the clever stuff and concentrate. Where did she live when she wasn't with her mother?'

'She had a snobby apartment on the Old Granary Wharf, overlooking the river, but she sold it when she moved home to care for Esther.'

'Friends? She must have had some.'

Cat grimaced. 'None that we can trace, ma'am. Not a single one. She's been a real loner since she came back.'

'Jesus! There must be someone we can talk to about her! And I *have* to know if she knew Oliver Kirton.'

'Ma'am?' Joseph pushed open the murder room door and dropped down into a spare chair. 'Any news while I've been out?'

Gill Mercer filled him in on what Jenny Jackson had discovered from the mandala. 'So what's the story regarding Dr Welland and Carla Duchene?'

Joseph shook his head dispiritedly. 'Nothing that leads me to believe he's our kidnapper. He doesn't like Carla because she was pretty much against her mother attending his "quack clinic," as she called it initially. Carla believed that the old lady should stick with the chemotherapy and radiotherapy. Esther felt differently, and after she met Helen Brooks, she became a regular at the Willows. After a while, Carla came around to her mother's way of thinking, end of story. Dr Welland says he simply never warmed to Carla. She was a very different sort of person to her mother.'

'In what way?'

'"A cold fish, with no spirit," was Sam Welland's description. The mother was well-known and well-loved, a warm, kind-hearted soul with a great love of nature and the more spiritual side of life. A true artist. He found Carla too pragmatic, too earthbound. He reckoned she looked to science and no further for all her answers.'

'And that's all? A difference of views?'

'More or less, although he did give me a name. Worth following up under the circumstances, I suppose. It's a nurse who was looking after Esther in the oncology suite at Greenborough Hospital. She was a bit of an ally of Carla's when Esther decided to abandon her treatment there. Carla spent a lot of time with her apparently, so she might know something that could help.' He sat down at his desk and picked up the phone.

Gill turned back to Cat Cullen. 'Get some details of exactly what Carla did in Africa. Who she worked for, and if she had anyone close to her — a friend, a lover, a close work colleague. We *have* to know more about her. Someone was with her when she left her mother's house, either a captor, or a friend. And it could have been Oliver Kirton. We *must* find her, and not just for her sake. If we find Carla, I'm certain we'll find Nikki.'

CHAPTER TWENTY-SEVEN

Joseph was close to collapse. Despite all his time in the military, he had never been so afraid for another person's life. Even when his own daughter's life had been threatened, he had felt confident that he could help her, and he had. But this was beyond his control. They were groping in the dark and he was helpless. When his phone rang he grabbed it, staring desperately at the display, seeing not Nikki, but Mickey.

'Is it true, Sergeant Joe?'

He dragged in a long breath. 'Yes, Mickey, I'm afraid it is.'

'Can I help?'

There was a catch in Joseph's voice. 'No, son. We are doing all we can. We'll find her.'

There was a deep sigh on the other end. 'You must, Joe. You have to. She's special.'

'I'll do my best. You know that.'

'I know.' There was a pause, then Mickey said, 'Listen, I have a message from Archie and Raymond. They have asked me to tell you to concentrate all your efforts on finding Inspector Nik, and to keep away from the Carborough.'

The emphasis on "keep away" was not lost on Joseph. 'Something is happening?'

'Joe, can you tell your people to let us alone? Just for one night?'

'Turn a blind eye to the Carborough Estate? Phew! That's a big ask.'

'It would be best for everyone, and you need every rozzer in the county out looking for Nikki, don't you?'

Joseph understood exactly what was being asked of him, and why. But would anyone listen? 'I'll do my best, Mickey.'

'We expect nothing less, okay? Take care, Joe, and let me know when she's safe.' The phone went dead.

Joseph drew himself up, straightened his tie and marched out of his office. He had an ally in the uniformed desk sergeant, who was a big fan of DI Nikki Galena. Joseph would lay it on the line, tell him everything, and hope and pray that uniform would suddenly become far too busy looking for a missing detective to get to some minor disturbance out on the Carborough.

* * *

With some reluctance, Superintendent Woodhall finally picked up the phone and asked to be connected to Superintendent Arthur Kirton. Better to go straight to the top, rather than skulk around trying to ferret out information about Oliver from dubious sources.

The call did not go particularly well, but at least Woodhall found out what he needed to know. Oliver Kirton did not own, rent or use any property. The bottom line was that all his money had gone up his nose, and he was forced to lodge at his aunt's house. Arthur Kirton had no idea where his nephew was, and his tone said that he cared even less. His young nephew was obviously a significant source of embarrassment to the high-ranking police officer. Woodhall hung up, wondering what his fellow officer was going to think when he heard that there was a warrant out for Oliver's arrest, on suspicion of murder and abduction.

* * *

Joseph replaced the receiver and stared hard at the worn surface of his desk.

Dave Harris' deep voice broke into his thoughts. 'Problem, Sarge?'

Joseph frowned. 'I've just spoken to that nurse at Greenborough Hospital. She remembers Carla Duchene very well. She reckons Carla didn't just disagree with her mother about going to a complementary healer, she was absolutely furious about it. She doesn't believe for one moment that Carla would have changed her views in any way.'

'Not even for her mother's sake?' Jessie asked.

'Her words were, "Not a cat in hell's chance."'

Gill Mercer approached, her eyes glinting darkly. 'Okay, so did this nurse tell you anything else about her?'

'Yes. She said she was almost obsessive about her mother. She idolised her, apparently.'

'So? Lots of children love their parents. I know most of the slimeballs that we deal with come from broken homes, but not everyone had a bad childhood.'

'The nurse said she agreed to support Carla when the old lady refused conventional treatment, but after a while it scared her a bit. She was too intense for it to be healthy.'

Before anyone could say anything further, there was a cry from Cat Cullen. 'Ma'am! I think you should see this!' She was taking several sheets of paper from her printer. 'It's from Africa, from the group Carla worked with.'

Joseph followed Gill and the others over to see what Cat had found, then he stopped and grasped the inspector's arm. 'My God! Ma'am! I've just remembered something!'

They stopped and stared at him.

'At the Duchene house. Her car, a little Peugeot, bright red, 206 model. It was still parked out front in the drive. The engine was cold. I checked the garage, and there was nothing there, but I've just realised there was a load of car stuff, you know, oil, screen wash, touch-up sticks, junk like that.' Gill Mercer began to shuffle impatiently. 'Ma'am, it was *diesel* oil. The Peugeot was a petrol model. And the touch-up stick was for a dark blue vehicle. I think she's got two cars!' Before he had even finished speaking, Jessie's fingers were flashing over her computer keyboard. 'Come on, come on . . . bingo! You're right, Joseph. Oh shit! The Peugeot was her mother's. She owns a navy blue Nissan X-Trail.'

'A dark four-by-four.' The colour drained from the DI's face.

'It gets worse, ma'am. Listen to this. Carla came home long before her mother was taken ill. She was considered unfit for work. She was unstable, traumatised, burnt out from years working in the field.'

Joseph's voice didn't sound like his own as he asked, 'What did she do? What was her job?'

'Field hospital theatre sister in the Congo. The war zone.'

'Perfect!' Rory Wilkinson strode into the room, his deep voice ringing out. 'Someone who would know all about drugs, and how to use them out in the field! Oh, yes, and probably specialising in anaesthetics. Dear hearts, I think we had all this back to front, don't you? Maybe our Ollie deserves an apology.'

Through the haze of his confusion, Joseph heard Gill Mercer barking out orders.

'Find out if either Carla or the mother owned any other properties! Esther was a professional woman. Did she work from home? Did she have a studio somewhere? A house, a retreat, holiday cottage?'

Jenny Jackson had followed Rory in. 'I can help there. Esther had two properties that I know of. A cottage on the coast, close to the bird reserve at Flaxton Mere, and one of the two small lighthouses out on the estuary of the River Westland. One is automated and still functions, the other went up for sale a few years back. Esther bought it and converted into a residential property to house her photographic studio and to watch the birds out on the marshes.'

'How far away are they?'

'Flaxton Mere. Twenty minutes' drive, max. The lighthouse is a fraction further.'

Joseph bit his lip. 'I know the places Jenny mentioned. Both are remote, with few passers-by, except the occasional rambler or bird watcher. DI Galena's office has the best map of the area. I'll show you where they're situated.'

'Here, and here, ma'am.' He jabbed his finger at the two locations.

'Right. Even I couldn't miss a lighthouse, but that cottage doesn't look too easy to find. Get me the exact coordinates. We'll need two armed response units, one for each location.' She turned to Joseph. 'We need to split up, Sergeant. You take Cat and Jamie with a large team of uniforms and get out to that cottage, okay? I'll take Dave, Jessie and a bunch of uniforms over to the lighthouse.'

The DI threw herself into Nikki's chair and grabbed the phone. 'I'll organise the armed back-up, you bring the super up to speed, then get to hell out of here!' She stopped, then added, 'Second thoughts. Jessie, you come in here for a moment.' She hurriedly made her call then turned to the detective, 'I need you to do something. It's very important. Look at this, I've only just noticed it.' She showed Jessie a photocopy of the warning note, the one ostensibly pushed into Carla Duchene's pocket prior to the vigil. 'Look, compare it to this. It's a phone number written on a scrap of paper I found sitting here on Nikki's desk.'

Jessie took the two sheets and compared them. The scrap simply said, *Carla Duchene*, and a local number. 'This one's her writing, guv?'

'Well, it's not Nikki's, so I reckon it has to be. Compare it with the C and the D on the threatening note.'

'They're identical! The scheming bitch! She never was in danger! She sent the note to herself.'

'Get that straight down to forensics to confirm it. Now I've really got to go. I'm leaving you in charge here, Nightingale. Man the phone, and remember, keep Joseph and I posted on anything that happens, anything at all. Understand?'

Jessie nodded furiously. 'Good luck, ma'am. I know you'll bring DI Galena back safely.'

As Gill ran from the office she wished she felt as certain. But this was their best lead yet. It might be their only chance.

* * *

Nikki leaned heavily against the door. What should she do next? There was some slight sensation returning to her legs, but she knew it would be hours before they would take her weight. Hours that she didn't have.

It was tempting to call out. She was convinced that the killer had brought another victim to this place. If they could communicate, maybe they could hatch some kind of escape plan. But if it wasn't another victim, who or what was it? And where was the killer?

As she thought, she heard the far door being opened again. Again, a cool draught of air, and with it . . . ? Nikki tensed. She was too anxious to stop and think about it. What was the person outside the door doing? Nikki shuddered. Well, she would go down fighting. Her legs were useless, but her hands and teeth were just fine.

A loud groan came from outside the room. This was followed by low curses and the sound of a scuffle. What was happening? Nikki eased herself down so that her ear was close to the gap at the bottom of the door, and strained to make out what was going on.

There was a scraping noise, then something heavy fell to the floor. The voices continued, swearing, muttering, growling.

There was a shout, and then Nikki knew exactly who was outside that door. From her position on the floor she had detected a hint of perfume on the draught that blew across her face. She had smelt that expensive oriental perfume on at least three occasions before. Each time she had been talking to Carla Duchene.

And the voice? She'd know that educated tone anywhere. It was Oliver Kirton! So he had not only abducted her, he had taken Carla as well.

Nikki tried to make sense of what was happening. He must have drugged her and dragged her in here, but she wasn't as far gone as he had believed, and now the poor woman was fighting for her life!

She had to do something! Surely any distraction could help Carla? Nikki took a deep breath and yelled.

* * *

In the murder room at Greenborough, Jessie Nightingale passed on her latest message from Joseph. 'Sergeant Easter's area is clear, ma'am. The Flaxton Mere cottage and all the outbuildings are empty. Joseph and his team are on their way to meet you at the lighthouse.'

'Thanks, Jessie. We're about four minutes away.'

'And ma'am, Eric Barnes rang in. He was in an accident on the A16. He's been taken to Peterborough hospital. Nothing too serious but he needs x-rays. He said he's sorry and he'll get a cab back here when they discharge him.'

Jessie heard the DI grunt with impatience. 'Okay, we'll worry about him later. Anything else?'

'Yes, I have managed to track down Carla Duchene's private doctor. He sent me a report on her condition when she first returned from abroad. It makes scary reading, ma'am. Go very careful with her. It sounds as if she's capable of anything.'

'Rest assured, Jessie, I will. Over and out.'

* * *

Evening was settling across the bleak fenland. All day a keen wind had blown in from the cold grey waters of the North Sea, and the officers that drove towards the lighthouse were chilled to the bone. Rory Wilkinson, who had insisted on accompanying the team, knew that the numbing cold he felt had nothing to do with the climatic conditions. As they drove, he asked DI Gill Mercer what they could expect.

265

'We're trying a silent approach. No sirens, no blue lights, no announcement of our arrival. If we've got the right place, we have to use the element of surprise in order to save her.'

'Will you use heat-seeking equipment to detect who's inside?'

'No time to wait for it, and I dare not send the helicopter up. The killer would know immediately what we're up to.'

She tapped the driver on the shoulder. 'Can't this bloody thing go any faster?'

CHAPTER TWENTY-EIGHT

Nikki slammed her shoulder against the door, hammered at it with her fists, and screamed her head off. She cursed Oliver Kirton with every name she could think of. She didn't expect a reaction, but at least she was doing something.

Suddenly a key turned in the lock. When the door swung back, and Nikki saw the scene before her, she finally realised that she had been wrong all along.

No longer Byronic and elegant, Oliver Kirton was crawling almost blindly towards the entrance door. He managed to swing round and look at her for one moment.

'Got it wrong, Detective,' he croaked. 'We both did.' Then he pitched forward, face down, and lay still.

'Carla?'

'Yes, Detective Inspector, Carla Duchene. Poor, helpless Carla, needing the police to babysit her all through the vigil.' She gave a harsh cackle.

Nikki saw the syringe in her hand and understood how she had managed to overpower Oliver Kirton. A flood of emotions swept through Nikki, to be followed by a feeling of hopelessness. She knew that no one was coming to save her now. None of them had even considered this woman as a possible suspect. Why would they? End of story.

Resignation descended over her like a damp, cold sheet. 'Okay, before you finish this, would you tell me why you murdered my friend?'

'Oh I intend to.'

Carla's face was utterly devoid of all trace of humanity.

'But first, I seem to have given you far too much freedom.'

'I'm hardly likely to bloody well leg it, am I?' Nikki pointed to her useless legs.

'Even like that, you are a dangerous woman, DI Galena.'

Nikki spread her hands. 'I won't try anything. I just really need to know.'

'Move back to the wall, and sit still. One move,' Carla gestured with the syringe, 'and you won't ever wake up again. Understood?'

'Just tell me.' Nikki dragged herself to the wall and leaned heavily against it.

'You never met my mother, did you? She was a brilliant photographer, passionate about the countryside and everything in it. She was an angel, a perfect angel. And your friend Helen Brook killed her.' She tapped the syringe with a finger. 'She killed my mother slowly. If it hadn't been for your friend and her phony cures, I would still have my dear mother with me now. With scientific medical treatment the tumours would eventually have been overcome. But Helen Brook stole her from me. Her silver tongue confused and beguiled my poor, ill mother. So you see now why she had to die.'

Nikki knew that this woman was beyond reason.

Carla was still talking. 'Using Helen's treatment table was perfect, terribly fitting, don't you think? It was right that she should die on the very table where she filled my mother's head with her mumbo-jumbo. God! I saw enough mumbo-jumbo in Africa!'

Nikki understood well enough why poor Helen had been targeted, but she was not sure what she herself had done to upset this mad woman so badly. What was all that about Africa? 'And am I to suffer the same fate? Have you got some arty-farty graffiti lined up for my bellybutton?'

The eyes burnt into her. 'Don't belittle my mother's beautiful epitaph! No, you are not worth the time and trouble. You will simply die, and then I shall place your dead body on the marsh edge and let the tide take you out for fish food.'

'Why me? What is it, guilt by association?'

'The vigil, Inspector! Think about it. It was *you* who allowed it. You who turned that evil fraud of a woman into a martyr! You ruined everything I'd set out to achieve. I'd avenged my mother's death, and you turned it into a farce. You had one chance to stop it, when I showed you that warning note. But you ignored it, and in doing so you sealed your own fate. You are to blame, Detective Inspector Nikki Galena, you and no one else.'

Nikki opened her mouth to speak, then she noticed a slight movement behind her. Years of drug abuse must have given Oliver Kirton a pretty high tolerance of chemicals. Now he was back in the land of the living, and silently holding a finger to his lips.

She needed to keep Carla Duchene's attention. 'How did you get into Helen's flat? Did she let you in herself?'

Carla tilted her head to one side, then she frowned. 'I was down in the treatment room, waiting for my mother to have one of her ridiculous "sessions." There were several keys on the conservatory keyring, so I stole the spare and had a copy made. I replaced it the next time I took Mother for another "treatment."'

'Lucky for you they were the only locks that poor Andrew didn't have changed.' Nikki tried to keep talking. She could see that Oliver was almost upright, though he was moving with agonising slowness.

'Even now the detective in me wants to get things clear, so one last question, Carla. Helen was being watched by the young man who was caught up in the Blackmoor Cross accident with her. Did you know about that?'

Carla gave another bark of laughter. 'Oh yes! Dear Helen was kind enough to share all her fears about her stalker with my mother. And Mother told me. Fortuitous wasn't it?

I timed her death perfectly so as to throw suspicion onto the peeping Tom.'

Nikki had almost run out of things to say, and Carla Duchene was inching closer to her.

'I suppose—'

There was a loud crash, then the sound of running and shouting. Nikki had been on enough busts to instantly recognise the noise and mayhem created by a dozen hyped-up coppers.

'Police! Down on the floor! Now! On the floor!' A black-garbed marksman grabbed Oliver Kirton and threw him down, pulling his arms up behind him and jamming the snout of an automatic weapon between his shoulder blades. 'Don't move a muscle!'

'As if I could? It took me nearly five minutes to get up the first time.'

'It's not him!' shouted Nikki. 'Get the woman!'

Oliver looked up from his position spread-eagled on the floor. 'Watch out! She's carrying a syringe, it's lethal!' Then he slumped forward, out cold.

Carla Duchene had plunged into the room where Nikki had been held. Before she could lock it, armed officers had forced it open and taken her to the floor.

'She's got a syringe! For God's sake be careful!' shouted Nikki. Then she heard the words, 'All clear! She's safe.'

Safe! Nikki began to shake. She was safe.

'Nikki!'

'The gang's all here!' Nikki laughed and cried, as Gill Mercer, Rory and Dave Harris burst into the room. 'I am *really* glad to see you guys!'

'No more than we are to see you, ma'am.' Dave knelt beside her and took her hand. 'Are you hurt?'

But even Nikki's useless legs felt wonderful. 'I'm okay, my friend — well, I am now.'

She watched Carla Duchene being led outside, and felt a stab of sadness. She didn't yet know what had sent her over the edge, but she was sure it would be a heart-breaking story.

Rory was busy going through the empty phials that Carla had left in a dish on a table. 'Nothing to give too much concern, thank heavens. Can you move your legs yet, Inspector? Once it starts to reverse, you'll be back to normal in no time.'

'Just about. They won't take my weight, but they are coming back to life.'

'And the head?' Gill Mercer added. 'We saw you get clobbered on CCTV.'

'I've got a tough skull, Gill. I don't think I've got more than mild concussion.'

Gill smiled at her. 'Ambulance is on its way, we'll get you checked out. It's over now, you can breathe again.'

'Nikki!' Joseph burst through the door and flung himself down beside her. 'I thought . . .'

She gripped his hand tightly. 'So did I. I really did.'

'I'm so sorry. I should never have left you at that damned vigil.'

'Bollocks! What are you, Joseph, my minder? I never liked reins, even as a tiny kid, and no one is going to tie me down at my age, that's for sure!'

'The super said you'd say that.'

'Well, honestly, Joseph. We're police officers. Shit happens, it's no one's fault.' She grinned at him. 'So if you really want to be useful, get me up. I feel like a sack of taters down here.'

Joseph scooped her up in his arms as if she weighed nothing at all. 'I hear the siren, so I guess your chariot is arriving.'

'Someone better go with her,' said Gill Mercer, 'Rory and I will sort out the SOCOs and a cordon for this place.'

'Where *is* this place?' asked Nikki. 'I've been wondering that ever since I woke up here.'

Joseph explained. Then he turned to Gill and added, 'Don't worry. I'll go to the hospital with the inspector.'

'Of course. And ring me with an update, okay?'

Joseph carried Nikki out to the ambulance and waited while the crew checked her over and made her comfortable on a stretcher. She saw him pacing impatiently outside the vehicle and smiled to herself. When she'd looked into Carla Duchene's empty eyes, she really hadn't expected to see him again. The thought had been almost too much to bear. Nikki always maintained that she was a loner and needed no one, but that wasn't really true. She *did* need Joseph — and the team. They were her family and her closest friends. Apart from Eve, they were all she had, and they meant everything to her.

Nikki settled back on the trolley feeling, all things considered, pretty lucky.

CHAPTER TWENTY-NINE

The hospital had reluctantly released her into Joseph's care, but under strict head-injury instructions. They had emphasised that Nikki must not be left alone for the next twenty-four hours.

Now they sat together in the kitchen at Cloud Cottage Farm and talked about what had happened.

'She was very sick, wasn't she, Joseph?'

'She spent years out in African warzones, saving lives. I guess she saw too much suffering. Some people can't take it.' Joseph stretched. 'And I can understand that, having been there myself.'

'I was hating her, but maybe I shouldn't. Maybe she's just another victim.'

'That's pretty magnanimous, considering she murdered your friend, and then proceeded to try to do the same to you.'

'As I said before, shit happens. And it isn't fussy. It happens to good people who don't deserve it.' Nikki yawned. She was exhausted and her head ached horribly, but she didn't want to sleep. She was just happy to be sharing a quiet time with Joseph. At least her legs were almost back to normal. She could stand and walk, although she felt as if she had been kicked in the small of the back by a large and angry horse. 'I never got around to asking about Oliver Kirton. How did he come to be out at the lighthouse? And what did she want with him?'

'That dramatic eulogy at the vigil was his downfall. His devotion to the woman that Carla believed had killed her mother was too much for her. So he had to go.'

'But how did she get him there?'

'She put a note through his door. She persuaded him to meet her out at her mother's studio on the pretext that she knew something about Helen's murder. She said she wanted to talk to him about something before she went to the police. Load of rubbish, but Oliver was obsessed with Helen, so he fell for it.'

'Poor Oliver. He was trying to rescue me, you know. God knows what would have happened if the big guns hadn't arrived.'

'Fancy a mug of cocoa?'

She smiled. 'I used to say that to Hannah when she couldn't sleep. Yes, I'd love one.'

As Joseph boiled the kettle, his phone, lying on the kitchen table, rang loudly. 'Hellfire, it's almost three in the morning!' He held it up and saw Mickey's name. He had already let the boy know that Nikki was safe.

'Mickey? What's wrong?' He switched to loudspeaker.

'It's Archie, Sergeant Joe. He wants to see you and Nikki, urgently.'

Joseph threw a worried glance across to Nikki, and she nodded. 'Okay, Mickey, we are on our way.' He closed his phone. 'Are you really sure that you are well enough for this?'

Her face told him to save his breath.

* * *

The Carborough was as quiet as Nikki had ever known it, to the point of being eerie. 'I don't like the feel of this, do you?'

'No, I don't.' Joseph didn't elaborate.

They drew up outside Archie Leonard's house. Mickey was waiting for them.

'Are we too late?' Nikki asked when she saw the boy's face.

'No, Inspector Nik, although he won't see the night out.' Mickey turned and went inside. 'Come up. He wants to talk to you.'

Nikki and Joseph eased between the silent family members, who seemed to occupy the whole house. Finally they made it to Archie's bedroom, and he indicated that they close the door.

'Let's not make too much of this, my friends,' the old man rasped. 'I don't have the breath for conversation, but I wanted to say goodbye and leave you with a gift.'

Oxygen tubes fed into his nose, and his breath was laboured. His chest heaved with the effort of talking. He held out a hand to Nikki, and she clasped it tightly. 'We've had some interesting times, Archie, haven't we?'

'We have indeed. And I know that Greenborough is a better place because of the two of you. I wanted to thank you both for the sensitive way you dealt with the death of my lovely niece, and for all you've done for my dear grandson here. I can never repay you for your care for this boy.' He fought back a cough and his whole body rattled with the exertion. 'Look after each other.' He gazed at Joseph, who nodded solemnly. 'Now, will you go with Mickey? I have left a little something for the two of you. I hope you will appreciate it.'

Nikki leaned forward and kissed the old man's forehead. 'I'll miss you, you old villain.'

Joseph took her place. 'Me too, sir. And I mean it when I say it's been a pleasure knowing you.'

They went slowly down the stairs after Mickey, neither daring to speak for fear of breaking into tears.

'This way. It's not far.' To their surprise, Mickey hurried back out onto the street and began to walk down the road.

'Where are we going?' asked Joseph, with a hint of anxiety in his voice.

'Just along here. A couple of minutes, that's all.'

A gift? Nikki trusted Archie, but even she was beginning to worry.

'Here. This is it. Go in, please.' Mickey's voice sounded strained.

'DI Galena, and DS Easter, Archie said you would come. Good. Come with me.' Raymond Leonard seemed taller and more menacing than Nikki remembered.

Raymond ushered them into a small untidy lounge. 'Sorry about this. It's a bit of a squat, although we have it to ourselves right now.' He pointed to two threadbare chairs and seated himself on a rather unwholesome-looking sofa. 'I wanted to talk to you away from the rest of the family. My father says this is personal between you and him, and it's his way of saying goodbye and have a good life.' He abruptly stood up and beckoned them to follow him.

He walked into the kitchen, stood to one side and pointed down to the floor.

The body was lying on its back on a thick plastic builder's sheet. There was very little blood, although it was obvious he had been stabbed several times.

Nikki swallowed and felt a tide of emotion engulf her. She reached for Joseph's hand and clung tightly to it.

'The scar-faced bastard won't ever hurt or threaten you again. He damaged our family, and he damaged you.' Raymond drew in a deep breath. 'Father said it was important that you see his body, or you would spend the rest of your lives looking over your shoulder. He said he owed you that much. And I agreed. Stephen Cox is dead and now you know that for a fact. Nikki? Joseph? I know you are police officers, and you have a job to do, but listen carefully.' His eyes narrowed. 'Now you have seen this, it will disappear. It never happened. In a very short while there will be nothing here, just an empty room with no evidence of anything more than mice. You never saw this, but you will sleep at night.'

Nikki stared at the once handsome face of the man that had haunted them for years. Stephen Cox, the man who had killed and tormented without emotion or mercy, who had brought Joseph to within touching distance of an early grave. Stephen Cox had been a truly evil man. And now he was gone forever. She knew that no matter what, she should never condone murder. It went against everything she stood for. She knew that she should reach for her phone and call this in. In those few moments Nikki knew a lot of things, but then, in that dirty, filthy kitchen, she saw the faces of people that he had hurt. She felt that she was surrounded by the dead souls that had cried out for retribution. And now they had it, not in the manner that she would have wanted, but they could finally rest. She blinked back tears, and saw, in her mind's eye, three beautiful girls. Three beautiful dead girls. All dead, because of this beast of a man. No, she wouldn't be ringing this in, she and Joseph were never here.

She shook her head in disbelief, then realised that Joseph's body was racked with silent sobs. She had never seen Joseph cry, but she understood why he was crying now. She put her arm around him, and gently said, 'Time to go. It really is over at last.'

As they walked outside into the night air her headache intensified. She wanted to be home and away from all this, but she paused and turned to Raymond. 'The two men who were in his pay? The ones who probably killed your relative? Fabian and Venables?'

Raymond's face was full of distaste. 'They were ghosts, Nikki. They disappeared into the twilight. And I hope they have gone back to the Continent where they came from, because I'd rather not meet them again.'

'Let's hope.' She drew her coat around her, 'Goodnight, Raymond, and thank you for letting us say our goodbyes to your father. We do appreciate it.' She took Joseph's arm and leaned heavily on him as they walked away. Over her shoulder, she called back, 'We appreciate everything.'

EPILOGUE

Just as Nikki was locking her front door, she saw Joseph walking up the lane from Knot Cottage.

'Just came to say have a nice evening, and you will give my best wishes to Eve, won't you?'

'Thanks. Of course I will.' She looked at him suspiciously. 'You're looking rather smug, what gives?'

Joseph grinned broadly. 'You know I've been trying to fathom out what on earth I can say to Niall about his relationship with my daughter?'

'I know you've been avoiding the issue like the plague, if that's what you mean.'

'Ha-ha! Well, I don't have to worry anymore, because Niall came to see me, and he did all the talking.'

'And?'

'He asked for her hand in marriage. All very formal. And he requested my permission before he approached Tam.'

Eyes wide, Nikki said, 'I assume you immediately filled out the regulation paperwork?'

'Well, I shook his hand and asked if he had the slightest clue what he was letting himself in for.'

Nikki squeezed his arm. 'That's brilliant! I'm delighted for the two of them. They are going to be such a great couple.'

'I hope.'

'They will. They are a different generation to us, with different goals and priorities. They will do well, I know it.'

Joseph wasn't totally convinced. 'As I said, I hope so.' Then he broke into a broad smile. 'Wouldn't I just love to be a fly on the wall when her mother hears about this!'

'Laura will love him when she gets to know him, but maybe they should hold off telling her he's a copper.'

'Oh no, that's the best bit.'

'Wicked man, Joseph.' She glanced at her watch. 'But hey, I have to go. I'll see you tomorrow and fill you in on Eve and her mysterious message.'

'Be sure you do.'

* * *

The supper was delicious, leaving Nikki in no doubt that this was one area in which she did not take after her mother. As soon as they had cleared away, Eve led her through to the lounge and they both settled into large leather recliner chairs.

'Sorry to sound so evasive on the phone the other day, but this is something for a face-to-face talk, not a few words over the phone.'

Nikki felt anxiety begin to nibble at her.

'I wanted you to have these.' Eve passed her a large sealed envelope. 'It is the details of my solicitor and a copy of my will. Not that I intend going anywhere in the near future, you understand. But as you are the sole heir, you should have them. They are all very straightforward.'

'I can't, Eve. Surely you have other relatives that are more deserving?'

'I have no one, Nikki. Just you.'

Nikki didn't know what to say. If this was the case, why was she going away?

'The thing is, I'm wondering whether maybe I should have stayed away? You have been amazingly kind and understanding, but I can see that you have such a full and rewarding life, I'm just not sure if I have a part to play in it.'

She smiled and went on before Nikki could say anything. 'I suppose, being in the RAF for so long, rather like you really, work was everything. I never knew where I'd be going or what I'd be doing next. Now, well, I can't be doing nothing. I'm just not good at relaxing, I need purpose. So, I've been offered a job of sorts, helping to set up an artists' retreat in France. You know, one of those holidays where you have classes and educational trips in the day time, then enjoy good food and good company in the evenings.'

'It sounds great, but do you have an interest in art?' Nikki tried to sound enthusiastic, but knew she had failed.

'I dabble. It's probably the only thing that holds my attention.' She pointed to a framed painting of a misty morning over the marshes. An old rowing boat nestled in one corner with a grey heron perched on it, watching the still waters.

'But that's beautiful!' exclaimed Nikki, and meant it.

'Thank you. I do enjoy it.'

'Do you go to classes, or is it a natural talent?'

'Both really. I needed something to occupy my time, and as I used to sketch a bit when I was a kid, I thought I'd try classes. I had no expectations of being good, but it turned out I do have an eye for colour and perspective.'

'I can see that!' Nikki said. Then she looked away from the picture and said, 'Don't go, Eve. You *do* have a place in my life and I really don't want to lose you again. You are my mother for heaven's sake! There are plenty of things to do right here. Please stay.'

Eve drew in a long breath. 'In that case, I'm not sure I like French cuisine that much anyway.'

'How about omelettes? They are French, aren't they?'

'I love omelettes.'

'Oh good! They're pretty much the only things I can cook.'

THE END

THE JOFFE BOOKS STORY

We began in 2014 when Jasper agreed to publish his mum's much-rejected romance novel and it became a bestseller.

Since then we've grown into the largest independent publisher in the UK. We're extremely proud to publish some of the very best writers in the world, including Joy Ellis, Faith Martin, Caro Ramsay, Helen Forrester, Simon Brett and Robert Goddard. Everyone at Joffe Books loves reading and we never forget that it all begins with the magic of an author telling a story.

We are proud to publish talented first-time authors, as well as established writers whose books we love introducing to a new generation of readers.

We won Trade Publisher of the Year at the Independent Publishing Awards in 2023. We have been shortlisted for Independent Publisher of the Year at the British Book Awards for the last four years, and were shortlisted for the Diversity and Inclusivity Award at the 2022 Independent Publishing Awards. In 2023 we were shortlisted for Publisher of the Year at the RNA Industry Awards.

We built this company with your help, and we love to hear from you, so please email us about absolutely anything bookish at feedback@joffebooks.com

If you want to receive free books every Friday and hear about all our new releases, join our mailing list: www.joffebooks.com/contact

And when you tell your friends about us, just remember: it's pronounced Joffe as in coffee or toffee!

ALSO BY JOY ELLIS

ELLIE MCEWAN SERIES
Book 1: AN AURA OF MYSTERY
Book 2: THE COLOUR OF MYSTERY

JACKMAN & EVANS SERIES
Book 1: THE MURDERER'S SON
Book 2: THEIR LOST DAUGHTER
Book 3: THE FOURTH FRIEND
Book 4: THE GUILTY ONES
Book 5: THE STOLEN BOYS
Book 6: THE PATIENT MAN
Book 7: THEY DISAPPEARED
Book 8: THE NIGHT THIEF
Book 9: SOLACE HOUSE
Book 10: THE RIVER'S EDGE

THE NIKKI GALENA SERIES
Book 1: CRIME ON THE FENS
Book 2: SHADOW OVER THE FENS
Book 3: HUNTED ON THE FENS
Book 4: KILLER ON THE FENS
Book 5: STALKER ON THE FENS
Book 6: CAPTIVE ON THE FENS
Book 7: BURIED ON THE FENS
Book 8: THIEVES ON THE FENS
Book 9: FIRE ON THE FENS
Book 10: DARKNESS ON THE FENS
Book 11: HIDDEN ON THE FENS
Book 12: SECRETS ON THE FENS
Book 13: FEAR ON THE FENS
Book 14: GRAVES ON THE FENS

DETECTIVE MATT BALLARD
Book 1: BEWARE THE PAST
Book 2: FIVE BLOODY HEARTS
Book 3: THE DYING LIGHT
Book 4: MARSHLIGHT
Book 5: TRICK OF THE NIGHT
Book 6: THE BAG OF SECRETS

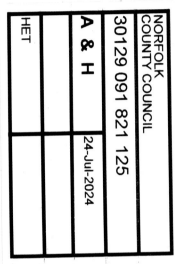

NORFOLK
COUNTY COUNCIL

30129 091 821 125

A & H

24-Jul-2024

HET

STALKER ON THE FENS a gripping
7063855

Milton Keynes UK
Ingram Content Group UK Ltd.
UKHW012332100724
445430UK00011B/165